In Too Deep

Daniel Brewster is standing in front of the rust-spotted mirror, running a battery razor back and forth along the line of his jaw. He's leaning over the sink, barely a couple of inches from the glass, peering intently at his reflection and frowning hard.

Nothing unusual about this, apart from the location. And the fact that he's standing there stark naked.

Dear Lord in Heaven, he's beautiful!

Unaware of my scrutiny, he stands relaxed, his limbs elegant, loose, almost classical. His form is muscular and compact, not an inch of spare flesh on him, and there's a delightful little tangle of dark hair adorning his chest.

My eyes skitter from one to another of his body's charms, almost painstakingly avoiding the place they really want to look.

But eventually, of course, I succumb.

In Too Deep
Portia Da Costa

BL

This book is a work of fiction.
In real life, make sure you practise safe, sane and
consensual sex.

Published by Black Lace 2008

2 4 6 8 10 9 7 5 3 1

First published in Great Britain in 2008 by
Black Lace
Virgin Books
Random House,
20 Vauxhall Bridge Road,
London SW1V 2SA

www.rbooks.co.uk

Typeset by Palimpsest Book Production Ltd, Grangemouth, Stirlingshire
Printed and bound in Great Britain by CPI Bookmarque, Croydon CR0 4TD

Addresses for companies within The Random House Group Limited can be found at:
www.randomhouse.co.uk/offices.htm

The Random House Group Limited Reg. No. 954009

Distributed in the USA by Macmillan, 175 Fifth Avenue, New York, NY 10010, USA

A CIP catalogue record for this book
is available from the British Library

ISBN 978 0 352 341976

The Random House Group Limited supports The Forest Stewardship Council [FSC], the
leading international forest certification organisation. All our titles that are printed on
Greenpeace approved FSC certified paper carry the FSC logo.

Our paper procurement policy can be found at www.rbooks.co.uk/environment

For my travelling companions, Valerie and Madelynne

CONTENTS

1 You've Got Mail

I hardly dare look again. But if I don't look, I must be imagining things, and I'm not sure I want to admit to imagining *this*.

It's slightly scary. And it makes me want to giggle. In about equal measures.

For the third time since I fished it out of the library's old-fashioned suggestion box, I flip open the eggshell-blue envelope and unfold the four sheets of heavy, high-quality paper inside it. The words written on them, evenly spaced in navy ink, are inscribed in an elegant, almost copperplate hand.

I blush, and it's as if my mind fills with a silent, thrilling voice. My heart beats hard and I get this stupid urge to press my hand to my chest, as if that could slow it.

It's an effort to sit still, but I manage to, even though I'm still in danger of sniggering.

I've been watching you, Ms Gwendolynne Price, did you know that?

Every day I observe you in the library. Every day I want to reach out and touch you. Every day I wrestle with my urges ... You pass me by and I want to grab you by the arm, drag you behind one of the book stacks and do unspeakable things to you. I want to slide my hands beneath your skirt and fondle you until you moan with pleasure. I want to bare exquisite expanses of your creamy skin right here in the public lending library, inches from those peasants who meander unaware around your domain. I'd like to unveil your sumptuous curves and kiss and caress you with my tongue until you're in such a state that you can't keep still. I want to suck your delicious clitoris until you whimper and buck and come. Come for me.

Don't be afraid, my lovely Gwendolynne. I mean you no harm ... I just want a taste of you. Or a touch.

Would that I could worship you chastely from afar, like some courtly knight pining in purity for his lady. I wish to God I could write romantic poetry, cataloguing your sweetness, describing every last facet of your smile and your grace, and outlining the way I long to kneel at your feet and then kiss your very footsteps as you walk away from me.

But it's no good, my darling. That's just not enough for me. I can't confine myself to the pure and high-minded. I'm too much of an animal, my dearest. A horny, uncontrollable beast. The sight of your curves gives me an enormous hard-on. The desire to fuck you senseless rules me. My cock turns to iron as you pass me by. I ache as I hear the way your skirt swishes around your thighs, and I almost wish that I could be that simple length of cloth myself. So that I could be close to your delicious cunt and drown in its fragrance and its taste.

I can't stop obsessing about what lies between your legs. The lush grove of your sex and its intimate pink geography. I'd love to spread you wide and stare at you for hours, caressing you with my eyes, savouring what naked vulnerability and exposure would do to you.

My fantasies about you plague my every waking hour. They screw up my work, but I don't care. My only comfort is imagining that similar fantasies might obsess you too. I dream about you dreaming about my cock. Picturing it and speculating about it, imagining how it would feel in your hand, or your cunt.

And it's not such a bad one, dearest Gwendolynne, as cocks go. In fact when I'm thinking about you, it can get pretty spectacular. It rises in tribute to your luscious, sensational beauty *and the promise of exploring every last inch of that beauty, plunging into it as we roll around on the Reference Library floor, half-naked and fucking like a pair of desperados.*

And yes, my glorious, erotic Queen of the Library, it won't surprise you that I've been masturbating like a maniac lately, thinking of you. I've been working and working away at my cock while I dream of what I'd like to do to you with it . . .

I keep seeing images of you in lingerie. Little scraps of barely anything at all that reveal more than they conceal.

Do you like silk and lace, dearest Gwendolynne, or are you a plain white serviceable cotton type of girl? I could devour you in either, or in nothing at all, but you know what we lustful, raving perverts are like. We fritter away hours of our lives speculating on what kind of bra and panties the women we long for wear.

In my imagination you're wearing high-end underwear today. Delightful skimpy wisps that embrace your glorious breasts and bottom like a second skin . . . Little bits of frippery that enjoy intimate body privileges that I can only dream about.

I see you in scarlet. Not any plain old red but a deep, rich, singing colour, the colour of a fine vintage wine or a rare and precious ruby. And there's white lace too. A piquant edge of innocence that only makes the red silk look more sinful. More decadent. More like the sort of thing a high-class hooker would wear.

Yesterday, in the library, you were wearing a pretty navy-blue shirt and a trim denim skirt that showed off your sumptuous arse to perfection. But in my mind you were dressed as a thousand-pound-a-night call girl underneath all that.

I loved your breasts in that shirt. In fact, I adore your breasts, full stop. They're rounded, abundant and magnificent. Worthy of the goddess of love herself. You're Aphrodite to me, you know that, don't you, Gwendolynne? And your splendid breasts command me to worship them in the most exquisite detail with my eyes and my fingers. Here in the sanctum of my imagination, they're a feast for my greedy, famished senses. They're high and pointed, a pair of delicious handfuls, a joy to behold. And the silky skin of their upper curves, above that teasing edge of lace, is as sweet and soft and mellow as milk and honey on my tongue.

Do you touch your own breasts, Gwendolynne? I'd love to know ...

Why don't you touch them now, as you read? Slyly and sweetly ... No one need see you do it, but I'd know, oh, I'd know ... I'd see an exquisite, embarrassed flush on your lovely face, and I'd know you were blushing for me, and me alone. That you were touching yourself because I wanted you to ... and to please me.

That's it, unbutton your blouse, slide your fingers inside, and run the tips of them across the lush curve, and around the nipple where it's hard beneath your bra. Do it! Do it now! Nobody will be able to see you if you pretend to reach down and get something out of the drawer in the desk.

It'll just be our private sex act, the first gambit in our game.

And later, at night and in privacy, you'll do it again, thinking of me as you roll the tip of your finger around the tip of your breast. Round and round, round and round, light as a feather. And when that excites you too much, perhaps you could gently pinch yourself? Punish yourself for teasing me by taking that dark juicy berry of a nipple and tweaking it this way and that while you begin to squirm where you sit, wet and turned on?

Do you enjoy a little pain with your pleasure, Gwendolynne? I think everyone should, at least once in their life. Not too much ... I'm not a brute or a sadist ... But it's a delicious, sophisticated spice on the sexual menu and you strike me as a woman whose appetites are voracious once they're whetted. I think you have the imagination to sample just about anything, don't you, my darling goddess?

I'm only guessing, but I'm not often wrong.

And you, you're a woman who's brave and bold and ready for adventure. A woman who's primed for pleasure and the chase.

Am I right? I think I am ...

Anyway, back to your breasts, your beautiful breasts ...

Now, I see you lying on satin sheets, your magnificent body framed in the luxury it deserves. I suppose satin sheets are a bit of a cliché, really, but who cares? They're the stuff of a million classic wank fantasies, not just mine. But perhaps your sheets are white rather than black? Mm ... that works for me.

'Nights in white satin', eh, my delightful one? What I wouldn't give for some of those ... Long, dark, scented nights in which to gorge myself again and again on the abundant pleasures of your body ... Well, that would be my paradise. My ultimate wish ... will it ever happen?

You lie there, a study in scarlet and white, creamy, honeyed skin and long, wild, tawny hair. No plaits tonight, sublime Gwendolynne. Your beautiful hair is another aspect of you that's almost become a fetish to me ... Would you be disgusted and repelled if I said I'd like to come in it? I imagine myself kneeling over you, your naked and rampant supplicant, and then folding the wild silky waves of your hair around my penis and caressing myself with it until I climax.

Oh, Gwendolynne, I'm hard as a rod of iron simply thinking about it!

And I think I'm going to do something about it. Right now.

Adieu, my glorious Queen of the Library, adieu ... Perhaps you could write me a little email to say you forgive me for being such a disgusting deviant? Or perhaps you could tell me one of your fantasies? And then I'd know that you're just as deviant as I am ...

Yours, in body and soul, especially in hard, aching body ...
Nemesis

Nemesis? Oh, please ... The man's a raving pervert, fond of purple prose and probably dangerous ... and he calls himself 'Nemesis'? It sounds like something a teenage gamer would call himself when playing online.

And yet, all the same, the note and even just the stupid word itself induce a shivery frisson. I imagine a tall dark figure, very mysterious, maybe masked even, maybe wearing leather, looming over me. Someone strong and hard and sexy, who makes me kneel and kiss his boots ... then kiss his cock.

I shake my head and it dawns on me that for the last few minutes I've been completely out of it, lost in Nemesis-land. And the worst of it is, I'm actually doing what he told me to. Well, not quite, but not far off. I'm touching my ribcage, just beneath my breast, through my cotton top.

Snatching my hand away, I make a big deal of folding the letter carefully and shoving it in the pocket of my skirt. And that makes me feel a bit turned on too, thinking of what he said about my skirt.

In a weird way, the letter *is* Nemesis and, in my pocket, he's nestling dangerously close to my pussy, just like he said. There are only a couple of layers of cotton between it and him.

Taking some deep breaths and trying to look like a perfectly normal human being, I scan all of the main Lending Library that I can see. Yet despite the fact that I feel as if I've got a neon sign flashing 'Whore of Babylon' over my head, nobody is looking at me. Everything's quiet and in the pre-lunch lull there's only a small handful of punters perusing the shelves. It's safe to pat my pocket and think again about my new 'correspondent'.

The weird and slightly sad thing is that, in spite of it being anonymous, pretentious, kinky and slightly disgusting in a good sort of way, this is actually the nearest thing to a love letter that I've ever received. Even when we were hot for each other, my late and not particularly lamented ex, Simon, never sent me love notes or even emails. And since we split up all I've ever received are terse 'communications' about the divorce and 'orders' about selling the stupid house. He's still trying to order me about.

Well, balls to him. I've got more immediate things to worry about. Somebody who sounds like much more fun trying to control me. And occupy my mind.

Who the devil is Nemesis? And where is he lurking? And where does he get off, telling me to touch myself? Judging by the letter, he must be a library regular, and that means he's probably quite close to me. Possibly even right now. What if he's watching me at this very moment? The library's quiet. He could be anywhere ... just feet away.

Did someone turn the heating back on today? I'm too young for hot flushes, but whatever it is I'm having certainly feels like one. Surreptitiously, I flap the neckline of my top. Then stop immediately. Nemesis will go mental if he sees me doing that. I glance around and the lobes of my ears prickle as if the possibility of being watched is an actual physical force.

Is he here? Looking at my nipples through my top and imagining what's beneath my skirt? My head fills with bizarre notions of X-ray vision and me walking through the library with transparent clothes on. The way Nemesis talks about my body, he makes it sound as if he's actually seen it naked.

Oh, why did I just think that?

Nemesis isn't the only one who can have porny fantasies. I get a flash image of me lying on the floor of the Reference Library, just like he said. I'm flat on my back and there's a gorgeous man pounding away between my spread thighs. The real Nemesis is probably fat and middle-aged with a comb-over or some such hideousness, so for convenience' sake – and because he's in my mind quite a bit anyway – I substitute my current major lust object into the action: the library's pet celebrity, who's working in the special collection in our archives for a few weeks, researching a project.

Now there's someone I wouldn't mind doing all the stuff in Nemesis's letter with!

I glance over my shoulder in the direction of the Ref. That floor in there is hard. But I still seem to feel it against my bottom, as I writhe.

Nemesis isn't the only one who's mental! I've only gone and made myself start getting wet now … Am I just as twisted and kinky as he is? I'm definitely horny, and at the same time I feel as if I've had the wind knocked right out of me. I've let myself respond to the ramblings of a pervert. Someone who could be dangerous. And sick. Someone who probably *is* dangerous and sick.

And someone, whoever he is, who's certainly been close enough to me to pop a sealed envelope in the Lending Section's suggestion box. Someone who knows the library's routines and personnel too. Who knows that it's my job to empty the box, and when I'm likely to do it. Who knows the times when the General Enquiry Desk probably won't be manned.

The desk is on a little platform, just a few inches above floor level, but it's still a vantage point. From here I can scope out quite a bit of the open-plan section of the library's new building. People are starting to filter in for lunch-hour browsing, and Nemesis could be any one of them. Hundreds come in every day during opening hours. There are several dozen in now, about half of them men, meandering round the shelves.

Over there by the sports section, there's a shifty-looking individual, a prime candidate. He's a regular and I've caught him looking at my breasts often enough. He's doing it now, the swine. Oh no, I don't want Nemesis to be him!

It's at times like these that I wish my boobs were a bit smaller. In fact, I wish that *all* of me was a bit smaller. Most of the time, I really don't mind being a curvy girl, in fact I quite like it, but ample flesh does seem to bring out the beast in a lot of men. And especially, it seems, a new breed of beast ... one who seems to be trying to make his basic instincts seem more acceptable and less gross by flinging in the odd bit of fancy talk about worship and courtly love.

Not that I've let any of the beasts get their paws on me all that often lately. Since my divorce I've been holding out for quality, not quantity. Maybe for some kind of hero. Being choosy seemed like a good idea at the time, but it's backfiring big time now because I'm just dying for some sex. I hardly dare admit it but, if Nemesis is halfway decent looking and not too deranged, I'm seriously tempted to give him a shot.

Which is the reason I'm probably not going to tell anybody else on the staff about my pervy letter. We get weird stuff in the box all the time, and the harmless items we have a good giggle about in the lunch room at break times. The sicker ones get reported to the Chief Librarian, although goodness knows what he can do about it. But they're mostly one- or two-offs and the pests quickly lose interest.

This is different, though. I just have a feeling. And this is *my* pervert too, and I don't want to share him.

I stare at the Hotmail address at the bottom of the page: N3m3sis@hotmail.co.uk.

Should I send a message? Tell him to leave me alone? Or maybe give him a shock and answer in kind? Make up the dirtiest fantasy I can imagine, about my lingerie, or some confection of lace and satin I haven't got and probably couldn't afford? Or maybe I should concoct an elaborate story about him and *his* masturbation? I was always good at composition at school. Maybe I should tell him what I want *him* to do?

Before I know what I'm doing, I've opened the email client on my terminal.

Oh, no, no, no ... that's just wilfully stupid and dangerous. But God knows I want to. I think I probably am as perverted and strange as he is and I just didn't realise it. My fingers hover over the keys, and it's only the thought that the library's computer system is subject to random monitoring that stops me. Even so, my heart flutters madly, and down below I feel a stickiness in my knickers. The higher brain functions don't seem to be working correctly, and my body has turned into an out-of-control mass of hormones.

Sports-section guy has lost interest now, and is actually reading a book. If it were him, and he's seen me with Nemesis's blue writing paper in my hand, his eyes should be out on stalks and he should be moving in. But instead he seems to be engrossed in the history of Yorkshire rugby.

Who are you, Nemesis, you sick devil? Are you here? Now? Within visual or even touching distance?

There's no way to know. I'm not on duty in the main Lending Library all the time, so anyone could come to the box during the course of a day. And this is the Borough Library Headquarters, and we've got the Scientific Library, the Audio Visual Library, the Children's Library, the archives and a variety of specialist collections. Nemesis could be anywhere in what's a very large and quite rambling building, much of it open to the public. He could be disguised as a bona fide punter.

Breathless panic wells up again. What if he *is* genuinely dangerous? I need to get out of here, and I release an inner sigh when I spot that the big clock by the entrance reads nearly noon. Thank heavens, I'm on early lunch today. Within minutes I can be out in the fresh air and thinking like a person who's *not* insane again.

As if she's a genie and I've summoned her, Tracey arrives promptly for her stint on the desk. It's not manned all the time, but we get lots of reader enquiries during the busy lunch-time.

'You OK?' she enquires, and it dawns on me that I must look as flustered and slightly off my head as I feel.

'Yeah, I'm fine,' I lie, fabricating what I hope is a normal-looking grin. 'I was checking the catalogue and the system went a bit weird again, and I thought I'd cocked something up … But it seems to be OK now.'

We chat for a couple of moments on routine library business, and I think I've fooled her into believing that this is just another in a never-ending series of mundane and uneventful mornings. I feel guilty not telling her about Nemesis, though. She's a friend and, under normal circumstances, she'd be the one I'd have a laugh with over all this.

Two or three minutes later, I'm heading for the back door on my way out to get some air. Clarkey, the building's main-tenance manager, and the visiting techie from Borough Hall who's supposed to be upgrading the computers were in the lunch room. Is Nemesis either of those two, I wonder? Greg, the computer nerd, is young and bright and cute, but yuk, the thought of Clarkey sending me sex notes makes my stomach curdle. Mind you, I hardly think he'd have 'greedy famished senses' for anything other than the enormous meat pie he was shovelling down his throat and, judging by the scarcely legible notes he tapes to the staff cloakroom's water heater when it doesn't work, I'm not sure he could manage copperplate hand-writing.

Security is tightish at the library, as we've got some rare and precious documents in the archives, but after my usual wrangle with the keypad and the deadbolt I manage to get the door open and launch myself outside, with the intention of heading for the small urban garden beyond the parking area, for some thinking.

But just as I'm hurtling out, someone else is hurtling in, and I run smack into a dark, bespectacled, heavily laden figure. He isn't moving fast, but his arms are full of his briefcase, a pile of books, several newspapers and a rolled-up map and we cannon into each other, sending his paraphernalia flying everywhere.

And I'm blushing again. It's only our semi-resident, semi-superstar eccentric academic I've gone and barged into. The adorably fit and lovely but rather bookish and haphazard Professor Daniel Brewster.

'Oh dear! I do beg your pardon,' he apologises as if it's entirely *his* fault and not mine for forgetting to look where I'm going due to woolgathering about perverts and blue notepaper. We both swoop down, fielding the books and papers, and, as I pick up several volumes that I know he really shouldn't have removed from the archive, I'm struck again by how scrumptious he is in a distracted, studious way. His curly black hair looks as wild as a gypsy's and as usual there's that gorgeous, swarthy hint of stubble darkening his cheeks. If he didn't have the rather etiolated look of someone who stays inside poring over books all the time, he could easily pass for an earthy Mediterranean sex-machine. Apart, of course, from the seriously studious glasses and the superannuated tweed jacket.

I get the shock of my life as I look up from retrieving a few sheets of typed paper, to meet the dark eyes behind those elegant specs ... and find them locked on to my cleavage like a pair of targeting lasers. It's clearly visible in the dip of my V-necked top.

Is *he* Nemesis? The notion makes me rock on my heels and nearly tumble over backwards.

Every part of me starts to tingle but, when he blushes a darker crimson than Nemesis's lurid underwear fantasy, it's seems unlikely that he's the man himself. Especially when, having been crouched down on his heels to sweep up his books and papers, he promptly *does* tumble over backwards on to the concrete path. All from the shock of having been caught staring at my ample bosom. I've only gone and knocked a minor TV celebrity, whom I just happen to fancy something rotten, over on to his arse! It's all your fault, Nemesis, for making me crazy!

'Oh, I'm so sorry!' I exclaim, graciously taking the blame for him falling, even though I didn't knock him over; he fell over while gazing at my breasts. Which he's still doing, his brown eyes on fire. His ears seem to be feeling the heat too, because the lobes have acquired a very fetching touch of pink. I suddenly wonder what it would be like to gently nibble them.

What? I don't know what's got into me these last few days but, what with Nemesis and Professor Hottie McHotstuff here, I seriously think I'm turning into a sex maniac.

Hauling in a deep breath, I reach out to help him rise, thus improving his view of my boobs, but he springs up with an unexpected athleticism, snapping to his feet in an almost panther-like leap.

'No, no! It was my fault,' he corrects, sounding both mortified and slightly irritated. He bends down again to scoop up more of his maverick paperwork, and then as he looks up from his search, his face is almost parallel to my crotch and only inches away from it. He doesn't tumble over this time, but sort of starts backwards as if proximity to my pubic parts has zapped him. The action's more like a startled gazelle this time than a sleek feline predator.

This whole episode is rapidly turning into a mini-farce, so I thrust the pretty professor's papers haphazardly into his hands and dash past him, flinging a smile and another 'sorry' and a 'see you later' over my shoulder as I run across the tarmac in the direction of the garden.

2 Time Out with Professor Hottie

What a ludicrous pantomime that was! As if I wasn't shaken up enough by Nemesis and his erotic ramblings, now I'm all of a lather over Professor Hottie again. I've been fancying the famous Professor Daniel Brewster since well before he became a temporary feature attraction at the library several weeks ago, when he arrived to research a new book and a possible television series. His popular history documentaries are frequently repeated on UKTV and, even though I've seen them repeatedly, I always watch them when they're on.

Now, though, I don't look back, and I keep moving at a trot, trying to pretend that none of our little prat-fall ballet on the back step happened. I don't stop until I reach my special place, a secluded bench in a small shady arbour, well out of the way of the main park area where people gather for lunches. Very few people seem to have found this little haven, which is sheltered by several large trees and a high hedge, so it doesn't get the sun. That probably explains its desertedness. Most folk round here still seem to be devoted to the active pursuit of melanoma. So this is a place where I can find peace and quiet, uninterrupted, in the middle of the day.

Not that I'm feeling in any way peaceful today. And my brain isn't quiet. It's whirling with the choice phraseology of Nemesis's missive and action replays of me almost exhibiting my breasts to Daniel Brewster.

I pull my bottle of water out of my bag, and gulp some down. It's icy, fresh from the fridge, and its cold bite on my tongue calms me down. Something clicks into place like a camera focusing. I look round, taking in the greens of the leaves and the dull grey of the gravel. This, and the fresh air, is real and normal, far from the heated world of explicit letters and speculation about handsome, quirky men who are way out of my league.

A few more sips and I feel centred again. Not ready for my sandwiches yet, but I'll tackle them shortly. For a while, I just sit feeling very Zen, at one with nature and all that. Then, just as I decide it's time to eat and sort out my blood sugar, I catch sight of the edge of those sheets of blue paper poking out of the side pocket of my bag. I slide them out and unfold the written madness.

Words leap out at me.

Do you take that dark juicy berry of a nipple and tweak it this way and that while you begin to squirm in your seat as you get wet and turned on?

Reading it makes me want to do it, and as I glance up momentarily I'm back in my murky parallel world of irrational lust. I'm not wearing one of those white blouses that Nemesis clearly has a fetish for, but, almost without conscious thought, I suddenly reach up and cup my own curve through the soft cotton of my top.

My nipple is hard, and doubtless, if it were exposed to the air, it *would* be dark and firm like a juicy berry. I give it a little strum through the layers of fabric – top and bra, cotton both – and a silvery flutter flies through my body. I'm convinced that Nemesis is a man, but he certainly seems to know all about the connection between tit and clit. I'm already hot between my legs, my pussy heavy and congested, even though it's the words that are getting to me most, not the touching. Words, and the sight of a dark-haired, slightly geeky but very beautiful man in a fluster of embarrassment.

I wonder if Professor Hottie's earlobes have cooled down yet?

I stare at the cool, green façade of the hedge that faces me – but I don't see it. Instead, I'm imagining a scenario, doing a Nemesis, I suppose. In my little drama I dropped this letter when I ran into Daniel Brewster, and somehow it got into his papers. He's reading it now as I sit here and dream about him.

I see those cute earlobes get even pinker, his dark eyebrows shoot up to his hairline to be masked by the kiss curls dangling on his forehead. He takes off his elegant frameless glasses and polishes them, and then wriggles in his seat, just the way I'm doing. Which is weird, because Nemesis's letter is written to a woman, and he's a man …

My fingers are damp where they clasp the blue pages. I know that if I had half a brain cell I'd shred this correspondence and ignore any further similar ones. That's the sensible thing to do. Sex nuisances are like plants: they die off if you don't water them with a response.

But the words and my collision with Daniel Brewster have got a grip on me and I just can't sit still. My mind is a jumble of Nemesis and silk and touching myself and the image of the divine professor, all blushing and tumbled on the ground, limbs akimbo. My body is hot, full of strange energy and blood in dangerous places. Surreptitiously, I part my legs, pressing my sex down against the hard park bench and spreading and opening it. But I'm not getting the pressure I need on my clit, and I bite my lip at the gnawing, sudden need.

Dare I touch myself? Right here, right now? Not just my nipple, I mean, but down there, down below, in my pussy?

What do you think of that, Nemesis? I've escalated the game and you'll never know about it. How's that for brinksmanship, pervert?

There's no one around. I've never ever seen anyone here. Theoretically, I should be able to do it. But still it seems impossibly crude and slutty to touch myself, out here in the open. And it's weak-willed too. I'm giving in to him, and I feel as if he *would* know, although God knows how. Since my split from Simon, letting men manoeuvre me into doing things is no longer a part of my playbook. I don't think I'd even be inclined to do what Professor Hottie wants me to do, if he were here. Although I don't know …

This is all getting exceptionally weird. And all I'm sure of is that Nemesis would come smugly in his boxer shorts, or whatever he wears, if he knew I was squirming around on a park bench, desperate to touch myself between my legs until I orgasmed.

In stealth mode and glancing around warily, I slide my hand from the rounded curve of my breast, down over my waist and my hip to my thigh. There's plenty of territory to cover but, as Nemesis obviously likes my acreage and Professor Hottie certainly isn't immune to my boobs, that's not a problem. In fact I'm beginning to see the advantages of my ampleness.

Even more sneakily, I begin to inch up the folds of my skirt with my fingertips, keeping it bunched so it drapes over my wrist and hand. With a degree of dexterity worthy of a conjurer, I craftily slide my fingers across my bare thigh, then wiggle them inside the boundary of my knicker-elastic.

Almost there. We approach the heart of the matter.

I flick at a wiry pubic curl then start to forge into the forest, searching for its hot, magic centre. As soon as I part the lips, the tips of my fingers are saturated. I'm swimming with juice, and it's a shock that there's so much, even though I knew I was pretty excited.

My clit gives a single hard deep throb as I reach it, saying 'hello' so intensely that I gasp.

I'm part horrified with myself, part bursting with excitement. I've never been much of a thrill-seeker and a risk-taker until now, but it suddenly seems as if I'm making up for lost time. I'm dancing on the edge of madness and, if I stopped to think about it, I'd probably run a mile back to the safety of the staff lunch room. But I've no time to think. I just feel.

After a tentative stroke or two, my entire body pulsates with captive energy. I'm an overflowing well of sexiness and every slight qualm I ever had about being curvy, chubby, plump or whatever you want to call it disappears. Every inch and every ounce of me is 'goddess' – just as Nemesis told me.

I gulp in breath. My legs tense and I push my heels out across the path, bracing myself. I'm desperate to climax, and even begin a little flutter – and then to my horror I hear something I've never heard here before. The sound of footsteps, swiftly approaching along the gravel.

I just manage to whip my hand out from under my skirt, and shuffle up straight into some kind of normal sitting position, when a familiar figure in tweed jacket, blue jeans and running shoes rounds the corner. It's Professor Hottie – and he's almost caught me touching myself.

'Oh, hi!' he says uncertainly. He blinks behind his spectacles and offers me a crooked, cautious smile. Then he purses his lips and darts forwards, and I have to edge along the seat. He compels me to allow him to sit down.

'I'm so glad I've found you, Gwendolynne. I was anxious to apologise to you for earlier.' He taps his long fingers against his denim-clad knee as if he's filled with unresolved energy, like me.

I'm so dumbfounded that it's difficult to grasp words from the swarm that buzz around me. But what can I say when my brain is still off in masturbation-land?

My new companion still seems acutely embarrassed and

pulls off his glasses, whips out a large pristine white handkerchief and begins to polish them with almost manic fervour.

'But why? It was me who knocked you over.' Amazingly, I've captured a few of those words. But they come out rather more abruptly than I would have liked.

He stows away the hankie, still looking ridiculously uncomfortable. Which is ironic, because it should be me who's more nervous, given how close he's sitting. Surely he can smell the musk on my fingers?

'No, I'm at fault. When I was down on the ground, I was looking at your breasts, and I know you saw me doing so. Please forgive me. It was inexcusable to ogle you that way.'

Aw, he's an old-fashioned gentleman on top of being a hunk of male pulchritude. I'm about to say 'no problemo' or something like that, but my attention's suddenly caught by his brow-crinkling frown and the way he pulls off his glasses and rubs wearily at his eyes. My sex mist clears like a shot as another sentiment grips me. I've seen him do this quite a lot in the library, as if he's bothered by eyestrain or headaches, and, even though I barely know him, I suddenly hate the thought of him suffering. Someone so gorgeous should always be able to smile.

'Are you OK, Professor Brewster? Is there something wrong? If you've got a headache I've some paracetamol in my bag.'

'No, it's nothing, thanks. I'm just tired. I've been working since early, back at my hotel, and I thought a change of scene and a change of light would buck me up a bit … but it hasn't. That was why I came out here to apologise instead of catching you in the library. I really need some air.' The frown unfurls and his beautiful eyes clear as he sets his spectacles back in place, 'And please do call me "Daniel" … I would appreciate that.'

'OK ... Daniel.' For a moment, I wish I'd not just been masturbating and that I wasn't all flustered and in a tizzy about Nemesis. There's something both sweet and perplexing about the good professor that makes me go all fluttery in a good but different way. It's like the crushes I used to have as a girl, the sweet, innocent ones before sex had ever reared its horny head. I was forever lost in daydreams of walking through flower meadows, holding hands with some sublime, unattainable hero. But the rose-tinted visions dissipate again, because the hand that romantic hero would be holding right now is all sticky from me touching myself.

And it reeks of sex. I can smell it, so Daniel surely can as well. But his handsome and every so slightly imperial nose doesn't wrinkle in the slightest. Even when he reaches for the offending hand and gives it a quick squeeze.

'I really am sorry, you know. You've been so helpful to me in the library, and I respect you as ... well, as a friend. I would hate to spoil an excellent working relationship because I've done something inappropriate.' His lips twist and he gives a little shrug. Irrational as it is, he seems really nervous, and I wonder why a man so handsome and accomplished gives the impression that he's unused to talking to a woman. Someone of his academic stature, who's been on television and has such a distinguished CV and a high profile, probably has whole battalions of groupies all ready and willing to lay down their knickers for him.

'Please don't worry about it,' I reassure him, rocked by the flash image of *me* removing *my* knickers for Daniel Brewster. What the hell is wrong with me? The fact that he seems to be shy is getting me horny now! Along with the thought of tutoring him, the great scholar, in the ways of women's lustiness ... which pushes strange sexual buttons that I didn't know I had. 'No harm done. I'm sure ... well, in fact I've got documented proof that you're far from the only man who looks at my breasts while I'm on duty in the library.'

His fine brow puckers again.

'Documented proof? Whatever do you mean?'

Uh oh, now I've done it. I'm sitting next to the very quintessence of an enquiring mind, a man used to searching out every clue and bit of background to any historical topic. To ferreting out facts from the skimpiest of sources.

In the same instant, our gazes flit to the pages of Nemesis's letter, still lying beside me on the other side of the bench from where Daniel sits. I feel as if I'm rocking on the tips of my toes on another of those precipices. The ones between behaving sensibly or doing something light-years beyond foolhardy.

Item. I barely know Daniel Brewster, and we've just had an awkward moment, skirting like a pair of fencers around the very edge of sex.

Item. This letter is tantamount to sexual harassment by a bona fide pervert, or even a deranged sex criminal. I should be careful, not flash it around indiscriminately.

Item. If I share this secret communication with another living soul, I'm betraying Nemesis. And how irrational a concept is that? I don't know the guy, and he's imposed his lust upon me. But, still, the feeling's there. I can't deny it.

Before I can think through the reasons why, I reach for the letter and hand it across.

'I received this today. If you read it, you'll realise that your accidentally enjoying a fleeting glance at my breasts is pretty mild stuff compared to what other men ... well, what *one* other man is thinking.'

He reads, and for a moment I just stare at his tapered fingertips holding the paper. Suddenly I'm all about hands, thinking of what Nemesis said he wanted me to do, and what I actually did, and what Nemesis *might* do if he got the chance to lay *his* hands on me. My heart and my gut somehow know that he doesn't mean me any real harm and that, if words were deeds, I'd only gain, not lose.

Daniel's hands are works of art. They're slender but strong-looking, hands that seem to settle into elegant, classical shapes. Every nerve-end in my body tells me that if *those* hands had a fraction of the skills that Nemesis lays claim to, they'd blow my mind, and then some, and some more. But now they're shaking as he holds those wild blue pages and reads their elegant blue script.

And not only that. He swallows repeatedly. His black brows shoot towards his hairline again. He gnaws his soft lower lip as his eyes widen and a touch of colour rises beneath his smooth skin and the delicious stubble around his jaw-line.

Like the unashamed trollop I seem to have every intention of becoming, I glance swiftly towards his groin. Life is stirring there too, burgeoning behind his zip. He's got a hard-on.

Now I've done it. Respectable librarian Gwendolynne chastises me for being unutterably stupid for starting all this, while Gwen the wannabe libertine and sensualist grins inside and thinks 'Oh boy! Oh, boy oh boy oh boy!'

Daniel shuffles the pages, apparently rereading. Or perhaps he's just unable to look up and meet my eyes? I let him carry on. Reading. Blinking. Getting harder. It just gives me more time to check out his package.

Judging by the way the denim at his crotch is bulging, he's deliciously big. As much a titan in the physical endowments department as he is in the realms of learning. As I watch, he shifts on the bench ever so slightly. I guess that he's uncomfortably positioned inside his jeans, but is fighting the urge to do something about it.

'Goodness me,' he says at length, earlobes a touch rosy again. 'When did you receive this? And how?' He folds the letter between his long fingers, eyeing it as if he's handling a rare and especially poisonous species of viper, yet is still apparently reluctant to let go of it. 'It's serious, you know … the sort of man who writes something like this could be very dangerous. It might be wise to report this to the library's security. Just to be on the safe side.'

He's right, but I'm not going to do it. And not just because I don't like being told what to do, or because those security thugs would have a field day of sniggering over it. No, it's because of my gut feeling about Nemesis: that, despite his kinkiness, he's fundamentally benign, and he genuinely likes me. OK, so maybe I am behaving too stupidly to live, but how often does a man tell you he worships and adores you?

'It was in the library's suggestion box, personally addressed to me.' I fold the sheets again, feeling a shimmer of arousal as if the very paper is drenched in an aphrodisiac. A potion that works on Daniel Brewster's loins just as it does mine. 'It was there when I opened it up at ten o'clock.'

He shifts uneasily in his seat and I watch the play of emotions on his face. There's indignation, excitement, puzzlement and perhaps, possibly, jealousy. I hide a smile. Does he wish *he'd* sent the letter? Has he been wanting to shake off his scholarly image and get frisky with me for weeks now, and he's furious because he's been beaten to the post by Nemesis? It's a delicious thought and, if true, great for my ego. He's a superstar of sorts, and I'm just a rather average, slightly overweight librarian.

'What will you do?' He gives me an intense look, eyes dark as espresso behind his elegant lenses. With a swift, agitated gesture, he sweeps a dangling black curl away from his brow.

'Well, nothing just yet. It's just one note. There may never be another.'

Now there's a thought. And one I should welcome. But instead it makes me feel deflated and depressed. There's been a scarcity of erotic excitement in my life for a long time now – in fact there never was much – but suddenly I've got a taste of it and my appetite is roaring. What will Nemesis say next? How far will he go?

'This could be a very dangerous individual, Gwendolynne.' Daniel's still frowning and edgy. But he's also still stiff behind the fly of his jeans. I sense that, as a man of reason and analysis, he's slightly cross with himself for getting turned on, and that only reinforces my fanciful idea that he might be jealous.

I wonder how he would approach a woman? And what ploys he'd use to get her into bed, or simply persuade her to allow him to touch her?

He steeples his fingertips as if he's debating with himself, and I feel like telling him he wouldn't have to try very hard with me. I'm all over his delicious, quirky male beauty and I'd succumb to him at the drop of a rare history text. No flirting, no dinner dates, no presents – none of that stuff required. Not even any saucy but delightfully poetic letters.

Shocking as it seems, I'd do him right now. If I got a chance.

'Don't worry, Daniel. I'm sure it's just a one-off. We get dodgy notes and rude pictures in the box all the time.' My fingertips tingle with the need to reach out and touch him, maybe pat his long denim-covered thigh to make my point. Yeah, right ... 'When you don't reply to the overture, they always lose interest.'

He clasps his fingers and his expression tells me he doesn't quite believe me. Or maybe it's just that he's sharp enough to read my signals and he's not sure he likes them, hard-on or no hard-on.

'Are you sure?' He heaves a sudden sigh, his chest lifting. And I know it's a very nice chest, because a week or so ago, during a brief heat-wave, he abandoned his tweedy jacket in the main lending library and just worked in a white tee-shirt that embraced his luscious pecs delightfully.

'It'll be OK. But thanks anyway. For worrying ...'

He straightens up on the seat, and somehow seems to grow from Clark into Superman.

'But you must promise me ... if there's any trouble with this ... this Nemesis, you'll call on me for help.'

He *is* Superman, and suddenly, despite the fact that I fancy him something rotten, I'm touched. And this time I *do* pat him on the thigh. And then lean over to kiss my 'thank you' on his cheek.

Well, that's what I meant to do. Instead, somehow, I miss his cheek and zero in, with pinpoint accuracy, on his lips.

At first, it's still a kiss of thanks, and Daniel's mouth is velvet-soft and quiet under mine. We're still OK. Nothing's happened. It's just a 'friend' thing and we can both get out of this without either the pink cheeks or the rosy ears of total embarrassment.

But then everything changes. In a suspiciously accomplished movement, Daniel whips off his glasses, tosses them on to the bench, and then his hands, those strong elegant hands I've been entertaining such spectacular fantasies about, come up and cup my face, fingers spread to hold my head and keep our mouths in perfect alignment.

His tongue presses against my lips, and there's nothing in the slightest bit diffident about it. As it explores and thrusts and tastes, I crumple Nemesis's letter and let it fall to the gravel, blue words on blue paper forgotten as I lift my hands to Daniel's shoulders.

His mouth tastes of peppermint as if he's been sucking Polos. I share the flavour but it's the man that's more delicious. And for someone who's projected such an image of composure and scholarly reserve all the time I've known him, he certainly knows how to kiss like a macho stud.

Attack. Retreat. Cajole. Beguile.

I'm putty in his hands, a melting heap of pumping hormones, liquefying both metaphorically and very physically between my legs. He doesn't touch any part of me other than my face, which he cradles, but he might as well have his hand inside my panties.

Me, I have less restraint and, as the mad hormonal messages ramp up and up, some of them bypass my brain completely and end up in my hand. Completely out of control, I lay my fingers across his crotch.

For a few moments, it's as if his conscious mind doesn't notice, and just his body responds, automatically pushing his erection against my touch. Then his grey cells catch up and he shoots back across the bench like a startled kitten, breaking our kiss and sending his spectacles skittering on to the gravel. He swoops over, scrabbling to find them, and we're in farce-land again.

In a flash, I'm mortified and angry, but I'm not sure who with. Me, for doing something reprehensibly stupid and forward with a man I barely know? Or with Professor Hottie for leading me on and then suddenly getting cold feet?

He blinks at me from behind his miraculously unharmed glasses, and doesn't appear to know what to say.

'Well, obviously that was a mistake of huge proportions.' I rise and swoop up my belongings – bag, water bottle, perv letter – from the ground where they've all ended up in the course of Daniel's wild retreat.

'Er . . . yes, it probably was,' he agrees softly.

Now I'm crosser than ever. I know it's mainly frustration, but still I lash out.

'So it's OK for you to look down my top and admire my cleavage, but it's not OK for me to make a move on you?'

He makes a little huffing sound, as if perplexed. He obviously does not like complications.

'That's not exactly what I meant by a mistake.' He's in control again now, although a glance downwards shows he's still perky. 'It's just that you and I have an excellent professional relationship. In the library. And I enjoy our interaction there.' He taps the tips of his fingers against each other, something that I think means he's nervous but trying to squash it. 'And I wouldn't want to spoil that or make things embarrassing for you.'

'Of course not, Professor, consider it unspoilt and me unembarrassed.'

Oh, please don't behave like a brat, Gwen. You're a grown woman, not a kiddie who's just had her lollipop stolen. I know it's a nice lollipop ... it felt heavenly to the touch ... but please act sensibly, will you?

'Good, I'm glad that's settled.' Tap, tap, tap, go the fingers, and while my wayward pussy throbs, craving their dexterity, another part of me suddenly wonders if it's all tactics, some kind of clever and devious act. 'Would you like me to walk you back to the library? Just in case?'

For a moment I wonder what the hell he's talking about, then it dawns on me. Is he concerned about me being stalked by Nemesis? Playing the chivalry card?

'No. Thanks. I'll be fine. I think I'll walk into the Cathedral Centre and do some shopping. There's no need to worry about me.'

This is doing my head in. I don't want to get involved in any more mind games. I hardly know Daniel Brewster any better than I do Nemesis. I have to get out of here.

'Right. OK. I'll see you later.'

With that, I twirl on my heel, crunching the gravel and speed away as fast as I can without actually running.

I manage fine. I get as far as the corner, and I can't hear him following me. But then I spoil everything. When I look back, he's still standing there. He should be frowning but he's actually smiling, nay, grinning. Which makes him twice as beautiful and ten times as infuriating.

And as far as I can tell he's *still* got an erection!

3 Self-indulgence Kit

Ah, my beautiful Gwendolynne ... do you have a lover? Much as I'd like to have you all to myself, I can't imagine that there isn't a man in your life. Or even men. Any male who crosses your path would get a hard-on.

It's another note. More copperplate seduction waiting for me when I got back from lunch ... As if I haven't got enough trouble.

Of course you have a lover. Why wouldn't you? And just to prove that I'm not jealous or possessive, I don't resent him at all, I just admire him for his sublime taste in women.

So, this stud of yours, does he visit you often? And do you wait for him in bed, heart beating in anticipation of a sweet new fuck? Does your delicious, trembling body warm for him and grow moist, ready for his cock?

If I were he, I'd come to you every single night. I wouldn't be able to resist. I'd let myself into your room, and pause for a moment on the threshold to savour that gut-kick moment of knowing that soon I was going to be inside you.

Ah, there you are, spread out on those satin sheets again, perhaps wearing the silk lingerie we discussed earlier. You're drowsing, dreamy, waiting ... Perhaps you're touching yourself, savouring your own readiness, your fingertips slyly tucked beneath the exquisite thong you wear? In the soft grove of your pubis there's a flowing well of moisture, oozing and silky. You rub yourself lightly, imagining the touch is mine – his – and preparing yourself. You want to be ready. Ready to rise to a swift orgasm, hungry for initial pleasure. For a delicious hors d'oeuvre to prime the sexual palate for a long banquet ahead.

As I stand at the door, welcome flares hot in your eyes, but you don't pause in your attention to your pussy. Your smile sears my loins as your fingers circle beneath the silk and lace, and you swirl your gorgeous bottom against the satin beneath you, breathlessly excited.

I beg you to allow me to approach, but for the moment you're in charge, and you forbid it. I stand at the door, every inch of my body enslaved as my cock aches and throbs. You close your eyes, locking your pleasure inside a personal, exclusive world, and as you rub faster and faster you begin to gasp and groan.

My need for you is unbearable. It's agony, like having my cock trapped in a tight iron cage. It strains in torment against the restriction of my jeans, pushing at the zip so hard my eyes start to water. Or is that just tears of joy at the rawness of your beauty, and your supreme sensuality?

As you climax, I can't hold back any longer. The sight of you is overpowering. I rush to your side, throwing myself on to the bed, stretching out alongside your writhing form, absorbing every detail of the way you move, the way you look, the creamy lustre on your skin and the adorable, agonised expression on your rapturous face.

I see everything. I see your pleasure. I see everything I want and need.

And now I must take care of myself . . . release the tension in my cock in the time-honoured way. Still seeing, in my mind, your fabulous body writhing.

Yours, Nemesis.

Crikey, this is intense stuff. I opened a bottle of wine a while back – for medicinal purposes only – and I suddenly realise I've drunk nearly half of it, mulling over this letter and the contrariness of Professor Hottie at lunchtime.

Men! They're all either perverts or control freaks or they don't really know what they want. Daniel Brewster seems to conform to all three of the above but, refreshingly, Nemesis at least seems to have some idea of what *he* wants, and he knows how to ask for it! The guy is obsessed, obviously, but I'm still getting that irrational impression that he's not just some heavy-breathing dirty-mackintosh merchant.

To compound my wine-swigging transgressions, I dive headfirst into a jumbo bag of Kettle Chips for comfort too. Stuff the diet. It's been a strange, strange day.

My bedroom is my sanctuary, and thankfully free of kitsch satin sheets. I feel both tired and energised at the same time. I have the telly on low and my self-indulgence kit all around me. Wine and crisps to feast on, a brown velveteen throw around my shoulders, and my freshly showered body all cosy in my soft, loose, brushed-cotton pyjamas.

There'd be far more creative scope for self-indulgence if I had a man beneath the duvet with me, of course, but Nemesis is only available via his perverse literary offerings, and the odds of getting Daniel Brewster here have lengthened considerably since I behaved like a complete imbecile in the garden at lunchtime, not to mention cannoning into him and flashing my boobs at him earlier.

I suppose we still might be friends, sort of, but only in the strictly-no-funny-business, professional-workplace sense.

That kiss was so ravishing and wonderful, it *ought* to have led to more. If only I hadn't grabbed his crotch ... but I just couldn't help myself. And in my defence, he did seem to be giving out signals that he wanted me to. Sticking his tongue in my mouth was a green light in anyone's language.

Bloody man, he's just as perverted and manipulative, in his

own crafty way, as Nemesis is. What about that bashful academic shtick for a start? Hell, the man's been on television enough … he must have more than his share of thespian skills.

Is *he* Nemesis?

If he is, the performance was pretty impressive. Those blushing ears – surely nobody can make that happen to order?

But then again, maybe all he has to do is imagine a picture of me with my curves just clad in sexy scraps of hot red silk?

My heart thuds hard inside my chest, and suddenly there's that strange sensation again. The reality shift from the garden. It's like a hidden door opening just a crack to show something bright and irresistible beyond it. A game. A wild game. A challenge of wits – and of sex.

It could be just a figment of my imagination but it's like nothing I've ever felt before, or even thought. I get a sense of the unreal, the surreal, as if I'd suddenly wandered into the middle of an art film or an existential novel.

But, draining my glass, I want the unreal to be real. I want an end to self-imposed ruts. I need to expand my horizons, both intellectual and sensual.

The Kettle Chips are gone now. Another appetite remains to be satisfied. With a weird canvas of Daniel Brewster and a dark faceless figure drifting in and out of focus before my eyes, I slither down in the bed and lay my hand on the rounded curve of my belly.

Now, I have time. Now, there's zero likelihood – alas – of being discovered. Now I can touch myself and do all the things I couldn't do in the library or the garden. Whether it's the truth or not, my mind coalesces Daniel and Nemesis into one totem of dazzling male fantasy.

We're back on the bench again and, wordlessly, he reaches for me, taking the hand that I'd been touching myself with in his. His eyes sly as sin behind his glasses, he raises the tips of my fingers to his lips, and then kisses them, one by one, his tongue swooping out to scour away the last remnants of my nectar. His lush, wily mouth curls archly as he conveys my hand to the stunning bulge that interrupts the smooth line of his jeans.

No flinching away like an outraged Mother Superior this time. Gently, but with authority, he folds my fingertips around the hot, sharply defined ridge, then leans back against the bench and closes his eyes. His cool, intelligent face, dark with manly stubble, relaxes. He looks like a fallen angel who's accepted the kiss of sin.

I give him a light squeeze and he drags in a long, ragged breath. I squeeze again, and his powerful hips bump upwards, inviting more attention to his cock. Unbidden, I reach for the buckle of his belt, then attack the button on his jeans. Within seconds I'm dragging down the zip, careful not to snare him. My caution was apposite, for beneath it he's bare and rampant.

His superb cock bounces into view, and my mouth first goes dry, then begins to water with sensual hunger. As does his glans. A pearly drop forms in the eye of his penis, sweet pre-come oozing to welcome and encourage me. Not daring to taste it yet, I reach for him instead, and smear the silky fluid over the hot head of his cock. The solid flesh is hard, like polished wood, the superfine skin stretched by his extreme arousal. This magnificent organ is a thing of raw, physical beauty, the very expression of primal maleness, the essence of man.

It's hard to look away from his rearing shaft but, when I do, I see his head tipped back to exhibit the heart-breaking line of his throat. He swallows hard as my thumb slowly circles, and his hands, beside him on the bench, curl into fists.

His body is a gift, a living sex toy, an object of worship. I fall to my knees on the gravel. Gravel that in fantasy is powerless to pain me. I kneel like a supplicant between his outstretched legs and go to my eager task with both hands now, intent on pleasing.

The scenario seems to shift and morph, and suddenly I'm in a darker place, an opulent room, scented with leather and lavender polish and lit by candles and the flickering glow from an open fire.

Whoa, where did this come from? It's popped into my head fully formed, perhaps materialising from images in certain books that are kept on the restricted shelves down in the library's archives. Pornographic volumes that masquerade as art photography, and are often pored over by us naughty library girls when we're shelving or cataloguing down there. The general public never get a chance to get to look at them.

I'm kneeling still, but now I'm naked – and bound, my hands behind my back so I can't touch the man I'm adoring. The heat from the banked-up fire licks over my body like a giant caressing tongue and, instead of looking up, I'm now staring at the carpet, my head bowed out of respect for my master.

My master? Am I a sexual submissive? It never occurred to me before that I might be. If asked, I would have said that was the kink furthest from my psyche.

'You may approach.'

His voice is strange, echoing, as if filtered. Is it Daniel? Or is this the way I imagine Nemesis might sound? It could be both of them, overlaid, or neither. Outside my fantasy world for a moment, I make a note to buy more of this wine I've been drinking. It's primo stuff. It packs the wildest of punches.

'On your knees.'

Tapping into knowledge from other books I've perused from time to time on the restricted shelves, I know it's important to be graceful. But that's a tough call when shuffling along on the carpet, trembling like a penitent in the grip of religious ecstasy.

He's wearing leather. A man – Nemesis? Daniel? Some other figment of my imagination? – is sitting in a great throne of a chair, his long thighs parted as Daniel's were a moment ago, but now clad in gleaming black leather jeans that are tucked into tall polished boots.

In my mind-world, I'm grovelling naked on the floor. In my real world, I'm wriggling about frantically, my hand in my pyjama bottoms, the velvet throw, the duvet and the Kettle Chips bag on the floor. I can't believe how wet I am, but suddenly noting this real, tangible manifestation of excitement disconnects me somehow. The fire-lit room fades and I moan in frustration as the orgasm I was reaching for drifts just a little way out of my reach.

'Fuck it!' I growl, and quickly roll sideways to fish around in my bedside cabinet drawer, searching for the last item in my self-indulgence kit. Ah, yes! Faithful vibe, there you are! Cheap and cheerful and effective, and, as I push down my pyjamas and slide the black plastic bullet into the red zone, my errant orgasm flits and flutters like a butterfly. Dancing from image to image, it returns to me and I sigh.

And as I lift my face from the dream carpet, and see the dream face of Daniel Brewster gazing solemnly down on me, my climax alights on the tip of my clit like a kiss of burning gold.

* * *

Being back in the library today is going to be embarrassing. Big time. The prospect of facing Professor Hottie after that kiss – and the concomitant grope – makes my ears blush ten times as pink as his did, and I haven't even set eyes on him yet.

And not only that. Even if the fumble and the kiss *don't* get my ears and cheeks simmering, how am I going to be able to look at him and not remember that I fantasised about him as I climaxed last night? Not to mention the fact that I've subconsciously assigned him – and me – a leather fetish.

It seems important to face my fears and potential embarrassment without acting like a shrinking wimp, though. It's also necessary to look hot. Or as hot as it's possible to look when you're a chubby chick in your thirties and you work in a public library.

Courting the Devil a.k.a. Nemesis, I pick a crisp white blouse that's slightly fitted and actually makes my bosom look pretty sensational in a tasteful sort of way. I team this with a slimmer skirt than usual, knee length, with a slight nineteen-fifties vibe, and, even though we can't wear heels in the library, I pick a pair of black flatties that have a classy Audrey Hepburn look.

And stockings. Yes, stockings. I don't know who these are for. Me, for my own self-esteem? Nemesis, who even now may be lurking around the corner and will probably go ballistic when he sees a hint of a suspender button through the fabric of my skirt?

Daniel, who might well pretend to cringe with embarrassment at the thought of such a suspender button and use that as an excuse to hide downstairs in the basement all day, to get away from the pathetic vamp librarian who had the effrontery to grab hold of his tackle?

The last seems likely. Our pet professor has an improvised carrel tucked away in the archives, and even though sometimes he comes upstairs and searches for items in the general lending area, and in the local collections that are available to the public, we haven't seen so much as a sniff of him so far today, and it's already halfway through the afternoon. After yesterday's debacle, it seems he's either not coming in or he's spending the day safe below ground.

Well, screw you, coward! I've got other things to occupy me.

I decide to open the suggestion box again. There was nothing in it this morning. Well, not of the flavour I was looking for.

Emptying the box involves coming round to the front of the Enquiry Desk and crouching down slightly to unlock a door in one of the wooden panels. It's all a bit antiquated in these days of computerised lending and multimedia this, that and the other, but we have a lot of older borrowers who like things traditional and old school. Being an old-fashioned girl myself a lot of the time, I know how they feel.

Anyway, dipping down as gracefully as I can, I feel as if there's a ten-thousand-watt searchlight beaming down on me. And that a thousand avid eyes, not just those of Nemesis, are greedily following my every move, my every breath, my every twist. I can almost hear a salacious collective grunt of approval as the gabardine of my skirt tightens across my bottom and outlines its well-rounded shape.

Sweat breaks out between my breasts as I reach in and pull out the wire basket. I've got one of my best bra-and-panties sets on today too. Not crimson satin, alas, just crisp white lace with delicate embroidery on the bra cups and accenting the knickers in a sort of 'Here it is! Get it here!' style. Why on earth I've gone to this trouble I don't know. Well, not consciously. My nasty subconscious is probably even now working out how

I can let slip a glimpse of this semi-fabulous underwear to Daniel Brewster – or even Nemesis, if I should happen to find out who he is.

But the contents of the basket knock the wind out of my sails. No blue envelope. Is it over so soon? All that talk about the pervs losing interest if you don't respond to them *is* true.

Oh shit, I really want this, don't I?

After locking the box again and retreating behind the desk, I stare blindly at requests for more shelving space to be returned to books and 'why do we have to have so much audio-visual crap these days instead of real literature'. Complaints about long waiting lists for the top romance authors. What about more Children's Book Club events? The usual stuff.

But it's like a foreign language, and the only tongue I want to read is the one that's written in copperplate on eggshell-blue paper. I feel like crushing all the legitimate, bona fide but irredeemably boring library communications and hurling the crumpled balls across the room at the tedious and most likely non-kinky browsers amongst the shelves.

I want excitement, something huge and breathtaking, a taste of dark compulsion I fantasised about last night. Nemesis hasn't shown that particular card yet, but my every screaming instinct says he will. Or he might have done, if I'd had the bottle to reply to him. His email address was at the bottom of each note, inviting me. But I was too chicken to answer. And now it might be too late.

I tear all the suggestions into tiny, tiny little pieces and then realise this is really not on, because we *are* supposed to read them and raise the issues at library development meetings. Will anybody discover my crime? I decide to cover it by slipping the bits into the shredded-paper recycling bags, down in the basement. I decide to raise at least some of these issues at the next meeting myself, to assuage my guilt. I jot down everything I can remember, but all the while there's the tick, tick, ticking of a compulsion gathering.

The shredded paper bags are in the basement, where the archive is. The archive is where Daniel Brewster's workstation is. If I can't have Nemesis, at least I can be proactive on the Professor McHotstuff front. He can only reject me again, and then, at least, I'll know for certain that fancying him is a dead end.

As one of the readers' advisors, I have carte blanche to secure my desk and go down to the stacks in search of books for subject requests. So I roll down the cover and walk smartly to the 'No Entry' door that leads downstairs. The Borough Library archives and the area housing the stacks are a strange place, much of it bearing no resemblance to the more modern buildings upstairs. These are cellars belonging to old houses that were bulldozed to make way for the library complex. The lighting is odd and yellowy, and there's an atmosphere part gentleman's club, part abandoned nuclear bunker. A lot of the staff don't like coming down here and will do anything to avoid it. But I'm rather fond of the place, especially lately.

Or rather I was, until, on a whim, I touched Daniel Brewster's cock.

There's old carpeting on the floor, so my steps are muffled to near silence. I discharge my ostensible reason for coming down, dumping the shredded paper and returning a couple of volumes I snatched up as a pretext. And then I pause, trying to frame a cheery greeting and a light, throwaway reference to yesterday that will get us over the hump of awkwardness and back on to a more promising path towards, well, towards something.

Daniel's carrel is empty. But he's been here, and he's clearly coming back. His tweed jacket is hung on a hook on the end of one of the stacks. Precious texts on the Wars of the Roses are lying open across the broad wooden table. You would think as a historian he'd be a touch more respectful of such rare tomes, but maybe he's got other things on his mind, eh?

There are also a lot of sheets of handwritten notes scattered hither and thither, along with two newspapers, each open at the crossword and Sudoku page. His high-end laptop is glowing with what looks suspiciously like a solitaire battleship game, rather than a learned treatise. Curiously, there are not one but two large magnifying glasses, set atop a heap of computer printout, and as well as a couple of roller-balls and some pencils there's a rather beautiful fountain pen lined up beside an open stenographer's notepad.

Fountain pen?

The area is awash with more light than illuminates the whole of the rest of the archive. Not for this scholar the ancient practice of scribbling and squinting by flickering candlelight. Several high-watt Anglepoise lamps shed clear bluish light provided by special daylight bulbs. Professor Hottie likes things bright and easy to see.

So do I. But where the hell is he? Probably ferreting about at the far end of the long complex of smaller archive rooms. So I take the risk of drawing closer and taking a better look at his things.

And the handwriting of the notes.

I don't know what I was expecting, but it's not a bit like the elegance of Nemesis's lettering. It's quite sharp, large and vigorous, expressing a hugely confident intelligence in its author. And the bits that are written by fountain pen are in black ink, not blue.

The archive is almost silent apart from the occasional tiny chatter of the laptop's hard disk and the distant humming of electricals, and the air is heavy with the weight of knowledge and dust. But suddenly I detect something else. A distinct buzzing sound. It's almost exactly the same pitch as my vibrator and instantly my mind presents the weirdest of pictures. Has Professor Hottie got a secret vice he indulges in, down here in the bowels of learning? Or maybe I'm not the only member of the library staff who's leading the life of a clandestine pervert?

Either way, I've got to know what's going on. It's blindingly foolhardy, and there's the potential for stunning embarrassment, both for me and for whoever's buzzing, but, walking on fairy-footed tiptoes, I steal in the direction of the noise. It's coming from the tiny and rather shabby washroom. It used to be a staff loo but now we have newer and far nicer facilities upstairs. It's handy, though, when you're shelving in the stacks for an extended period.

I inch forwards until I can see round the corner. Judging by the sound, whoever's in there has left the door open. And then I have to cram my knuckles in my mouth to stop myself squeaking like a startled mouse. Daniel Brewster is standing in front of the rust-spotted mirror, running a battery razor back and forth along the line of his jaw. He's leaning over the sink, barely a couple of inches from the glass, peering intently at his reflection and frowning hard. Nothing unusual about this, apart from the location – and the fact that he's standing there stark naked.

Dear Lord in Heaven, he's beautiful!

Unaware of my scrutiny, he stands relaxed, his limbs elegant, loose, almost classical. His form is muscular and compact, not an inch of spare flesh on him, and there's a delightful little tangle of dark hair adorning his chest.

My eyes skitter from one to another of his body's charms, almost painstakingly avoiding the place they really want to look. But eventually, of course, I succumb. And his cock is just as beautiful as the rest of him. Hanging soft and unaroused, it's still impressive, and swings meatily against his thigh as he steps back and puts the razor out of sight.

I have to flatten myself against the plastered wall to keep from inching forwards and maybe revealing my presence. I feel just like Nemesis, observing the object of my fantasies and willing the imagined vision not to evaporate. But the reality of Daniel Brewster's nudity far exceeds any of the day and night dreams I've been entertaining about it since he arrived here. My heart thuds and bashes about, and I'm half afraid that, even if I don't move a muscle or breathe ever again, he'll still detect its tremendous clamour in my chest.

With a little sigh, he runs water into the sink, and then sets about giving himself what my dear old mum would have described as a 'strip wash'. He rubs a soapy flannel all over his arms and shoulders and torso, then rinses the cloth out and wipes away all traces of lather.

Then he soaps the flannel again and applies it to his genitals. At first he's just getting clean. But after a few moments, and inevitably, I suppose, all that changes. Under the ministrations of the flannel, his penis begins to lengthen and thicken, rising up. With a grunt he tosses the washcloth into the water and takes himself properly in hand. His smooth, freshly shaven jaw tenses as he manipulates his cock with his fingers, pushing and pulling in long strokes, working the fine, rapidly blushing skin over the hard, blood-filled core that keeps on swelling.

Fully erect, he's astonishing, magnificently fulfilling the promise I felt yesterday, when I touched him through his jeans.

He breathes deeply, raggedly, his fine chest heaving as he

really throws himself into his pleasure. With his free hand bracing himself on the sink, he pitches forwards, pressing his forehead against the mirror. I can see his lips moving, but I can't hear what he's saying for the hammering of my heart.

His body is like a perfect engine and he's pumping it, priming it. I send up a silent prayer of thanks when he adjusts his position, widening his stance for stability, and presents me with an even better view of his erection and his hand upon it. Up and down, up and down, he's merciless with his own flesh. He rubs his forehead against the mirror as his corded thighs flex and work in time to his masturbation.

I wonder how long he can keep this up. I certainly can't last much longer. Not without whipping up my skirt and pushing my hand into my panties to share his gasping ritual by rubbing at my clitoris. My sex feels wide and wet, as if welcoming the beautiful male organ just a few yards away. I clasp my crotch, cupping it hard through my skirt, and just as I'm about to reach for my hemline Daniel lets out a broken groan ... and comes.

Semen spurts out of him, shooting from his tip in intense little jets that splatter on the porcelain pedestal and slide down it like liquid pearls. He seems to go on and on, as if he's been abstinent for weeks, even months, and only now has he been forced to seek release. His face is agonised yet celestial and his voice is desperate as he swears and snarls, wordless and incoherent.

I don't know what to think or how to react. I barely *can* think. I'm dumbstruck, thunderstruck, mind-struck. This is the most erotic thing I've ever seen, so perfect and intimate it's dazzling.

It's too much. My head reeling, I back away as fast as I can without making any commotion. But as I reach the corner I trip and scuff my shoe and the sound seems enormous, resounding through the entire basement, even though really it's tiny. I spin and launch myself towards the stairs, up to the world of normality, but not before an image imprints itself momentarily on my eyes: Daniel's head coming up, turning, following the sound.

Has he seen me? I hurtle up the stairs, issues of sound forgotten. I must get out into the library as fast as I can. I burst out of the door to the archive and nearly run into Tracey, carrying an armful of fiction.

'You all right?' Her eyes are wide as I stand there, panting. I'm not out of breath from running, but from the impact of what I've seen.

'Yeah ... well, no, bit of claustrophobia, I think,' I babble, as she frowns in concern. 'I'm usually fine down there, but it's hotter than usual somehow.' I fan my face, and it's not for effect. I must be bright pink, and I'm convinced my ears are far rosier than Daniel's have ever been. The image of his penis, also rosy, makes me sway on my feet.

'Look, why don't you take five in the staff room?' Tracey shifts her books to one arm and pats me on mine. 'I'll keep an eye on the desk for a bit. Nobody will mind.'

She's a kind soul, and I take advantage of her offer. But it's not the staff room I rush to. I pile into the ladies' cloakroom and lock myself in the nearest stall, the disabled persons' cubicle. As I collapse on to the lowered lid of the loo, I realise that I'm still breathing heavily.

Did he see me? And if he did, do I even care, right at this moment? All I want to do is bring myself off, release the tension, come as he did. I haul up my skirt and thrust my hand into my panties. No niceties. No slow build-up. This is desperation. Does Nemesis do himself as urgently as this when he's watched me in the library?

It doesn't take long. I rub roughly, messily, slipping around in a great puddle of silkiness, parading stark images through my head at the same time. Daniel's hand on his cock. His heart-stopping profile as he grimaces. Semen, jetting, jetting, jetting.

I roll my head to one side, my own neck arching back as I come, riding the heavy, wrenching pulses.

Afterwards, I feel like a wrung-out dishcloth and it takes a long time for me to compose myself. And to clean myself up too. I mop ineffectually at my crotch with damp toilet tissue, trying to get rid of the telltale smell of my arousal. But that only gets me going again, and I rise to another quick, hard, guilty and not entirely satisfactory orgasm, biting my lips and wishing suddenly that I'd never gone downstairs in the first place.

It's quite a while before I return to Lending, and Tracey swoops in on me to see if I'm OK.

'I'm fine now,' I lie. 'Just needed a drink of water and a breather. It can get so stuffy down there in that hellhole.'

'I thought you liked it?' Tracey gives me a sly smile. 'I thought you liked the view?'

It's well known that I fancy Professor Hottie, but then, so do most of the female staff. And even one of the male staff too.

'I do, normally, but he wasn't around.' More blatant lies. 'Maybe it was disappointment that made me come over all funny?'

We chat for a moment more, then I see a rather uncertain-looking old gentleman approach the Enquiry Desk. Duty calls. What follows is one of those classic library misunderstandings. In a rather wavering voice he asks to be pointed towards books on 'rearing carnations'. Or at least that's what it sounds like. But when I lead him to our well-stocked gardening section, and find *Cultivating Carnations* by Reginald Blair, the pensioner looks at me uncomprehendingly, blinking in confusion. I'm not quite sure what's going on either, until, after closer questioning, it transpires that he's actually seeking info on 'reincarnation'. The mysticism and spirituality shelves yield exactly what he wants, and his effusive and rather sweet thanks are genuinely touching. It's all a good distraction for me, and I feel the simple glow of professional satisfaction as we return towards the desk with a clutch of books to check out. I tell him there's always the library's request system if he can't find exactly what he wants in this haul.

But the happy-librarian glow instantly dissipates, to be replaced by all sorts of other smoulderings, when I see Daniel Brewster standing waiting there, right in front of the suggestion box.

Even though the image of him naked and masturbating is now probably forever seared on the inside of my brain casing, the clothed Daniel is still quite a sight. Especially as he seems to be dressed up for some kind of gala event. Gone is the tweed and denim, replaced by a very, very sharp midnight-blue suit and a matching tone-on-tone shirt and tie combo. His crazy black hair is somewhat tamed, and he's holding his briefcase and has a dark mackintosh over one arm. Which makes sense. He was obviously having a wash and brush-up downstairs in preparation for going somewhere straight from the library, bout of self-abuse notwithstanding.

He appears to be waiting for someone and, when he turns my way and his dark eyes warm, it seems to be me. My face flames. He saw me! He knew I was watching! And yet his own face is composed, open and confident. There's nothing in his expression to suggest he knew he was being watched. He seems perfectly untroubled by anything that's happened today. Or even yesterday.

'Hello, Gwendolynne. You're looking very nice today. I like your hair like that.'

Compliments? Social niceties? What's going on? Even if he didn't see me watching him, that farcical little interlude yesterday should make this apparently casual meeting at least a little awkward.

'Thanks ... I thought I'd try a change.' I'd almost forgotten that I decided to do my hair differently this morning, another pathetic ploy to have an effect on either Nemesis or Daniel. It's still fastened back, but in a lower bunch, off to one side and more loosely. And I've left a few tendrils curling around my face. I was going for something a tad more sultry to contrast with the businesslike blouse and skirt.

I start blushing for a quite innocent reason, the simple female pleasure of being politely admired. But moments are ticking on, and I realise I've got to say something.

'You're looking very smart yourself, Professor Brewster. Are you going out somewhere?'

His sudden smile is a picture, and bizarrely it's almost as exciting in its own way as his naked body was. He touches his hair compulsively as if he's not used to being so gussied up. Even when he's been on television he's usually looked quite casual.

'I'm speaking at a dinner. I'm just waiting for my taxi.' He stares down at the polished toes of his shoes, then looks up again, making me realise that something else is different. No glasses today.

'What happened to your specs? Don't you need them when you're not working?'

A strange, almost angry expression flits across his face for a moment and his mouth twists. What have I said?

'I need them all the time, more or less, I'm afraid.' His voice sounds odd, flat. 'But I've got my contacts in tonight. Better for the old image, don't you know.' The crimp in his lips softens and he gives me a grin, as if embarrassed by his own vanity.

What the hell would he say if he knew I'd seen him naked? I'm convinced now that he doesn't know he was watched.

He smiles wider, gives a little shrug.

'Look, I'm sorry about yesterday lunchtime. I was abrupt and far too prissy. I shouldn't have been "off" with you.' His voice drops to a whisper and becomes quite thrilling. All the nerves that have just been settled by my session in the cloakroom start to quiver again. 'That was a delicious kiss. I really enjoyed it.'

Shiny behind their invisible lenses, his eyes glitter.

'Me too' is all I can manage.

His look is so intense I almost feel faint, and in its depths strange messages shift and flow. Is it him? Is he Nemesis? I find myself wondering again, and I feel a flutter of fear in my chest that he could be so clever and so devious and such a bloody good actor.

He checks his watch. 'Taxi'll be here any minute, and I won't be back until late. But maybe we could have coffee or something tomorrow? Or a drink? Or lunch?'

Crikey, is Professor Hottie asking me out for a date?

'Cool, that'd be great.' Don't sound so enthusiastic, Gwen!

'And, before I forget, I meant what I said about those letters. You must be careful. If any more arrive and you're worried about them, give me a call, won't you?' He whips out an austere white business card with his contact numbers on it.

'Thanks, but they don't worry me. Not really. I think he's pretty harmless.'

'Are you sure? I don't want you to do anything foolish.' His voice drops low, and he seems just about to say something else when there's the toot of a horn from the library's forecourt. 'That's my cab. Time to go. I'll see you tomorrow.' He reaches out, touches my arm, and even through my blouse his fingers feel as if they're made of flame. 'And remember, be careful. It's often the quiet and apparently harmless ones who turn out to be the most dangerous.'

He turns and walks away, but just before he reaches the main door of the lobby he looks back. Did he just wink? Surely not ... I must be imagining things.

4 Contact

Was it a wink or wasn't it? And if it was one, what did it mean? That he was acknowledging he'd sounded a bit pompous? That he knew I'd seen him downstairs, naked and masturbating? That he's actually Nemesis and he's fully aware that I suspect him?

It could be all of those or none of them. It could be just *me* that's imagining things. It seems to be my normal mode right now. But I do need to find out more about Professor Daniel Brewster if I'm to go out with him, either seriously or just as friends, with a unilateral no-crotch-grabbing policy.

I'm in bed again now. It's late. I can't sleep. So I fire up my trusty laptop for some Googling. Surprisingly for someone who's been on the telly, he has no personal website. There's just a page at the site of the University from which he's currently on sabbatical, but even that's simply a bare-bones bio, basic contact info and an impressive list of his qualifications and honours.

But further down the first page of search results, I hit pay dirt: a fan site for Professor Hottie groupies! I pour myself another glass of wine and dig in.

There's a treasure trove of photos, most of them screen-caps from his three television series. And whoever runs the site is a wizard with the capture software, because in most shots he looks far more like a pin-up than a professor. Here, his shirt has come slightly unbuttoned, and there's a hint of his delicious dark chest hair. Here, his sleeves are rolled up, showing his muscular arms. Here, he's actually wearing shorts, wahey! And here, the way he's standing, with one foot up on the tumbled blocks of some historical ruin, shows his elegant chinos stretched tight across his package.

Swigging a mouthful of supermarket plonk, I wonder vaguely if I'm turning into an alcoholic, drinking two nights on the trot. I wonder how the besotted girlies who've put this site together would react if they'd seen what I saw this afternoon? They'd probably expire of ecstasy on the spot. I wasn't far from it myself, and I'm starting to veer in that direction again right now, just from thinking about it. I try to put it out of my mind, and start clicking on other pages in the site. Soon I'm feeling almost as dirty and voyeuristic as I did this afternoon. Where have they dug all this personal info up from? Doesn't anyone have any secrets these days?

What a hypocrite I am. This is just the sort of intimate background skinny that I'm after. According to the 'dating history' page, Daniel doesn't have a girlfriend at the moment. Unable to stop myself, I check the 'date last updated' and see it's only a few weeks old. I shouldn't be sighing with relief, because I don't seriously believe there can be anything between us . . . but I am.

But he has had a rather colourful series of relationships. Lots of beautiful and quite high-profile women have succumbed to his charms, the most notable Larena Palmer, a socialite with whom he lived for several years, and whom he was expected to marry. I wonder how hurt he was when she ditched him for the son of a duke and became part of the landed gentry? Horrible bitch! How could she?

Am I feeling sorry for him? I think of my own defunct marriage. I was glad to be out of it, really, because once we got back from our honeymoon my ex-husband quickly developed the annoying habit of believing he was right and telling me what to do all the time. But it still stings a little to have failed in something that once meant so much to me. Frowning, and not sure whether it's over my own relationship history or Daniel's, I turn away from the screen and top up my glass. No alcohol tomorrow, and that's a promise.

The family background proves interesting too. His mother was a brilliant scientist, as much a luminary in her field as her son is in his. But she gave it all up, ditching her career to nurse his father when he became ill with a chronic condition. There's a picture of her with Daniel and, even though it's a candid, it's acutely revealing. Her face is sad and lost, even though she's trying to smile, and the expression is somehow reflected in her son's, as if he comprehends the bitter impact of her sacrifice.

He's got issues. Stuff in his life that's scarred him. People like that do strange things. But are they quite as strange as sending secret, floridly erotic letters to women they barely know, and then bluffing denial?

I flick back to the Uni site and click the email link. Does he still check this one? Will he answer if I mail him? Thunderbird opens and immediately I close the new message window. No, I'm not going to email him. It's too risky because when I'm online I have a nasty habit of saying far more than I mean to.

My glass of wine calls to me, and so does the strangest little frisson of fear-slash-excitement. I click 'check mail'. A couple of spam messages and a newsletter from Amazon arrive, and then …

'You have a message from Nemesis.'

It just sits there, almost pulsating on the screen. I go hot and cold, terrified for a moment, wondering how he's found me, and then I realise it's come via a social networking site I signed up to a month or two ago and never did anything with. If Nemesis is obsessed enough with me to leave me erotic love notes in the library's suggestion box, he's certainly going to search for me on the likes of MySpace and Facebook, isn't he?

Maybe I should just delete it. It might be safer. Even if Daniel and Nemesis *are* the same person, to engage in direct contact with his 'dark' side is just getting in too deep. Far too deep.

I open the email and click the link because I'm just certifiable and far too curious to resist. I find myself in the networking site's message centre, staring at a link saying 'Hello, Gwendolynne', flanked by an avatar that's just a picture of a quill pen. A historical writing implement for a historian who writes secret notes?

The 'online now' legend is showing. There's still a chance to step back. I don't have to click this link either. I can always check the box beside it then click 'delete' . . . can't I?

Telling myself 'No! No! No!', I open the message. Bracing myself for more of the deliciously purple prose in the letters, I look away from the screen. But when I turn back, I simply see a button to open an instant message system and the 'N3m3sis' email address I already know.

I feel as if there's a vortex in my chest, whirling madly. I can't, I just can't 'talk' to him in real time. That really *is* getting in too deep, and far too soon. Well, for me . . . He's probably gagging for it!

I click the email link and Thunderbird springs to life again, a new message open with 'him' in the recipient line.

Hello? I type, then reach for my wine again, staring at the white expanse of the open message window. I take a few sips, deliberately keeping my hands clear of the touchpad and the keyboard. I can still hold back. But my glass is empty and, taking a deep breath, I click 'send'. Too late, it dawns on me I've sent it from my personal email address, so he'll *know* it's from me. If I'd half a brain cell I would have used a more anonymous Hotmail or Google identity. Stupid! Stupid! Stupid! I feel like slamming shut my laptop and never opening the bloody thing again. Now I've done it.

Heart fluttering, I shove the lappie to one side on the bed, leap out and run to the bathroom. I'm such a coward. I squat on the loo, pee, blot myself – and instantly feel a keen jolt of pleasure. I'm running a river, I'm so aroused. How the hell did that happen? I wasn't even aware of it. I consider doing something about it, but I sense the computer waiting. Waiting as if Nemesis is in the room and tapping his fingers, impatient with my craven wimpishness.

On my return, I find that Thunderbird has automatically checked for new mail and there's a reply. I hardly dare open it but, when I do, there's the link for the instant messenger again, and the words.

Afraid to 'speak'?

Not giving myself a chance to falter, I send a reply saying '*no*' and open the IM software in a full-screen window.

And here's the quill-pen icon again, and mine, a very unimaginative picture of a book alongside my handle 'librarygirl'.

The cursor flashes and flashes. Has he got cold feet? I start to type.

LIBRARYGIRL: Are you there?

Still nothing, so I pour more wine. Obviously he's all talk and no action. I don't think Nemesis and Daniel can be the same person, after all. Professor Hottie may be a lot of things, but he doesn't strike me as a coward.

Then the connection icon starts to flicker ... and here it is.

NEMESIS: Hello, Gwendolynne. How delightful to actually speak to you at last. I've been waiting so long for this moment.

Is this a clue? Is he a library regular who's been fantasising about me for months and only just escalated to putting pen to paper and fingers to keys? Now that *is* really scary.

LIBRARYGIRL: How long?

NEMESIS: Since I first saw you, delicious one. Since I first saw you and my cock stood to attention at the sight of your gorgeous body.

LIBRARYGIRL: Really? And how long is that?

There's another aching pause, and I realise that I'm holding my breath. I drag in a great gasp, feeling light-headed, spaced and unreal.

NEMESIS: Now that would be telling. Let's say plenty long enough for me to become utterly besotted with you.

A pause.

NEMESIS: Long enough not to be able to count the nights that I've masturbated myself to sleep dreaming of you beside me . . . naked.

Uh oh, here we go.

NEMESIS: Or perhaps I should say beneath me and naked?

The minute it appears on the screen, I want it. It's been too long since I've had actual sex, rather than just playing with myself or using my vibrator. Bed wasn't especially spectacular with my husband, but it wasn't all bad, and a girl can compensate with fantasies. But now I feel as if I've been zapped by lightning. It dawns on me that Nemesis is pretty much what I was fantasising about all along while I was having sex with my ex-husband: a dark, mysterious, faceless lover who may or may not be real. Suddenly it doesn't matter all that much *who* he is. It's the fantasy I'm connecting with, not the reality.

I smile, ready to enjoy myself. All my fear, or most of it, has been melted by the gathering excitement, both mental and physical.

LIBRARYGIRL: So, who are you, Nemesis? Are you afraid to tell me?

There's another long pause, but somehow I know he's smiling too. Along with the horniness, he feels the same sense of challenge that I do.

NEMESIS: Not afraid . . . just reluctant to explode the game so soon.

Now it's my turn to make him wait. Should I push or hold back? Dare all or hedge my bets? My chest feels as if I'm having a mild apoplexy or something. I press my hand to my breastbone, as if that might settle my heart.

LIBRARYGIRL: Fair enough, but did I see you in the library today? Did you see me?

Vague enough. And a miracle of self-restraint, considering the question 'Are you Daniel Brewster?' is careening around in my brain.

NEMESIS: You saw me. I saw you. You looked magnificent. Elegant. An icon of groomed, professional sexiness. I wanted to fall to the floor, kneel at your feet, and then slide your skirt up and rub my face against your stocking tops, while I breathed in your perfume and the scent of your cunt.

If he goes on like this, I'll be able to breathe it in myself. In fact, I already can. I'm welling and flowing again, all damp and silky. I wish he was here, whoever he is. I see that image of a masked man again. Mysterious and threatening. Deceiving.

That image of him kneeling before me is just a mind trick. Submissive is the last thing on earth he is.

LIBRARYGIRL: You want to worship me?

As the cursor blinks, I imagine a dark figure rising to his

feet and then looming over me. In my mind he's wearing black, and that mask – it's leather and covers a lot of his face, reminding me of an executioner's hood and just as menacing.

NEMESIS: Sometimes . . .

Oh, what a wealth of promise in that single word. My mind is populated with images from the 'forbidden' photography books, and imagined scenes from the erotica I've read. Nemesis surely lives right up to his forbidding title, even though in mythology the name belonged to an avenging female goddess. He seems combative, dominant, out for some kind of retribution, although for what I really don't know. Maybe for all that fantasising. I suppose I was cheating on my hubby by not thinking about him while we were in bed.

LIBRARYGIRL: And what do you want to do with me at the other times?

NEMESIS: I want you to obey me . . . to allow me to educate you and expand the horizons of your experience and sexuality.

Bingo!

LIBRARYGIRL: Why would I want to do that? What if I like my horizons where they are now? What if I know more than you think I know?

NEMESIS: I think we'll both find there's much, much more to learn when we get going. You're enjoying yourself now, aren't you?

Pause.

NEMESIS: And I've managed to get you to obey me tonight by engaging in this conversation. When I'll wager the whole idea of it runs counter to your quiet-living librarian's good sense.

LIBRARYGIRL: Who says I'm quiet-living? I could be a raver

and have dozens of boyfriends and masses of sex all the time.

Just how much does he know about me? Has he been spying on me outside the library? Is he a *real* stalker?

NEMESIS: Well then, I just hope those dozens of men realise exactly how lucky they are. Will you obey me?

I'm trembling. I'm aching. I've never felt this excited. My nipples are so tight and erect they're almost sore, and my pyjama bottoms are wet through at the crotch, almost as if I've peed myself.

NEMESIS: Will you obey me?

The repetition reminds me I'm dithering. The remnants of what he quaintly calls my librarian's good sense are dying embers, ready to be rekindled by a 'Bring it on!' But I don't give in that easily. The defiance of a lifetime doesn't die in the space of a single online chat.

LIBRARYGIRL: Yes . . . but how will you know? If you told me to do something right now, how would you know I've done it? It's not as if I've got a webcam.

Which is, thankfully, true. If I were to see him, and him me, this would disintegrate. It's the anonymity – or the pretend anonymity if it *is* Daniel – that's so thrilling.

NEMESIS: Trust, my dear. I'll take it on trust. Which puts the onus on *you* not to cheat.

I close my eyes for a moment and seem to see his, framed by that mask. They're dark and glittering and playful. I wish I could draw so I could record their dangerous beauty.

LIBRARYGIRL: I'm not a cheater.

Ah, but I am one, and I'm such a liar too, considering all that fantasy cheating on my husband.

NEMESIS: I believe you. Now, what are you wearing?

I purse my lips. It's the old, old phone-sex/cybersex ploy and I'm almost disappointed in him. But not quite. Shall I fib?

I'm getting so excited and nervous I could explode. I'm like melted toffee boiling over on the stove, and almost literally so between my legs. I decide to compromise. Tell a bit of the truth, but with a bit of misdirection. After all, he's barely giving me anything from his side of the puzzle.

LIBRARYGIRL: Silk pyjamas . . . red. Very slinky.

Actually, they're brushed cotton and blue-and-white-striped.

NEMESIS: Ah, a secret seductress . . . fond of silk and satin . . . I was right about you. Imagining the exotica beneath your oh so appropriate attire in the library. You're making me hard, very hard . . . but I expect you realise that, don't you?

Ah hah, so he's not quite the mindreader or remote viewer I was so afraid of. I have a small advantage over him, a bargaining chip in the game. We're *both* fooling around with each other. And I like it.

LIBRARYGIRL: Well, I was kind of hoping you *were* hard, otherwise there's not much point to this, is there?

Silence for a minute.

NEMESIS: We could just be friends . . .

He follows it with a smiley face.

LIBRARYGIRL: But with extras?

NEMESIS: LOL Of course . . . Are you wet?

I was close to saturated almost before we started.

LIBRARYGIRL: Yes.

NEMESIS: Oh yummy! I thought you might be. Tell me how wet. Are you seeping all over your pyjamas? Is your luscious honey running down into the crack of your bottom?

I let out a moan. I can't help myself. My juice *is* running down. It's overflowing my pussy, like the nectar of a flower, brimming and oozing. I move slightly, adjusting the laptop across my thighs, and a trickle slides into the crease between the back of my thigh and my bottom. I've never been so wet before in my life.

LIBRARYGIRL: I'm very wet. There's a big damp patch in the seat of my pyjamas and it's trickling down. I can feel it on the insides of my thighs.

I hesitate only a fraction of a second.

LIBRARYGIRL: Does that make you even harder?

In my mind, I hear a soft, very masculine laugh, and the lips beneath the imagined leather hood curve into a smile that's half sultry, half menacing.

NEMESIS: Of course it does. You know it does. And you're getting above yourself, Ms Sexy Librarian.

Now that should make me annoyed, indignant. But it doesn't, it just makes me hotter and more sexualised than ever. My pussy feels pouched, puffy, wide. Needy. I edge my thighs apart, wishing I could shove the laptop aside and just communicate with Nemesis by telepathy, untrammelled by electronics and technology.

I wish he was here so he could reach down and touch my clit.

LIBRARYGIRL: What about you? What's your cock like? Are you big?

I feel as if I could say anything to him, and yet at the same time I'm actually liking this sense of being under his control. I feel as if my personality is splitting into two, the way his must have done, and the idea of being both real and a fantasy figure makes me feel giddy and lightheaded.

NEMESIS: And still you push me, Gwendolynne. You're a very daring and stimulating woman. If I describe my cock to you, I'll expect you to pay a fair price . . . do you understand that?

My heartbeat races again, and I press myself down against the mattress. I'm saturating my pyjamas *and* the sheet now, but I couldn't care less.

LIBRARYGIRL: Yes. I do. I understand. That's fair.

NEMESIS: Very well then.

He pauses and I imagine him looking down at his own body, formulating the words to describe it. I wonder if he's like a lot of men – prone to skewed assessments and exaggeration when it comes to his precious equipment.

NEMESIS: I'd classify myself as 'presentable'. Not humungous, but I'm happy with what I've got and the way it works. And I love the way it feels when I touch myself and think about you. The way it feels now . . .

The vision of Daniel in the washroom floats before me with aching clarity, then somehow gets jumbled with the man in the leather mask. I see Daniel in a leather mask, naked on a bed, working himself furiously, writhing on the very same white silk sheets Nemesis raved about in his letter. And Daniel is more than presentable.

But one thing doesn't compute. I'm having trouble combining typing with the grinding, gouging urge to touch myself. How the devil is Nemesis managing?

LIBRARYGIRL: How can you type and toss yourself off at the same time?

NEMESIS: LOL.

LIBRARYGIRL: No, seriously. I'm having trouble here, so you must be as well.

NEMESIS: Perhaps I'm using voice-activated software. Have you considered that?

LIBRARYGIRL: You mean like VOIP? Voice chat? Is that what you want?

The cursor blinks and blinks. Suddenly I don't want that. Hearing his voice will dissolve the suspense. If it's Daniel, or someone else I've had a face-to-face with in the library, I'll know them, and this weird game will be over. And not knowing, even if I have my suspicions, is somehow freeing. I know I can say anything to Nemesis while I don't know who he is, whereas if I *did* know I'd clam up. The magic might disappear, and I might not even *want* to play any more.

NEMESIS: Perhaps, some day . . . but not yet. I rather like these little pauses when I can't touch myself. It cranks up the anticipation, and makes the touches all the more pleasurable when they occur.

For a moment, I almost stop thinking about sex, and sense the intimation of something deeper, more profound. A different communication. Synchronous thinking . . .

LIBRARYGIRL: Yes! That's how I feel!

NEMESIS: Good. I thought you'd understand. But now it's time for you to pay that price I mentioned. You hadn't forgotten it, had you?

LIBRARYGIRL: No. Go ahead. Do your worst.

Again, I hear that strange, soft, anonymous laughter in my head. It's a voice but not a voice, yet so real that it's like the stroke of a feather across the tip of my aching clitoris. My pussy flutters and I squash myself down again while I wait for Nemesis's 'price'.

NEMESIS: Remove your pyjama bottoms. I want to know that your pussy is exposed. Available to me if I were there with you. I like that. I like the idea of it being constantly at my disposal, always touchable. At my command.

I can't breathe. My head feels as if it's lighter than air. It's a sort of faintness, but not faintness, as if I've drunk the whole bottle of wine without any ill effects and only the dreamy, liberating, intoxicating ones. My sex throbs hard, acknowledging its master.

NEMESIS: Gwendolynne? Are you ready to obey me?

LIBRARYGIRL: Yes, I'm doing it now.

NEMESIS: Good girl. Your sex belongs to me. Bare it for me.

I *am* in too deep now! Shoving the laptop aside, I wriggle

out of my pyjama trousers. The crotch is soaked and I can feel dampness beneath me on the sheet. My pussy is flowing for its master. I look down at the flossy little patch of tawny hair, then close my eyes as if I can send the image of it across the ether to Nemesis.

I know he's waiting to hear from me but I feel rude and wanton. I want to play. The area between my legs is my toy as well as his. I haul up my knees and part my thighs wide so I can see more. See the glistening, peachy redness, my lips and my clit and the inner cleft, awash with juice.

Here it is! See it! It's yours, I call to him silently, stretching wider. Constrained not to touch his possession until he gives me leave, I reach beneath my pyjama jacket and touch my nipples instead.

Mistake. Stroking my breasts only does diabolical things to my clit. It swells, throbs, engorges. Tears squeeze out of the corners of my eyes and I pinch my nipples to punish myself. Moaning aloud, making noises I can't remember ever making before, I turn to the side and see the screen.

NEMESIS: Gwendolynne?

In acute discomfort, I twist around and start typing.

LIBRARYGIRL: Sorry. I . . . I got too excited. My pussy is bare now.

NEMESIS: Did you touch it? You know that I've not yet given you permission. I shall be disappointed in you if you've anticipated my instructions.

I gasp. I'm drowning in desire, aching to come, but the idea of disappointing Nemesis crushes me.

LIBRARYGIRL: No! I didn't touch my pussy. I wanted to . . . I'm aching to . . . I don't think I can last much longer . . . but I *didn't* do it.

My body arches of its own accord, tormented by denial. I scream silently for permission as I feel more juice sliding down my cleft, coating the delicate tissues there and flowing into the groove of my bottom.

NEMESIS: But you did do something.

I could swear that he's watching me, but I don't have a webcam. Perhaps he just knows me better than I know myself?

LIBRARYGIRL: I played with my nipples. Next best thing.

He smiles. In my mind. I just see a mouth, strong and sculpted, but also lush. White teeth glinting. Absolute joy. I see a naked man leaning over my body, beautiful tousled dark hair hanging over my thighs and belly. It's Daniel because he's the only naked man I've seen recently. His lips are pursed.

NEMESIS: Perhaps in some ways the same. Still a transgression. One day, perhaps, I'll make you come without touching your clit. I'll toy with your nipples until you're beside yourself. I'll touch everything but your pussy . . . and then when you're halfway off your head with frustration I'll blow on your clit . . . and then you'll come.

Right! That's it! I've had enough!

Or nowhere, nowhere near enough. I clamp my hand to my pussy and dive in with my middle finger. It takes just two rough strokes and I'm coming like an express train, momentarily blind, deaf and dumb, unable to think of anything but the white heaven between my legs. I flail wildly and the side of my hand strikes the edge of the laptop screen. There's a twinge of pain, but it's a thousand miles away and can't touch me.

Seconds or maybe minutes later, I'm still gasping. My chest heaves like a bellows and my pussy still feels as if it's in another place entirely. I fight to focus, and blink to see the laptop screen. Amazingly I haven't shattered it in my transports of ecstasy, and in the chat window words glare at me accusingly.

NEMESIS: What are you doing, Gwendolynne?
They repeat and repeat.
NEMESIS: What are you doing, Gwendolynne?
NEMESIS: What are you doing, Gwendolynne?

5 Forfeit

It's the next day and it's as if I've got a hangover. But not from booze. I didn't drink all that much wine. No, it's a new phenomenon – a sex hangover. I've got the same sort of vaguely uneasy, blurry, guilty sort of feeling that I always get after I've got completely wasted. Coupled with the same spaced-out sensation of unreality.

Did last night actually happen? It feels like a dream, or something on the television that I half watched as I was falling asleep. I don't really see how it could have been real. I just don't *do* things like that.

But I must have. There was a damp spot: the bit of sheet that I dripped on when I was too aroused to think straight. And what's more, there was the chat transcript. I've printed it out, but I get the collywobbles when I try to read it. I suppose I must be harbouring some vague idea of challenging Daniel with it. But really, I'm not sure I want to. If I call Nemesis's bluff, it's game over. Before we've really started. And today I've got to deal with the forfeit he imposed on me when I admitted I'd had a climax.

NEMESIS: You're wilful, Gwendolynne. Now you must pay.

I shift on my stool at the Enquiry Desk. I feel uneasy. Not actually uncomfortable, but very, very strange. My forfeit is to come to work without panties. It's slightly scary – and very draughty. And, wouldn't you know it, it's turned cooler today and there's a frisky chill blowing around my nether regions that makes me constantly aware of my hidden nakedness.

I'm glad of the distraction, though, thankful for the excitement. There was some far less fun correspondence in the post this morning: another in an interminable series of letters from my ex's solicitor. Yet another salvo in his campaign to shaft me over the sale of our house. I would have liked to have parted thinking at least benignly of the man, but he's making it fucking difficult with his unfair demands.

All of which makes the Daniel/Nemesis/naughty-letters-and-dares situation a delicious gift. Not even my wildest imaginings could have come up with a better way to take my mind off my troubles. A gigantic turn-on. An insane game. A battle of wits that makes me crazy-alive and excited. I feel deliciously exposed and available, even though my skirt is a sensible knee-length work one and primly modest. It's as if every male in the library has suddenly developed X-ray vision and is ogling my pussy.

Every man I meet today seems to have a smile with a sinister edge to it. Even the most innocuous greeting sounds like a barely coded double entendre. I must have encountered at least ten men today who *could* be Nemesis, although by mid-morning the prime suspect hasn't yet put in an appearance. He might be down in his lair, but I've been too busy to visit. And the more the day progresses, the more nervous and jiggly I feel inside. Because the forfeit has a rider.

It isn't mandatory, but Nemesis has dared me to do something. Something absurd. Mad. Dangerous. And it'll probably get me sacked if it goes wrong. I have to *reveal* my commando status during the course of the day. Either by accident or design, I've got to flash somebody.

With a full complement of staff on today, Tracey arrives to cover for my coffee break, and even she gives me a strange, complicit look.

'Going down into the archive?' Her eyes narrow as I slide

awkwardly off the stool and pick up a few books that need shelving downstairs. 'Mustn't keep your boyfriend waiting.'

'What do you mean? He's not my boyfriend.'

'Professor Hottie ... Josie saw him heading off towards the garden the other day, not long after you left, and he was obviously following you. And then last night he stopped to talk to you as he was leaving.'

'So? It's a public garden ... and he was just being sociable last night. There's nothing more than that. I wish there was!'

She chuckles. 'And it's been noted how often you seem to find things to shelve in the basement these days.' Her pointed glance drops to my pile of books.

Now this is slightly alarming and my face must show it.

'Oh, don't worry, it's just me and Josie who are keeping tabs, not the big cheese. Your secret love affair is safe with us.'

'There is no secret affair!' I hiss at her as she settles on the stool. Oh, it must be so much less disturbing to sit there with your panties *on*. I'm relieved about the news concerning Mr Johnson, the Chief Librarian, though. I don't think he approves of any outside-work fraternisation with our celebrity guest.

'Whatever you say,' Tracey purrs, logging on to the Enquiry Desk terminal. 'Now get yourself off down there. Your prince awaits!'

I give her an old-fashioned look and speed off. I close the door to the main Lending Library behind me and lean on it, breathing hard. It's only my knickers I'm missing, but it might as well be my skirt, my blouse, my everything. I feel as if my pussy is a cauldron of seething hormones. I'm going off my head, I swear it.

After a moment or two, I begin to descend, trying to fool myself that everything is perfectly normal and I'm just heading down for a bit of shelving. But all the time I'm thinking, 'Is he here? Is he here?'

I nearly hyperventilate when I see the soft pool of light at the end of the stacks. He *is* here. Daniel? Nemesis? Both?

I pad quietly to the end of the long lines of tall book-stacks. Daniel's work area isn't nearly as brightly lit as normal and there's no sound at all. What the hell is he doing? Immediately, I imagine him masturbating again. I see him sprawled in the old manager's chair he's purloined from somewhere, his flies open, his magnificent cock rearing up out of his trousers like a fat red spear clutched in his sliding fingers.

I'm creeping now, inching, inching forwards. Then I slide around the corner, not knowing what to expect, but hoping for something like yesterday's awesome spectacle.

He's lying in the chair, legs spread, head tipped back. He isn't masturbating, but he's wearing a mask. He's wearing a bloody mask!

I sway and nearly drop my books as I try to work out what I'm seeing. But alas, it's not the kinky leather fetish mask from my fantasies, but what appears to be a pale-blue cool-pack pressed over his eyes like in *American Psycho*. He's holding it in place with both hands and they look tense, white at the knuckles. His body looks uncomfortable too.

'Gwendolynne?'

Slowly, as if it pains him, he lifts the mask away from his face, lays it aside and rises to his feet, looking a little unsteady. His eyes, usually so handsome, look red and irritated and he blinks furiously as he stares in my direction, his head tilted as if he's not quite seeing me. He runs his fingers through his hair, ruffling it as he massages his scalp, then cups the back of his head as if it's made of glass.

What the devil is wrong with him?

He reaches for his spectacles, which are lying on the table, and once they're in place he seems to focus and brace up, and gives me an uncertain smile.

So not Nemesis.

'Are you all right?' It's a redundant question. He looks all wrong. Almost as if he doesn't realise what he's doing, he pushes up his glasses again and rubs his eyes. 'Is there something wrong with your eyes?'

'No. Nothing. They're fine. I'm just a bit tired, that's all.'

It's more than that. Any fool can see he's in pain. Those beautiful eyes themselves make him a liar. He's worried, perhaps even afraid. There are shadows, dark shadows in those brown depths.

'Are you sure?'

'Absolutely. Don't fuss,' he says crisply, his entire body coming to attention and casting off the last signs of weakness. 'How are you? Any more secret letters?'

For perhaps a fifth of a second I think of the solicitor's letter, but I quash the thought viciously. The way Daniel's mouth curves and his whole expression brightens makes that task easy. If there's one thing that's guaranteed to take a man's mind off his aches and pains and worries, it's sex. And it works just as well for a woman's murderous thoughts about her ex-husband too.

'Well, not so much a letter as a "correspondence",' I answer, deliberately vaguely, to tantalise him.

He gives me a very professorial 'please expand your answer, recalcitrant pupil' look.

'An online chat. I had an online chat with Nemesis last night.'

'Really?'

Oh, if he's Nemesis, he's even cleverer than I already thought he was. His voice is perfectly neutral. There's nothing affectedly uninterested about it, or salaciously enthusiastic either. The pitch is perfect for someone who's mildly curious, perhaps slightly concerned, but observing the phenomenon from the outside.

'Do you want to talk about it? Or is it something you'd prefer not to share with a third party?' He purses his lips and looks a bit put out. Is he jealous at being excluded now? Or is this just more of his phenomenally accurate performance?

'Yeah, it's all right. No biggie.'

Actually, it's a huge deal, and I'm stark, staring crazy to share this with him, regardless of whether he's Nemesis or just a less than innocent bystander. If he isn't, the words are far too revealing, and if he is, well, I'm just getting myself more and more entangled with a seriously devious game player. But there's no way back now, for my body or my mind.

'Are you able to stay a while?' He's already walking round his cluttered table and pulling out a chair for me, another of those battered old executive jobs on wheels with bits of stuffing hanging out of it here and there.

'Yeah, it's my tea break. They're pretty flexible. They owe me some hours.' Which is total bollocks, but Tracey will cover for me. She seems determined that I get off with Professor Hottie.

'You can always say you were assisting me with my research.' He dips down to his bag, fishing round for something, but not before he's flashed me one of those ever so slight, maybe/maybe not winks. When he pops up again, he's holding two little individual apple juice cartons, complete with straws, and a large bag of crisps.

Oh goodie, a picnic! Technically, we're not supposed to bring food and drink into any part of the library other than the staff room, but who cares? Daniel is an honoured guest, after all, and allowed some latitude.

'Wow, thanks!' The sweet apple juice on my tongue seems to loosen it. 'Yeah, it was pretty wild last night. I've never done anything like that before. The anonymity makes you feel as if you can do or say anything ... it's really liberating.'

'But how on earth did he find you? Your email address or whatever ...' He takes a long pull on his straw and slurps like a schoolkid. The way he smirks over the top of the box is adorable. 'I'd say that's rather worrying.' He frowns. 'You're playing with fire, Gwendolynne. You ought to be more careful.'

Yeah, fire indeed. And I'm roasting on the griddle right this minute.

'He found me via MySpace, sent me a message. A chat invitation.'

Daniel shrugs and shakes his head as if despairing of that imbecile student again.

'Look, Professor Know It All, I know this probably sounds foolhardy to you, but it's ... it's *exciting*! And if you had to work in this gulag of a place all the time, you might feel like taking a few risks too. Plus ...' How to explain it? And dare I challenge him? How do I tell him that, even if Nemesis *isn't* him, I know the guy won't hurt me? 'Well, whoever Nemesis is, I don't think he means me any real harm. He's a freak, but somehow he still seems benign to me.' I slurp my own juice now, and we both laugh.

'Seriously, though, I've no intention of saying or doing anything I don't really *want* to.'

Daniel absorbs this, and I can see him mulling it over. Frowning slightly, he pulls open the crisps and offers them to me. I refuse, my stomach knotting in strange excitement. This den in the bowels of the library is as much a cocoon of unreality as the one I inhabited last night when I chatted with Nemesis.

'Whatever you say ...' His tone is one of pointed resignation, like someone who thinks I'm a blithering idiot but is refraining from saying it. Which could be how he really feels, or a command performance by a supremely gifted thespian.

'Yes, whatever I say ...' I look him in the eyes, trying to plunder his secrets. But I get nothing, except a hint of humour deep in there somewhere, possibly imagined. I reach into my pocket and pull out the folded transcript. 'And here it is – what I said.'

He cocks his head on one side, eyes narrowed behind his spectacles.

'I saved a log of the chat. Here's the transcript. Do you want to read it?' I tweak it at him, teasingly. 'It's not copperplate on Basildon Bond or whatever, but it's, well, pretty damn hot in its own way.'

He reaches out, long fingers elegantly extended, then pauses. 'But these are your words too ... are you sure you want me to read them?' He retreats an inch or two.

'I don't care. Go ahead.'

The paper is suddenly out of my hand and flicked open. No chance to change my mind, obviously. Daniel switches on a couple more of his Anglepoise lamps.

For the next few minutes, the atmosphere down here in Professor Hottie's hideaway seems to thicken as if we're in a pressurised chamber. We sit in silence, apart from the occasional rustle of the paper and the discreet background hum of the building's air conditioning and pipework. And Daniel's breathing, which seems to punctuate the rapid gathering of tension and desire. I'm excruciatingly aware that I'm not wearing any panties, and that within seconds the dark, beautiful man sitting just feet away from me will be aware of that fact. When his eyes flick momentarily in the direction of my pelvic regions I almost faint.

Finally he lays the sheets of paper aside and draws in a deep breath. His body sits uncomfortably in its chair now, and the slight hitching to and fro of his hips while he was reading only adds to my mental picture of his erection. His crotch is slightly in shadow from where I'm sitting but I know he must be hard.

He taps his soft lower lip with his fingertip and then says, 'Wow ...' Continuing to tap, he sits back in his chair, staring not at me now but into space.

Wow? Is that all? God, you're a cool customer, Professor Hottie.

'What do you think?' For some reason his studied lack of interest and his denial of his own body's reaction irk me. I decide to shake him up. 'Does it turn you on as much as it turns me on?'

Hah! His eyes snap back towards me and he adjusts himself in his seat again.

'Well, yes, of course it does. It's a very erotic scenario. Very intense.' He makes a little harrumphing sound, quintessentially academic. 'But I still think you're skating on very thin ice with this fellow.'

Skating on thin ice? Playing with fire? Well, at least I've got him seesawing between metaphors.

'How so? He's probably completely harmless. All talk, no action. If I were ever to confront him, I bet he's the sort who'd run crying home to mummy.' There, put that in your Oxbridge pipe and smoke it!

'You don't know that. He mentioned "one day", didn't he? I'd say that meeting you and, um, fucking you is definitely on his agenda.'

Ooh, he said 'fuck'. It sounds so exotic on his lips, and so incongruous. I imagine him growling it as he does what he's just said, cursing as he ploughs the furrow between my legs.

Oh, I want him so much. Him *and* Nemesis. Even if they're *not* the same person. My feelings are so perverse that they scare me.

'And that's a bad thing?' Despite my qualms, I seem pathologically incapable of not trying to provoke him.

He's avoiding looking at me, playing with his hair, twirling a curl around his fingers in a way that makes me think of those fingers twirling around other things.

'I still think he could be dangerous.'

'So can I.'

He looks up. 'I don't doubt it, Gwendolynne. I don't doubt it. I find you very dangerous indeed. You're a serious threat to my concentration.'

I'm on my feet in an eye-blink. 'Right, I'll go then. I'm keeping you from your work.' What is it with him? Most men would be all over this like a cheap suit.

'No!' Now he's on his feet too, and the erection I suspected of him is huge!

'It's just, well, this situation we're in is so unusual.' He makes a graceful gesture, indicating that I should sit back down. It's courteous, yet there's a command in it too, one that's hard to defy. I resume my seat, wondering why I'm giving in so easily. 'We barely know each other, yet we're talking about sex. And somehow we seem to be involved in what amounts to a *ménage à trois*. It's most ... most perplexing.'

'You started it,' I point out, wondering if he'll confess and the mystery will be over.

Instead, he frowns in a way that seems to make him even more handsome than ever and places his laced hands on the table in front of him. Is he doing that to stop them doing something that he doesn't want them to? Like touching himself? 'I don't know what you mean, Gwendolynne. How can I have started it?'

Such a display of innocence. It's very convincing.

'Well, you looked down my top, and then made a big deal about following me to apologise for it.' I reach for my juice box but it's empty now, so I fiddle with the straw. 'If you'd just perved me like a normal man who doesn't feel he has to say sorry for it, I would never have shown you the letter ... and we'd still be confined to polite "hellos" and "how's it goings" when we ran into each other in the library.'

He shrugs. Seems to concede. Graces me with the most exquisite, quirky little smile that makes my nerves tingle and my uncovered pussy flutter with longing.

'True ... very true.'

I'm tapping the juice box, full of excess energy. This is the weirdest situation. I'm losing the ability to work out what to say next.

But into the silence comes Daniel's voice again, raw and husky.

'So ... did you do what he asked? Or were you just playing a game with the poor slob?' He straightens his fingers, flexes them, straightens them again, in a sort of flapping action. 'Were you *really* wearing red silk pyjamas?'

'No, they were blue-striped brushed cotton.'

His jaw drops and his mobile pink tongue sweeps round his lips. 'But all the rest is true then?'

'Pretty much so ...'

He shakes his head and his curls fly wildly. Suddenly I feel as exposed as I did last night. The letters from Nemesis were one thing, but now I've laid my sexuality and even my orgasms out on a plate for this man I barely know. I'm in free fall to terra incognita, and the fear only arouses me even more.

'Are you disgusted with me?'

'No! Oh, believe me, no!' His eyes, which looked so tired and imperfect when I arrived, are brilliant now. 'I'm in awe of you, Gwendolynne. Afraid for you in some ways, but in others I'm thrilled to the core. That you'd display your ... your sexuality, laid bare like that, for me. It's a privilege.'

Suddenly he laughs, free and happy, like a naughty boy. '*Is it laid bare? Like the forfeit?*' He flashes a glance to my crotch area again, his long lashes flirty.

'Of course.'

My heart's going thumpata-thumpata-thump.

'You know ... if you showed *me*, you wouldn't have to show anyone else. You could pay your forfeit in perfect safety. Without any risk.' Those lashes are wicked. This is the friskiest I've ever seen him. It's as if we've taken a step somewhere, passed into that other reality without even realising it. 'In fact, I'd hardly even look, so you wouldn't really be exposed.'

We've come a long way from the prissy choirboy act when I touched his cock in the garden. He's on for this. He's ready. His eyes, his mouth, the total package is nothing short of devastatingly seductive.

But then, so am I. I've got my stockings and suspenders on again and, even though my thighs aren't quite as svelte as I'd like them to be, the dark charcoal bands of my lace stocking-tops more than make up for a little extra flesh. And my suspender belt, as red and satiny as my pyjamas weren't, is a perfect frame for the tawny floss of my pussy.

The sight's going to have an impact on him. Daniel is an intelligent and glamorous man in his cool, bookish way but he's still a man. Show a man your naked sex and you're talking to his primitive brain, not the part with an encyclopaedic knowledge of history or science or whatever. On the level of sex and bodies, he isn't out of my league, no matter how learned and famous he is. I can make him mine.

'All right then.'

Not giving myself time to falter, I stand up, pushing back my chair and sending it bumping against the book-stack to the rear of me. As Daniel shoves his chair back for a better view, I place the flats of my hands against the surface of my skirt, and slowly, slowly begin to raise it. I'd planned to flash him faster than the eye can see but, now it's come to it, I'm putting on a show.

Behind his spectacles his eyes widen at about the same speed as my skirt is creeping upwards. About as fast as his sweet red mouth is falling open. He sighs again as my pubis peeks into view beneath the hem of my skirt.

I feel supremely sexual. And I know I was right. In this moment, I've got him in the palm of my hand. He's mesmerised by a triangle of soft reddish-gold hair, and I allow him to stare at it for a few moments longer, his mouth still open and his eyes wide and glittering. Then I drop my skirt again and he looks as if it's Christmas and I've just stomped on his new PlayStation.

'This doesn't mean we're engaged or anything.' I smooth the fabric over my thighs, and he follows every minute movement. 'It's just a case of a friend helping out a friend … and a man getting a flash of what a man likes to look at as a reward. Fair enough?'

'Um, yes, yes, I suppose so.'

Does he want more? The definite bulge in his jeans says he wants something.

'Are you OK? Daniel?'

He hauls in a huge breath as if he's just run a marathon.

'Yes … yes, I am. It's just that I thought I could remain dispassionate and detached about this. And just offer assistance.' He shuffles in his chair and plucks at the denim of his jeans to ease his obvious discomfort. 'But I seem to have got rather more *affected* than I anticipated.' He offers a rueful grin, his soft lips curling, his expression befuddled.

Oh, who is he kidding? Even if he isn't Nemesis the Arch Pervert, he's a guy in his thirties who's famous and charismatic. He's probably had more women and played more sex games than I've had hot dinners.

'Surely you've seen a woman's crotch before? Don't try to kid me that you're some kind of born-again virgin or something.'

'No, of course not,' he answers *very* crisply. Is he cross? 'It's just that I don't usually see them in circumstances like this.' Then he smiles. 'It's usually a case of a few dates, dinners, theatre, maybe an exhibition. Then the "would you like to come up for coffee?" route. You know. Standard operating procedure.' His shoulders lift in a lovely little shrug. 'And only *then* do I get to see what you've just shown me.'

'You were the one who suggested it,' I point out.

'Yes, I know. I can't help but admit that I've been admiring you in the library since I got here, and I did sort of ask you out yesterday.' He frowns again, but it's not crossness. It's more a strangely sad, wistful expression. 'But now I'm wondering whether it's best not to complicate a good working relationship. Especially as I'll be gone before long, back to London. And ...' He pauses, sighing gustily again. 'Well, I don't know how to say this without sounding supremely arrogant and conceited and full of myself ...'

'Try me.'

'The thing is ... I'm not looking for a relationship right at the moment. I can only offer a, well, I suppose you might call it a "fling".' His handsome face works as if he's grasping at a way to express himself – which is downright peculiar in someone who's an acknowledged communicator. 'But that's not because of anything lacking in you. You're lovely. You're delightful. A dazzling woman. It's just I'm simply not a good prospect for anything long term. It wouldn't be fair to you.'

Suddenly he looks almost distraught and, despite the fact that my heart flutters foolishly at words like 'lovely' and 'delightful' and 'dazzling', and that my body is still on red alert, wanting him so hard it hurts, I feel suddenly worried for him and curious to know what the deep trouble is that's bugging him. Because there *is* something. Every nurturing instinct in me screams so.

'Like I said, this doesn't mean we're engaged or anything.' Feeling daring, I pat my crotch in the general direction of my pussy. 'And I'm not sure I want to give up this thing with Nemesis just yet.' I expect a reaction to that, but he doesn't bat an eyelid. 'But maybe we could get to know each other a little better while you're here. Nothing heavy, just fun. Maybe see each other. Maybe a bit of sex? Pursue this, this dalliance with Nemesis together somehow?' His face brightens. He clearly likes the idea. 'No declarations of undying love or commitment, just a temporary arrangement. Like you say, a bit of a fling. No strings. No ties. But no inhibitions either.'

I don't know what the hell's got into me, but bloody hell, I think I like it!

'You're a remarkable woman, Gwendolynne,' Daniel says softly, his face a complex tapestry of emotion. 'I don't think I've ever met anyone like you. Anyone so ... so adaptable. So brave and also slightly crazy.'

'Thanks ... I think.'

'No, believe me, it's a compliment. I *love* adaptable and brave and crazy.' He gets up and comes towards me. He's still amazingly hard. 'You're a beautiful woman, too. Your body is sensational.'

'Get away with you. I'm just a fat provincial librarian.'

I'm trembling though. And despite my bravado, I don't know what to do. How fast does one usually progress in the case of temporary-arrangement-type flings? I suppose we could start by kissing again, but the way he's standing in front of me, almost flaunting himself ... well, I suddenly just want to see his cock. That would be something really naughty to tell Nemesis about next time we chat. Something that I can pretend is just a fantasy, but which I can laugh to myself about because I know it's real.

But if Daniel *is* Nemesis, he'll know that already, of course. This is so complicated, but I love it, I love it!

His mouth twists slightly, as if he knows my every thought.

So, you think I'm brave and slightly crazy then, do you, Professor McHotstuff who just might be Nemesis? Well, watch this!

Before he can stop me, I reach for the belt on his jeans, grab it by the buckle and pull him towards me. Trying not to fumble, I unfasten his belt as fast as I can, whizz down his zip and reach inside.

Daniel gasps, then goes with the flow, reaching out and first putting his hands on my shoulders, then sliding them up and cupping my face. For a moment he looks down into my eyes, sort of half wondering, half arrogant, and then he slides his fingers round to the nape of my neck, slips the soft band out of my hair and shakes it loose.

As he frees my hair, I free his penis. Ah, beautiful old friend, I've thought about you almost constantly since I first saw you.

He's so hard. And getting harder. Weeping sumptuous silky fluid, the head plump and shiny with its stretched skin and its tiny pouting love-eye. And all in this fierce state from just a few moments' glimpse of my pussy? I fold my fingers around him, cradling him gently. Like an eager puppy he presses forward into my grip, making a low, very masculine rumbling in his throat. His fingertips burrow into my hair, cupping my head, pressing on it, pressing downwards.

Of course I know what he wants. Don't all men want it? The only thing that astonishes me is that we've reached this place so fast. One day it's a polite 'good morning, how are you?' in the library. The next, I'm sliding to my knees and preparing to give head to this man I barely know in any real sense.

I flick a glance up at him, but his eyes are closed, his head tipped back, his expression an ecstatic replica of the way he looked in the washroom. Unbearably touched and moved by his beauty, I swoop forwards and engulf his glans with my mouth.

He's fine and hot and salty, his flesh firm and latent with power. I lick him quickly, flicking and teasing with enthusiasm. Maybe I'm not a virtuoso, but I've got instincts, and a beautiful dick like this invites excellence and invention. I soon have him groaning and swaying and gouging at my head, fingers flexing like points of fire against my scalp.

I brace one hand on his denim-clad thigh, loving the hard, tense muscle beneath the coarse fabric. He feels toned and defined, and I remember his naked body as he stood before the sink. Beneath his comfortable T-shirts and his tweedy jackets and his fairly average jeans, there's the body of a stud, an Adonis. I try to ease down his jeans to get at his balls and cup them and taunt them as I work him, but he's suddenly frantic, pushing into my mouth, wild and rough.

Am I going to gag? No! From somewhere I find a calm and a relaxation within myself. I seem to have the capacity to accept him and love him to the nth degree.

For long moments we rock and sway and my lips and tongue caress him. Eventually, though, I feel his excitement increase and sense the rising of his spirit and the gathering of his ecstasy. He pushes, pushes, pushes, and I can almost hear the cry of pleasure that must be poised upon his lips.

He breathes hard, grips my head, and gasps, 'Gwendolynne,' but, before he can shout out, another sound freezes our incriminating tableau like an ice sculpture. Muffled footsteps, at the far end of the long complex of cellars, but steadily approaching. What to do?

Daniel starts to pull back, but I grab his buttocks and then plunge my mouth down deep on him. At the same time I press firmly on the denim seam that runs down the crease of his bottom, and force my finger as hard as I can against his anus. With one hand he continues to dig into my scalp but the other is ready to stifle his groan of ecstasy.

Semen, rich and thick, spurts into my mouth. He tastes delicious, the perfect man, and his come is plentiful. I swallow it down as fast as I can as the footsteps grow nearer. Then, in a most unseemly shuffle and grapple and struggle, between us we get Daniel back into his jeans and zipped up in double-quick time. And I'm on my feet, wiping my mouth with the back of my hand and then reaching for a pile of books from the table as a figure comes around the corner.

'Yes, of course, Professor Brewster, no problem,' I pronounce cheerfully, feeling the tickling of wild laughter start in my throat. I transmute it into a soft cough, then continue, 'I'll shelve these for you, and put in that request to Library Interloans. It shouldn't take much longer than a week.'

Daniel and I turn towards the newcomer. It's Greg, the computer tech, who's carrying a coil of cable and a tool pouch.

I *think* we've covered our tracks, but there's something so knowing and insolent in the young man's smile as he reaches us that I'm convinced he knows exactly what just went on here.

'Oh hi, Prof, Gwen, sorry to disturb you.' He waggles his eyebrows suggestively, and when I glance at Daniel he's regarding Greg with an almost complicit look of male bravado.

'I think I can run an extension from the Library's network for you, if you like, so you can get a faster internet connection down here while you're working. The Wi-Fi must be almost non-existent down here. It won't take more than a quarter of an hour or so.'

'Thanks, that would be great.' Daniel's smile is still subtly smug, and suddenly I want to punch him. The bastard! He's showing off! Letting Greg know that some kind of sex thing has taken place.

'Right. I'm off, Professor, see you later,' I snap out smartly, and without looking back I stride away in the direction that Greg just came from.

Men! They're all the same . . . bragging about their conquests and taking advantage of women they're supposed to care about. Fuckwits! So much for temporary-fling-type arrangements! I feel like stomping back to the carrel once Greg's finished working, and buttonholing Daniel for our first big row.

6 Compensation

I spend the rest of the day fuming. Especially when Professor 'Look at me, I just got a blow job' doesn't put in an appearance at lunchtime, or even come up into the main library during the day at all. All that talk about 'lunches' and 'honesty' and 'not being a prospect' and all that – was it really just a ruse to get his cock into my mouth?

But still, I'd rather be cross about being bamboozled into giving Daniel Brewster a blow job than cross about my dreary domestic problems. And it's not as if I didn't want to fellate him. Hell, he's Professor Hottie McHotstuff, famous television historian, and I had a crush on him even before he arrived at our humble library. There must be thousands of women out there who'd give anything to do what I've just done, with or without the offer of a 'fling-type thing'.

There's more, too, I know it. Something's bothering him, something serious. He's trying to distract himself with pleasure and games, but beneath that there's an anxiety in him, I can sense it. And if I can help him deal with that, then it's all right by me. So I spend the rest of my day pondering on that too, and I'm putting on my jacket, ready for home, when a notion literally stops me in my tracks.

Has Daniel Brewster got something wrong with him, some illness or other, and is that why he thinks he's not much of a long-term prospect for a woman? He does get bad headaches, after all. It seems a bit drastic, but I have the sort of imagination that can take things to the extreme sometimes. I rack my memory for possible signs, but there's nothing about him that looks ill. His body is magnificent, he's in peak condition and, if his sexual constitution is anything to go by, he's about as far from an invalid as a man can get. His cock was harder and more vigorous than any man's I've ever seen. Not that I've seen dozens and dozens, but a woman just knows about these things.

I'm still mulling all this over as I let myself out of the back door. And find Professor Hottie leaning on the railings, with a taxi standing a few feet away, driver reading a paper, apparently waiting for him and – it seems – for me.

'Good, I've been waiting for you. Let me give you a lift home. I, er, well, I feel that certain things were left unresolved and we need to discuss them.'

My jaw drops. Surely he doesn't think we're going to discuss our little fumble-di-dee in the basement in the back of a cab? And why a taxi, for that matter? I'd always assumed that Daniel drove to the library from wherever he's staying, but now I'm not so sure. I've never actually been looking out of the window when he pulled up.

'It's all right. I get the bus. It's only a short hop.' Which it is, and the reason I use it. Sometimes I even walk, carbon footprint and all that.

Daniel heaves a sigh, crosses his arms and gives me that 'professor impatient with a dense student' look that he's so infuriatingly fond of. I feel immediately both ungrateful and mulish in approximately equal proportions.

'OK, then. Thanks. That would be very kind. I'd love a lift.'

He rolls his eyes in a 'finally!' sort of way, and then darts forwards to open the car door for me, before handing me into the back seat as if I'm some kind of elderly, arthritic duchess. Either that or he's simply making sure I don't change my mind and bolt for the bus station.

'I'm sorry about earlier. It was unfortunate that Greg turned up like that,' he begins as the cab pulls smoothly away. 'I wanted our little interlude to end rather differently.'

Unbelievable! Now it's my turn to roll my eyes furiously, and I nod repeatedly in the direction of the taxi driver, who already seems to be riveted by our conversation.

'OK, OK,' Daniel concedes, but he's grinning wickedly as if he might just expatiate further at any moment, despite my objections. I imagine that Nemesis would probably just go ahead and describe every last detail of getting a blow job in glorious Technicolor detail, regardless of whether I wanted him to or not.

We make small talk. About the library. About Daniel's book on the Wars of the Roses and the great families from that conflict who lived round here. He asks where I live, so he can tell the driver. He seems about to pursue the subject of my flat a bit further, and having no intention of getting into the position of saying that I used to have rather a nice house, and what I thought was a nice husband, I ask where *he's* living while he's up here, in order to steer him away from that.

'The Waverley Grange Country House Hotel. Do you know it?' He leans back in the seat, relaxing, but with a strangely challenging air about him. 'I really like it. It's very comfortable and the service is excellent.'

'Yes, it's one of the best hotels in the area.'

The Waverley? Now there's intriguing. The place is indeed one of the most well-appointed and well-known hotels in the Borough. I've never been there, but I've heard that it's Olde Worlde, quite chintzy, but discreetly luxurious. It also has a bit of a reputation that doesn't match its straight and establishment façade at all. Mutterings. Murmurings. Apocryphal stories told by a friend of a friend of a friend that strange and rather sexy things go on there. I wonder if Daniel has seen any evidence of this risqué rep while he's been in residence?

I open my mouth, wondering whether to ask, but suddenly, out of the eye-line of the driver, Daniel grabs my hand and gives it an urgent squeeze. I glance into his eyes and they're on fire behind the lenses of his spectacles. Suddenly we're back in the library basement, man and woman, steeped in sex. And all I can think about is the fact that I'm not wearing panties and he's fully aware of it.

Why does it not surprise me when he lays a hand upon my thigh and slides it upwards, gently stroking through my skirt? Immediately I feel myself getting wet, ready for his touch or his flesh. My skin is like a charged electric field, and tingles of sensation race along my nerves and head directly for my clit.

'Perhaps you can join me there for a drink or dinner, one evening?'

'What?' I blurt out vacantly. I've completely forgotten what we were talking about. All I can think about is the way the heat of his hand is warming me right through my skirt. His fingertips are barely moving, but the way they drift to and fro is infinitely provocative.

'At the Waverley, remember?' He isn't actually laughing out loud, in fact he's barely smiling, but his body language is alive with impish mirth.

I shake my head to clear it. Twitch at my skirt, jerking it and my thigh away from beneath his touch.

'Yes. Great. OK, that would be nice.' My voice sounds tight, unfriendly and flustered. I didn't want to seem cross, but I am cross with myself for seeming that way. 'I'll look forward to it,' I add with more enthusiasm.

Daniel removes his hand and lets it rest lightly on the seat. He seems relaxed, unperturbed. 'Me too,' he murmurs, then astonishingly returns to the small talk, asking me about various buildings that we pass on the way to the house where my flat is.

Eventually we pull up in front of Merivale House. I reach for the door and pop it open, not sure what to expect by way of a parting. A handshake? An air kiss? A hug? A full-on tongue assault with grope? But Daniel just pops his own door and dashes around to help me out of the cab. I'm amazed how fast he can move when he puts his mind to it.

'I'll see you in,' he says, all domineering and male. He guides me forwards, his hand light on my ribcage as, over his shoulder, he instructs the driver to wait.

'It's all right. I'll be OK.' Which is true. The building is quiet and very safe. I could just do with some more money, so as to be able to afford my flat without such a struggle.

Daniel doesn't answer, but stays with me as I half trot to the front door and then punch in the code on the keypad. Yeah, the building is safe, but I'm not sure *I* am at the moment.

We step inside and the foyer is deserted and cool, smelling of floor polish. Again comes the thorny question of handshake, hug, kiss, or more, but suddenly there are voices from above and the sound of feet on the open staircase. Expecting him to step away from me and begin some kind of fabricated conversation, I catch my breath when Daniel glances quickly around, grabs me by the hand and hauls me into the little maintenance alcove at the back of the foyer, beyond the staircase. It doubles back on itself, and contains assorted cleaning equipment – mops and buckets, and watering cans for the building's ornamental potted plants.

The voices are in the hall now, so I can't cry out and protest when Daniel edges me backwards, moving deep into my personal space and owning it completely. His left hand shoots out, cupping the back of my neck as he pulls my face to his and presses his lips on mine. While his tongue possesses my mouth, that tricky right hand of his is back on my thigh, sliding, sliding, rubbing the fabric of my skirt against my skin.

His mouth is voracious, compelling me to open mine and accept his tongue. The taste of his tongue makes my pussy flutter and yearn for his cock. Its thrusting action is blatant, delicious, intoxicating. I try to give back as good as I'm getting but he's a tyrant, he subdues me, he's in control.

And not just with his mouth. He's not an awesomely tall man, but he's got power and momentum and a hunger to match my own. He drives me back against the wall, only just preventing us cannoning into a galvanised mop bucket and making a huge commotion. As I hit the plaster, his hand whips down, then up again, sliding my skirt right up my thighs and insinuating his fingers between my legs.

I gasp, but the inhalation draws his breath into my mouth. I feel as if his spirit rushes in with it, another possession to match the invasion of his tongue.

And his fingers.

He finds my wet heat easily, weaving his fingertips through the floss of my pubis and separating my labia. Another gasp later and he's flicking at my clitoris. He flicks. He rubs. He circles and massages. I circle too, working my bottom against the wall, but he doesn't miss a beat.

I think I'm going to faint. My belly and my sex are pulsating with heat. I drag in air again, gasping for breath, and Daniel frees my mouth, peppering little kisses across my cheek instead. A moan rises to my lips, but he slides the hand that was holding the back of my head around to my cheek, pressing his thumb into my mouth for me to suckle. His own mouth settles against my ear.

Someone out in the hall is wittering on at their companion to hurry up or they'll miss the film, but all I can hear is a low, barely audible whisper against my skin.

'Relax, Gwendolynne. I owe you an orgasm. Let me pleasure you.'

I can't speak. His thumb is in my mouth. But even if it wasn't, I'm beyond all speech as my sex quickens and grows heavy with expectation.

His voice sounds so strange. It's dark, intent, not quite earthly. And when he edges back a little, and I get a bit of distance and can look at him, his eyes are weird, spaced, almost somewhere else. He's looking at me, but is he really seeing me?

'Relax,' he urges me again, his circling finger working harder, 'Let me give you something to tell your friend Nemesis about tonight.'

The words 'you're my friend Nemesis ... I know it's you' flitter through my mind but it's as if another person is thinking them, not me.

I can only give myself to pleasure. I part my legs a bit more, then bear down. Daniel laughs almost inaudibly, and I come.

My mind's gone. Well, most of it. There's a tiny bit, somewhere, that's still thinking and thinking. As Daniel swoops in for a kiss again and I almost swoop out of consciousness, my body throbbing hard, the thought 'this is a game ... this is a game ...' seems to throb too.

His tongue is in my mouth again as he does a swivelling and flicking thing with his middle finger and I almost have to bite him. Except that he pulls back just before it happens and presses his lips against my throat instead. My head fills with a cool blue scent, the odour of his shampoo that still lingers on his curls.

He takes me up again, and again, then slowly lets me down, cupping my whole sex with his hand as if to calm it. We stand in silence, wound together, our breathing matched.

It *is* a game. It has to be. I don't really know why he's playing it but I'm with him, step by step, ploy by ploy. Even if it's basically just a lot of sexual fiddling about.

The movie buffs in the hall have gone now. The coast is clear, but still we stand here. I feel a change in our embrace. What was fierce, frenzied, almost animal a moment ago has suddenly become infinitely more tender. Daniel's hand continues to curve lightly around my pussy, but there's a feeling of nurturing and protection in his touch now. It's as if he's cherishing the feminine centre he's just pleasured. His lips are very soft against my neck. There are no words between us, but his warm breath and the way he nuzzles his nose against my hair speak more than eloquently.

'You are astonishing,' he murmurs at last, stepping back a little, then dipping down to smooth my skirt carefully back into place. Before I can stop him, he presses a kiss upon the front of my skirt, right over my sex. Which stuns me more than any of the orgasms.

When he straightens up again, he drops a light kiss on my lips, then pulls back, looking down into my eyes. His own are still dark, strange, hazy, complex. His face works for a moment as if he's searching for words. 'Are you all right?' he asks, stroking my cheek and my jaw-line with his thumb. It's as if he's searching for something, the answer to a question he doesn't even understand. And neither do I. Then he purses his lips and the weird little moment is gone again before I've even time to try to frame a response.

'I have to go, Gwendolynne. I've got a video conference with some American historians on a Tudors project, then a paper to prepare.' His voice is raw, genuinely regretful, but I can already sense him creating distance between us. Seconds ago we were closer and more in tune than I've ever been with anyone in my life, but he's in leaving mode now. Even though, when I lurch forwards and kiss him again, his erection still rubs against my belly.

'Can't you come up for a minute?'

Fool! Fool! Fool!

Don't beg, Gwen, you moron! This is a fling, remember that, nothing more. Don't go all soppy over the man. If he's Nemesis, he's still a cynical manipulator, no matter how tender he might seem.

To my absolute horror, I feel tears brim in my eyes. It's the orgasm, the release. I'm not crying like a baby for what I can't have. At least I hope I'm not.

Daniel catches a tear on his thumb and looks at me, perplexed. Then he strokes my face again, with utter gentleness, and pulls me to him, cradling me in his arms.

'Screw it,' he mutters, holding me tight. 'I'll do the video thing some other time.' His fingertips flutter across my skin. 'Bloody academics.'

He holds me against his body, soothing me, calming me. He's still got a hard-on, but it's as if he doesn't notice it. His embrace is exquisite, but I know I can't keep him. As he reaches for his mobile, I wriggle away from his hold and say, 'It's OK. Go to your conference thing. I'm all right. And I'm sorry for being a wimp.'

'Are you sure? Are you absolutely sure? I don't like leaving you, you know that, don't you?'

'I'm fine,' I reiterate, and, with a shrug, he seems to believe me.

God, I'm such a fibber.

'OK then. If you're sure.' His voice sounds convinced but his eyes are wary. He takes me by the hand and leads me out of the alcove and back around the corner into the open foyer, breaking the crystal circle of our intimacy.

Holding me by the arms, he looks into my eyes, all businesslike and sensible and rational. 'Look, tomorrow, maybe we can make plans to do something a little more normal. Like I suggested before. How does that sound?'

I shrug. I'm beginning to find it difficult to know what to make of dear Professor Hottie. His identity is shifting and morphing, sometimes merging with Nemesis, sometimes not. He's an unfathomable hybrid and I'm not sure how to handle him.

'Too boring?' He cocks an eyebrow, his mouth teasing.

'No, not at all. Boring is fine. Less scary.'

He opens his mouth to either agree or disagree with this, but suddenly the cab driver honks his horn and we both jump. I'm amazed he hasn't honked before, but maybe he has and I was just too out of it or soaring too high in the stratosphere to hear it.

'Look, I'll see you in the library tomorrow.' The horn blares again. 'Or maybe I can pick you up?'

'No, it's OK, I'll see you there. I like my bus trip in the mornings to get into "work" mode.'

'OK, very well. I'll see you tomorrow.' He bends, gives me a peck on the cheek then turns and walks smartly to the door. When he gets there, he turns and winks and calls, 'Have fun with Nemesis tonight!' Then, for just a second, he looks more serious. As if almost on the point of saying more, he bites his lip and gives me a tiny little wave.

Then, before I can shout back that I might not even bother to turn on my computer, he's unlatched the door, he's out, and he's gone.

'This is such crap!'

In disgust I get up from my easy chair, march into the kitchen and throw my reheated frozen 'dinner on a tray' into the waste-bin. These lazy meals are a guilty pleasure of mine as a rule, but tonight the one I've been picking at tastes of nothing.

I'm restless, edgy, wound up. If I hadn't had all those orgasms earlier, downstairs in the mop alcove, I could swear that frustration was my problem. Maybe I still need to come – again, more, whatever. My mind is a whirl of thoughts and variables and things that perplex me, a lot of them to do with Daniel and Nemesis and a few about my ex and the house money.

I eye my laptop, sitting on the desk, challenging me. If Daniel is busy tonight, there'll be no Nemesis around to play with. And if there is, it isn't him ... and I *want* it to be him. I think ... Do I? Round and round and round we go!

Well, fuck you, mystery man, you're as screwed up with issues as I am.

I need some air. I stuff my feet into my sneakers, grab a cotton jacket and my shoulder bag and in a few minutes I'm out the front door, heading into the soft, mellow evening for a stroll. I need to expend some energy, some tension, some calories, and a brisk walk seems like the perfect head-clearing therapy. Especially if I pick up some fish and chips on the way back home.

An hour or two later I'm back. And my head's still not clear. In fact I'm more confused than I was when I started.

At first, everything went to plan. Instead of a casual amble, I decided to take a brisk thirty-minute yomp into the centre of town and then have a mooch around the Piazza. This is the Borough's effort at urban regeneration and the development of what they laughably call 'café culture', an open square that borders on the canal, surrounded by bars and coffee bars and a variety of trendy boutique outlets that are open in the evening. It's not Paris or Milan but it's not turned out so badly, and I felt quite cosmopolitan, sitting on a bench eating my pommes frites and drinking a citron pressé while I watched the fountains and the mating rituals of the Piazza's inhabitants.

After a while, though, the novelty wore off, and I started to feel a bit conspicuous on my own. It's the sort of place you really need to visit with friends, or have a chap with you to enjoy properly. I started to fantasise about sitting there with Daniel, being admired and envied for my famous, handsome companion. I started to think how nice it would have been to be kissing him the way a lot of couples around the square were kissing.

Just kissing. Nothing more than that. No groping and fondling and showing one another our naughty bits.

What's the matter with me? He's told me what's on offer, and I thought I'd accepted that. Instead I'm hankering for more ... For romance? For ... ?

The thoughts were scary and suddenly the Piazza wasn't the distraction that I'd hoped it might be. I decided to get the bus home instead of walking, for quickness. Taking a rash shortcut down an alley to get to the bus station, I happened on a scene that might easily have come from my own life right now.

In a bricked-up doorway, dimly lit by the glow from a street-light further along, a couple were fucking. Right there. Up against the wall. Going at each other like a pair of rutting dogs, humping and moaning and rocking against the brickwork.

She was blonde and pretty. He was big. A big man in a dark jacket, his trousers and boxer shorts pushed down and just a bit of strong, hairy thigh on show at the back. He was holding her by her haunches, lifted on to him, his sturdy pelvis going like a jackhammer as she scrabbled at him, holding on for dear life, her head thrown back against the wall as he buried his face in her neck like a vampire.

Lost in their passion, they didn't see me. To them I was on another planet, even though I exist in a universe they'd understand. The realm of mad sex and doing crazy things on the spur of the moment.

I couldn't move away. I had to watch, my own loins suddenly aching and aching.

The girl was vocal, moaning and gasping and urging him on, while he punctuated his thrusts with a series of low, happy grunts. As they twisted sideways a little, striving for deeper penetration, I got a better look at him, at his profile. And I seemed to know him.

I still think I might have been hallucinating, but I could swear that the horny stud in the alley was Robert Stone, the Borough Director of Finance. I've seen him in the library quite often, striding in to attend meetings in our lecture theatre, and he always causes a flutter of female attention. He's stocky and greying and middle-aged, but he's just one of those men you know is an animal between the sheets. And in alleys too, apparently. Because pretty soon his girlfriend let out a cry, her eyes rolled up and she came.

I felt like a thief, committing grand theft sexual for clandestine thrills, but I still couldn't tear my eyes away from the sight of their jerking bodies. I forced myself to back off, but just as I did the big, handsome, dark-clad man looked round and seemed to see me in the shadows . . . and winked. I just ran.

So now I'm home again, and no more sorted out than I was before. If anything, I'm more shaken up and mixed up than ever. Daniel? Nemesis? One? Or two? And which one of them would I have wanted to be in the alley with? Oh hell.

I look through my wardrobe and lay out my clothes for tomorrow. Ignoring the laptop. I get undressed and wash and clean my teeth and moisturise my face ready for bed. Ignoring the laptop. I turn my little bedroom television on and get comfortable to watch a bit of late-night telly. Ignoring the laptop.

'Bugger!'

I turn on the bedside lamp, reach for the power supply unit, plug both ends in, and turn on the laptop.

At first I resist firing up the instant messenger, and kid myself I'm checking my usual round of news, movie sites, funnies, Wikipedia, Amazon. But after only a very few minutes I load IM, hoping it'll spring into life with some desperately sexy communication from Nemesis. But no, his avatar is dimmed. No sign of life. No rude and breathless sex talk.

In some ways, though, that's important. Daniel is busy tonight. He's got his video conference and his paper to work on. So this should be a tick in the 'Yes, Daniel is Nemesis' box. But I'm still wondering if I want them to be the same person. I want to trust Daniel. I want to get close to him. I want ... well, I want something *real* with him. But is that really a sane and desirable thing if he's also a perverted, devious stalker who plays twisted sex games from behind the protection of a mask?

That scene in the alley just stirred everything up again. Yearnings that are simmering in my blood constantly. I feel as if I've got a mild fever and I can still hear the pretty blonde girl's moans and gasps. And I can still see that knowing wink from the big, dark man who might just have been the Borough Director of Finance.

'Bastard!' I hurl the insult at a sort of vague amalgam of Daniel, Nemesis and Robert Stone, and shove my laptop aside on the bed. Some mindless late-night viewing might distract me. It's a vain hope, but I roll on to my side and try to immerse myself in a programme. I'm into my second segment of *Police*,

Camera, Action! and actually giggling at the antics of a drunk driver magnificently failing a sobriety test when the laptop beside me goes 'Bing bong!'

Nemesis wants to chat.

7 The Tale of a Random Man

It's like I'm in a lift with the cable cut. Reality falls away in the darkness as I drag the laptop across my knees and open the chat window.

NEMESIS: So, do you have something to tell me about?

Ah, right to business, eh? No pleasantries. No pussyfooting around. My heart slams in my chest. My mind fills with an image of Daniel.

LIBRARYGIRL: Yes.

I see a triumphant smile, so typically male. Yeah, you'd just love me to fall into line and spill all the dirty little details, wouldn't you? Even though you know it all already, I know you do.

Suddenly, I want to mix things up, surprise him, come out of left field with something he *doesn't* know about.

NEMESIS: Splendid! My splendid, bold Gwendolynne . . . I knew I could rely on you. Please, go on.

Cheeky sod! He's so convinced that he controls me!

I smile, and regain my centre as some of the unreality clicks back into a more real place. I can play him at his own game. I can match him. There's nothing to be scared of . . . I know him.

LIBRARYGIRL: I went out for a walk this evening. And I saw a man and a woman in an alley, fucking. It was one of the hottest things I've ever seen in my life.

Yes, second only to watching a beautiful academic tossing himself off in the downstairs washroom at work. Maybe

I should tell you about that one, Daniel/Nemesis? See what you think about it, eh?

The cursor blinks. I can almost hear him saying, 'Er ... what?'

Will he accept my gambit? Play along with my direction? Or be like my ex-husband, and get pissed off when things don't go his way? But I can't see him behaving like a spoilt brat somehow. He might be devious, and a major perv, but he's still a grown-up.

He's taking a damned long time to reply, though.

But eventually ...

NEMESIS: Really? Well, that's not exactly the story I was expecting, but it sounds intriguing. I'd love to hear more about your rambunctious friends in the alley. Please expatiate.

Rambunctious? Expatiate? Oh, yes, you definitely *are* Daniel ...

LIBRARYGIRL: I went out to get some air. I needed to clear my head. I have a lot on my mind at the moment.

Make of that what you will ...

LIBRARYGIRL: I decided to get a bus home. I was hurrying to the bus station and I took a short cut. I heard a sound and I saw them. He had her up against a wall and he was shagging her. She had her ankles around his back and his trousers were at half mast. He was really putting it to her and she was moaning and groaning, writhing about and giving just as good as she was getting.

And I was envious, I almost tell him. But I hold back. I'm not handing him all the goodies on a plate at once.

NEMESIS: That sounds like a delicious scenario. You're very lucky, Gwendolynne. I wish I'd been there with you. Perhaps I might have dragged you into the next alley and done the same to you. Would you have liked that?

But you did, didn't you? Or something like it? The image of the alley lovers fades in my imagination, replaced by the far more vivid, the full sensory memory of being overwhelmed in the mop alcove by Daniel. Kissed and caressed by this strange man I hardly know, brought to orgasm, subjected to his whim, yet also gently cherished.

NEMESIS: Gwendolynne, are you there? Would you like to be in an alley somewhere, fucking me?

Hell, yes! Right now, nothing more so.

LIBRARYGIRL: Yes . . .

NEMESIS: If I sent for you, to meet me somewhere, would you come? If I sent for you now, would you let me fuck you? Against a wall?

If I did, the game would be over. Am I ready for the new game?

LIBRARYGIRL: It's late. I need to get up for work in the morning. It's not that I don't want to. It's practicalities, Nemesis. Boring, but a fact of life.

I've killed it. I've spoilt it all now. I can almost taste his disappointment in the air, across the Wi-Fi, along the ADSL. I'm chicken girl.

NEMESIS: You're right, my Queen of the Library. I'm being ridiculous. I'm letting my obsession with you get the better of me, and forgetting that you have a life to lead. Perhaps I should let you get some sleep now?

Yikes, so serious. So sensible. I'm touched by his consideration but, contrarily, I *want* ridiculous now. I want the thrill again, the teetering-on-the-brink-of-madness feeling

LIBRARYGIRL: I didn't say I didn't want to chat. And anyway, I never answered your first question. About the forfeit.

Moments tick past and, just when I'm about to query again, words stream on to the screen.

NEMESIS: Bravo, my beautiful Gwendolynne. I knew you wouldn't disappoint me. Did you do as I say? Did you show yourself to a man?

I slump with relief against the pillows. I feel loose again. Sexy. Still heart-thuddingly nervous, but also relaxed, as if in the company of an old friend. And he feels like an old friend, this dual-natured, tantalising playmate of mine. Even though in truth I barely know him in either of his guises.

LIBRARYGIRL: Yes, I did. In the library. Just briefly.

NEMESIS: And who is this lucky fellow? Is he worthy of you? Does he appreciate the gift he was given?

Putting his real name into our chat feels risky. It's like getting too close to collapsing the game again.

LIBRARYGIRL: He's just a man, a random man – a pair of eyes to look at me. That's all.

There's another long, long silence, punctuated by the blinking cursor and the commentary on the television. As the tension builds I reach for the handset and press the mute. Insanely, I'm afraid I'll miss Nemesis's answer if I'm distracted by the box.

NEMESIS: How lucky he is. To see your beauty. To see your sex. Every detail of it. Did you exhibit yourself to him? Allow him to see the sweet flower of your cunt . . . the perfect pink folds . . . your clit? Ah yes, how fortunate he is . . . to be able to see it.

I wish I could hear his voice. Those words. They're just pixels on a screen, but impossibly there's an unmistakeable nuance to them. What is it? Irony? It's ridiculous, but I get a fleeting sense of bitterness somehow, a sadness about that phrasing.

And he keeps repeating the word 'see'.

LIBRARYGIRL: Don't worry, he only got a quick flash. You know just as much about my pussy as he does.

Especially as you've touched it.

I type in the words 'are you Daniel?' then delete them. It's too soon. He'll tell me in his own good time.

NEMESIS: How did it make you feel? To do something so daring, so naughty? Did it turn you on?

Did it? Hell, yes! It's turning me on now. Sex in my marriage was nice, but pretty safe and ordinary. Not a bit like all this.

LIBRARYGIRL: Yes. Yes, it did.

He wants me to elaborate, that's obvious, but he's bloody well going to have to *ask* if he wants more details. I can sense him smiling, wherever he is, but I don't see his face this time, just the ghost of a pair of beautiful lips curving and the glint of white teeth. God, this is so weird! It's almost as if Daniel and Nemesis are separating again, and the tiniest whisper of doubt about my conclusions nags my brain.

NEMESIS: And did you do anything about that? Did you proposition this random man of yours and ask him to fuck you and ease your frustration? Or did you sneak off to a secret place and attend to yourself?

Ah ha, clever clogs, neither of those!

I almost type that but, for a moment, I'm shaking too hard. This is a strange dance. A game of cat and mouse. I should speak out, demand clarity, demand his identity. But I know I won't. I'm prevented from doing that, and my gut tells me he's bound by the same inhibition. A bondage of the mind that he's wound both of us into without either of us realising it. I was never like this before. I've never even imagined such a sensual and intellectual joust. But now it's as essential as drawing breath.

LIBRARYGIRL: No, I didn't. I didn't do either of those things.

A pause.

LIBRARYGIRL: Although I wanted to, either one of them. Or both!

Now I hope that he's drawing breath. Or something. Either way, he takes a minute to absorb what I've said and, as the seconds tick, the need to 'attend to myself' right now grows and grows.

NEMESIS: What? No release for my delicious Gwendolynne?

That's a crying shame. A beautiful woman like you should never be left wanting. You shouldn't deny yourself, ever.

It's his turn to pause, and leave me on tenterhooks.

NEMESIS: Unless, of course, I tell you to deny yourself.

LIBRARYGIRL: I never said that I didn't come.

Yeah, make what you will of that one, Mr – or should I say Professor – Know-it-all!

The cursor flashes and flashes and I consider my options. Shall I make a cup of tea? Shall I turn up the sound on *Police Camera, Action*? Shall I slip my hand into my pyjama bottoms and attend to myself? It would be stealing secret pleasure right out from under Nemesis's unknowing cybernose, and beating him at his own game. Yet I have the eeriest feeling that he'd know if I touched myself. He'd just know.

Despite that, I'm tugging at my drawstring waistband when words start to stream into the chat box again.

NEMESIS: Dear Lord, you are the most tantalising and wayward woman, my Gwendolynne. You really do seem to delight in perplexing and teasing me.

Pot, kettle, kettle, pot!

NEMESIS: I expect you to give me total frankness and you evade and deceive me at every turn. I really should punish you with another forfeit. Or maybe we should elevate our game to the next level?

LIBRARYGIRL: What's that?

Can he hear my heart pounding?

NEMESIS: On the next level we meet, and I *really* punish you.

Oh my God. That's what I want, I think. But I also don't want it. I'm afraid of the new game, and yet I'm starting to get frustrated by the subterfuge. My playmate's contrariness is starting to rub off on me and I don't think either of us really knows what we want now.

But fantasies of punishment make me push my hand defiantly between my legs. I will have my pleasure now, and screw him! I groan as I discover swimming wetness.

Visions of Daniel standing over me, clad in black and with his features half covered by a leather mask, set me squirming against the bed with my laptop rocking on my knees. I keep Nemesis waiting deliberately while I strum and flick at my clit. The two personae are fused in my mind now, regardless of reality. Nemesis has Daniel's beautiful face as he looms over me like a prince of sensual menace.

My clitoris is so sensitive, I can hardly bear to touch it, but still I go on pushing myself – punishing myself – by relentlessly going back and forth and round and round. I keep expecting the demand 'Gwendolynne, what are you doing?' Especially when I take the tiny bud of flesh between my fingertips and gently tug it. I hover on the brink. Teeter over the crevasse. Stand, metaphorically, on the tips of my toes at the top of the ski jump. And then, amazingly, I pull back. Because of him.

My fingers are pungent and glistening with my arousal as I apply them to the keyboard and start to type.

LIBRARYGIRL: When did I ever say I was definitely going to give you total frankness? I don't remember that.

NEMESIS: Touché!

Is that all? No more words appear for a few moments, and I start to panic. What if he's not interested in anything less than total frankness? But then, that's BS. He's not being open with me, is he? All this masquerading behind silly names!

I'm virtually certain that Daniel is Nemesis and, what's more, I'm willing to bet that he knows I know. So what if we do begin the new game? I can take it! Hell, I *want* it!

Not thinking too deeply about the consequences, I start to type again.

LIBRARYGIRL: I think I ought to be frank though. I need to confess some more stuff. It's preying on my mind, and who can I tell if I don't tell you?

In either of your guises.

NEMESIS: That's better. Now we're getting somewhere. You said that you came after you showed this random man of yours your pussy. Tell me more details. I want to know everything that happened. Hold nothing back.

Well, I suppose he'll enjoy it from a different perspective this time. And maybe I *will* cheat? That'll add a bit more spice.

LIBRARYGIRL: When I showed him my pussy he got excited. He got all stiff in his jeans and I thought, seeing as how he'd seen mine, I wanted to see his.

NEMESIS: Seems fair.

LIBRARYGIRL: So I sort of leapt at him and unzipped him and got him out.

NEMESIS: You mean that you unfastened the trousers of this random man you barely know and exposed his penis? Where on earth did all this happen? Not in the Lending Library surely?

LIBRARYGIRL: No! Of course not. Even I'm not *that* crazy.

NEMESIS: Where then? I asked for details, remember, and I'm getting very few of them. Remember that forfeit?

How can I forget? There's a partitioned bit of my brain that won't stop thinking about it. Imagining punishment. Delicious mock humiliation that makes me melt and quiver. The ministrations of some as yet unencountered and mysterious facet of Professor Daniel Brewster.

LIBRARYGIRL: There's this place in the library. Down in the basement. It's very secluded, a secret librarians' hideaway. Perfect for that sort of thing.

NEMESIS: What sort of thing?

LIBRARYGIRL: Hold on, I'm getting to it.

I so want to touch myself again, but he's forcing me to type. The bastard, he's the one who deserves to be punished. For a moment I drift off behind my partition into a fantasy of me in a leather outfit. I've lost a bit of weight and I look amazing – and he's kneeling before me. I see him as an idealised male form, an archetype of smooth muscle and gleaming skin, but his hair is dark and wild, Daniel's hair. I see no face as he has his lips pressed to my shiny polished boot.

My fingers float over the keyboard, and I almost start describing the subjugated man, then I remember what I'm supposed to be telling Nemesis about.

LIBRARYGIRL: He was beautiful and big and I sucked him. He filled my mouth and he was salty and fine and delicious. I sucked him until he came and I swallowed the lot. It was yummy.

NEMESIS: You mean that you performed oral sex on this stranger, this random man?

LIBRARYGIRL: He's not a stranger. I know him slightly. I fancy him. In fact he's just the sort of man I'd give a blow job to anyway.

I seem to taste Daniel's flavour again, and it's blended with an aroma of raw sexual excitement that hums over the telephone network, shooting at bits or bytes per second from Nemesis to me. It's as if I can feel the energy and blood that's stiffening his cock.

I'm spiralling down into a dark and luscious world, and he's beside me. Smiling. I smile back, watching the cursor pulse like a heartbeat or the throb of my clitoris.

NEMESIS: So how often do you administer blow jobs to men that you fancy, then? Once? Twice? Three times a week? What do you do? Single them out in the Lending Library then lure them off to this hideaway of yours and suck their cocks? You're beginning to sound like a bit of a hussy to me, Gwendolynne, a trollop even. It seems to me that you're a woman of wild appetites and very little control over them.

I rock my hips against the mattress. He's right. I can smell my own arousal, clinging to my fingers and pooling between my thighs. My appetites *are* wild, but it's him that's whipped them up to this intensity. Because of him, I feel as if I've been reborn, or shed a skin. I feel totally different. Before, I was quiet. I lived safely. I was happy, but in a smooth, unruffled way. Now I'm all over the place and I like it, I like it. No, I bloody love it!

And I love being described as an old-fashioned hussy and a trollop.

LIBRARYGIRL: Well, I don't get the chance to give blow jobs as often as I'd like. That's why I jumped at the chance with my random friend. It was a perfect opportunity. I can't do you so I thought I'd do him instead.

No words appear, but I hear joyous male laughter in my head. I've tickled him, I know, and yet out of the blue I suddenly feel a little wistful. I wish, how I wish he were here in the bed beside me, so I could shove aside my laptop, roll towards him and we could make love. Maybe I could even give him another blow job first, at least to start with. Then, after that, I'd love to push him on to his back and climb astride him, taking control of the situation and of him.

NEMESIS: You'll get your chance, my dear. Don't you worry. I'll have all the pleasure of your mouth that I want, beautiful Gwendolynne. And sooner rather than later, mark my words.

Bring it on, macho man! I can take it! I feel like jumping up and punching the air, but I settle for shouting 'Yes!' to my empty bedroom.

LIBRARYGIRL: Is that a fact?

I pause, and let that sink in, then hit him with a daring foray.

LIBRARYGIRL: Maybe you've had it already?

Long silence. Long, long silence. Oh bugger, I've spoilt everything.

NEMESIS: I think you're tired, my dear. You're talking in riddles. Maybe I should let you sleep now?

My heart races again. He's not denied it and he's not confirmed it. Shall I push?

No. Not yet. Not yet.

LIBRARYGIRL: I'm fine. I'm not tired. In fact I'm horny. You can't wind a girl up this way then decide you've had enough.

Again, the phantom peal of laughter, and the ghost of a very beautiful smile. I sense a tacit admission. He *does* know that I know, and that I know that he knows that I know. I want to hug myself and laugh and roll about on the bed. But more than that, I want to come – and he knows that too.

NEMESIS: You're very impertinent and forward, Gwendolynne. I thought I was in charge here. If I indulge you and we play a little longer tonight, there will be a bigger forfeit. I might have to compel you to take the next step and risk a bigger game.

You know I want it, Nemesis, don't you?

His words and the patterns of pixels seem to stream across my clit like electricity. Just the thought of that bigger game, that higher level, that greater involvement, makes my head feel light, as if it's foam-filled. I showed my sex this afternoon to a man who's still a relative stranger. What more can I be manoeuvred into doing? Daring? Risking? I'm entering a velvet-lined cage of sin.

LIBRARYGIRL: Do your worst. I can take it. Let's play.

NEMESIS: Push two fingers inside yourself. Work them in and out as if I'm on top of you and thrusting into you. Do it for five minutes. No typing. Just finger-fucking.

LIBRARYGIRL: OK.

NEMESIS: Can you imagine me as you do it? Make up a

picture of me in your mind, or choose a face you know and pretend it's me?

Crafty sod.

LIBRARYGIRL: I can manage that. I'll use my random man. He's very cute.

NEMESIS: Well, do it then, and be quick about it, or I'll make you use three fingers.

LIBRARYGIRL: All right, all right.

I can't wait for his answer. I throw the laptop sideways, with scant regard for its fragile components, and wrench the covers away from my hips. My pyjamas twist around my thighs as I push them down in a bunch and wriggle on to my back at the same time, rubbing my bare bottom on the mattress as I go.

The ceiling is a screen for my fantasies as I jam my hand between my thighs, seeking the portal of my sex. I'm a seething swamp of heat and moisture. Two fingers slip in as if plunging into butter. Shall I try a third? Shall I pre-empt him?

It's more difficult than I anticipated. Three is a lot. But I breathe deep, gulping in air, and take myself to another place ... the library basement ... and I'm on the table, being mounted by Daniel. My three fingers become his magnificent cock and slide right in.

Being ravished by him is a dazzling ordeal. I'm speared, laid waste to, opened and stretched. I know that it's me, really, but somehow it's also him, huge and breathtaking.

I swear one day I'll make this dream come true.

Legs thrown wide amongst the papers and precious, irre-placeable documents, I writhe and squirm like a monkey. I'm a shambles, a mess, skirt all bunched up, knickers round one ankle, formerly crisp white blouse ripped open and bra pulled askew. Daniel/Nemesis is atop me, shoving hard, his own clothing similarly disarrayed. I'm grabbing at his bare bottom as he thrusts and thrusts, my hands beneath the tails of his black cotton shirt. His dark jeans are pushed halfway down his thighs.

As I work myself, I spiral down deeper and deeper into my imagination. Daniel is holding me down with one strong arm while he's fondling my breasts roughly with his free hand. He tweaks and twists my nipples and I'm loving it, loving it. It's the rawest and most uncomfortable sex I've ever had, but still it touches my heart and moves my soul.

Oh, I want you, Professor Hottie. Oh, how I want you.

Pounding at myself like this only leads to the inevitable. A performance like this can't be held out against for long. My body convulses and I shout with pleasure, coming brutally. My harsh breath rasps the air as if I've just run a marathon. A few feet away the chat window waits in empty silence. Then, as if I've summoned him, the words appear again.

NEMESIS: So, Gwendolynne, have you done it? Have you done what I asked?

I haul myself upright, wiping my fingers on the duvet cover. What a slut I am. What the hell is that box of tissues beside the bed for? I really am getting sleazy.

Feeling as if I've been put through a mangle backwards, I reach for the laptop and barely have the energy to pull it towards me. My arms flop like a rag doll's and I just want to sit here panting for a bit longer, but Nemesis's words pulse as if they burn permanently into the screen.

LIBRARYGIRL: Yes.

It's all I can manage.

NEMESIS: Yes? Is that all you can come up with? I want details, young lady, details! I want glorious Technicolor and precise terminology, or it'll be another forfeit for you, and this time a big one.

Greedy swine! Always making his demands and issuing

threats. I see him smile as he teases and goads me. And I smile back. I want to play longer, but I'm tired, I'm so tired.

LIBRARYGIRL: You've worn me out. I'm exhausted. I'll take the forfeit.

His whoop of triumph seems to sing along the miles of telephony and through the Wi-Fi. This is exactly what he wanted, and now he's the one who's going to be fantasising as he takes himself in hand. Imagining *me* doing whatever outrageous erotic act he comes up with.

NEMESIS: It's going to be a bigger one. I'm going to ask a lot of you, my darling. A quantum leap this time.

My heart thuds with energy and, despite the lethargy in my body, I begin to feel aroused again.

LIBRARYGIRL: Bring it on.

And he does, how he does ... But all I can think of is the word 'darling'.

8   A Quantum Leap

I can't wait to tell Professor Hottie about this! I want to watch his face as I outline the next forfeit. I want to see the hidden smile, the secret complicity in his eyes. I want to see how far I can tease this out before he gives in and concedes and I win. Because it's definitely a contest now. To see how far we can go, and who'll cave in first.

Will he say, 'All right! I give in! I'm Nemesis!' Or will I say, 'Admit it! Just admit it! You're Nemesis!'

There's still the tiniest notion, behind another of those partitions of mine, that I've got this all wrong and he *isn't* Nemesis. And that I really am playing the most dangerous game with a very seriously twisted and perverted individual. But right in my heart, where rationality is a most infrequent visitor, I know, I just know that Daniel Brewster is my Nemesis. Or Nemesis is my Daniel. Or whatever.

Either way, I'm determined he'll fold first.

I've pulled out all the stops at the library today, and I must admit that the looks I've got from Techie Greg, Clarkey and even Mr Johnson the Borough Librarian have been priceless. Like the frosting on a yummily exciting cake.

I've gone with my nineteen-fifties Nympho Librarian persona again. The fitted blouse, the slim skirt, the stockings. Once again, I lament that I can't wear high heels in the Lending Department and the other public areas. The floors have been redone recently and stilettos are strictly forbidden.

I've done a slightly different thing with my hair today. It's in a very loose plait, asymmetric again, but with a lot more of those self-consciously seductive tendrils trailing down the side of my face.

I really think this office-sex-bomb look suits me, and it's definitely working. No more moping around in baggy clothes for me. From now on I'm going to hark back to the days when it was OK to have plenty of curves. Hell, Monroe was a plus size by today's stupid standards, and she had grown men grovelling on their knees to adore her.

Part of me wants Daniel to grovel too. Yes, indeed. But quite a lot of me keeps having these other disturbing and knicker-moistening fantasies about me grovelling to him – and much, much more. The leather mask and sometimes even a pair of high, black leather huntsman's boots seem to figure quite a bit.

The suggestion box yields no blue letters today. Disappointing, admittedly, but I console myself that we've moved on to more interactive modes of communication now. Nemesis has even given me a mobile number to ring, which I have to call when I've made my decision. Although, when that'll be, I don't know. It's one mad challenge he's posed, this so-called quantum leap.

He wants me to proposition another of my 'random men' in a bar. He says he might – or might not – watch me from a distance, in disguise, while I pick up a horny male I've never set eyes on before for anonymous sex. I wonder if he's been reading one of those notorious call-girl blogs?

Smiling, I stare out across the library. We've only been open a short time but some of the regulars are already drifting around the shelves or settling down with the papers. What would they think if they knew what their familiar Miss Price was up to? Maybe some of them suspect? It's not just the eyebrows of staff members that have shot up again this morning. One of the unemployed blokes is stealing sly glances at me over the top of the *Sun* and the boring local rag.

For my hooker gig, Nemesis says I have to choose the hotel, and I've a shrewd idea which one he'll expect it to be. I suppose I ought to oblige him, but it would be fun to shock the living daylights out of him by suggesting a scummy old dive like the Horse and Jockey or the Master Bricklayers' Arms.

Speaking of Nemesis, where is the prime suspect this morning? I managed to snatch a minute to sneak down to Professor Hottie's cubby-hole before opening time, to see if he'd let himself in by the back door. But there's no sign of him. Which, of itself, isn't unusual. He's an honoured visitor here, and he isn't on the clock. He doesn't even have to come in every day. Although I would have thought there was a rather piquant incentive over and above the Livesey Archive and its irreplaceable documents.

The thought of *not* seeing him has an extraordinary effect on me. I'd always believed it was just a figure of speech when someone described their heart sinking, but I'd swear mine plummeted southwards at the idea of not seeing his adorable face today.

Adorable? What the hell is wrong with me? Have I fallen for him, other than just fancying him something alarming and wanting to play demented sex games with him? Are there finer feelings lurking in the lust? Now that *is* wilfully stupid.

This alarming implication sends the day into a downturn, but I try not to show it to my public. I pin a smile to my face and launch myself into reader advice with almost manic enthusiasm, going the extra mile or several for everybody who essays even the most diffident enquiry. At break time I race downstairs, but it's all in darkness, and I return to the light still carrying the basement's forlorn emptiness inside me.

I've just got to take my mind off men with beautiful mouths, magical fingers, perfectly demonic thought processes and twisted imaginations. I daren't allow my wayward musings to go down those very, very dangerous paths.

He only wants a temporary fling. And that's what Nemesis wants too. Oh, this is more screwed up than a very, very screwed-up thing! But still, I'm itching for it to be lunchtime so I can hurtle downstairs again and check if he's there.

Just when I'm about to go off duty, and have abandoned all hope, he arrives. Through the front door and with a woman! And she's beautiful … They pause just inside the vestibule, and she stares into his eyes, this vision, her own full of tender concern as she pats him on the arm, and says something quiet and solicitous, leaning towards him.

With molten lead in my gut, I want to scratch her eyes out. She's older than me, and older than him. Forties, but glowing and prime-time with it. Her hair is expensive, with high- and lowlights, and she's wearing this gorgeous suit that screams 'designer'. She ought not to be Daniel's type, but he returns her fond look with a shrug and a twist of his lips that's strangely intimate. Now I want to scratch *his* eyes out too.

I wish I could hear what they're saying, but from their body language I can make out that she seems to be worried about him and trying to reason with him over something, and he's doing the 'man' thing, shrugging it off, even though he pulls off his glasses for a moment and rubs his eyes and the back of his dark curly head.

There's a bit more of this to and fro, then she leans in and kisses him softly on the cheek. This deposits a touch of soft pink lipstick on his skin, and in another possessive gesture she wipes it away.

As she disappears, Daniel glances towards my desk, but, just as he begins to approach, a reedy and rather worried voice to one side of me asks, 'Please, can you help me?'

I want to shout, 'No! Fuck off! It's my dinner break,' but I turn and smile. It's a young and very harassed-looking woman with a child in a pushchair, and she looks close to tears. Haltingly she describes a school project her older kid is doing, which needs to be completed by tomorrow. Not everyone has the internet yet, it seems, and she's found her way to the public library for the first time in her life, looking for resources. Ten minutes later, and with a deskful of books from the four corners of Lending, she's thrilled and touchingly grateful. Even her pushchair babe seems to have calmed, sensing the sudden lift in his frazzled mum's spirits. Her thank-yous are effusive and, despite all my fretting, behind the partition, about Daniel, I too feel better. There's a solace and a satisfaction in getting to the essence of my job, instead of going through a bunch of bureaucratic motions. I encourage her to come back any time and ask for me.

This feeling of missionary professional wellbeing quickly dissipates, though, when I think of Ms Designer-Suit-and-Lowlights and her divine right to kiss Daniel in public. As there's one of the library's perennial rota glitches and nobody to relieve me this lunchtime, I close the desk, make for the staff area, slam my card through the time clock and scoot down the back stairs to the basement.

Nothing like a bit of confrontation to release the growing tension. Well, I can think of better things … and hey, maybe I'll get them if I don't pick a fight instead.

My heart bounces like a rubber ball as I bound down the steps at a foolhardy speed. If Old Johnson happens to be around it'll be a reprimand, for sure. But who cares? I've simply got to find out who that woman is.

I know my jealousy is ridiculous. Professor Hottie and I aren't an item. We haven't even had sex together, properly. A bit of fiddling about and a blow job do not a steady relationship constitute. Temporary fling, remember? Although the woman in the foyer just now didn't look temporary or fling-like.

I slow down. I need to cool it. It's just a game.

He's not in his cubby-hole. Books and documents are spread out as usual, with the laptop glowing softly to one side. Another of his strategy games is running, I notice. Does he ever actually do any work down here? His tweed jacket is draped over the back of his chair. I wonder if he's slipped to the washroom and I'm rocked in my flatties by the memory of what I saw last time I followed him there. So elegant. So beautiful. So male.

A tiny sound breaks me out of my lustful reveries. Was that a groan? It certainly sounded like one to me. Is he at it again?

I pad along to the end of the basement where some weather-beaten old furniture is stored, from earlier times and a more genteel library experience. Back then, the library had an elegant reading room with leather upholstered settees for passing gentry to sit and read copies of *The Times* on. These venerable seating arrangements are losing their stuffing nowadays, but I discover Daniel stretched out full length on one of them, his arm thrown across his face, covering his eyes. His other arm hangs down, almost brushing the floor, spectacles dangling from his fingers. He looks like a cross between a fallen archangel and a Victorian poet trashed off his face on absinthe and laudanum.

'Are you all right?'

At the sound of my voice, he shoots upright, then grabs at his head again.

'Yes . . . sort of.'

'Liar!'

His eyes look like two dark wells in this shadowy, ill-lit corner of the basement, and he's obviously in pain. This is the second time I've caught him down here not exactly in the shining prime of health.

He swings his legs down to the floor, making a space for me on the settee. I sit but he's making a bit of a thing of replacing his glasses, and still doesn't look at me directly. Like the elegant woman earlier, I place a hand on his arm. His flesh feels hot and feverish through the dark-blue cotton of his shirt.

'What is it? Something's wrong.'

'Just a headache. It's nothing. Don't fret.'

His voice sounds strained, raw.

'You seem to get them a lot. Have you been to a doctor?'

He squares his shoulders and sits up straight, and now he *does* look at me, the twinkle returning to him.

'I'm just working hard. It's nothing.' He places his hand over mine, his fingertips light, moving slightly. 'How are *you*?'

In bits now, because he's touched me. These same fingers drove me to madness yesterday evening, and their delicate movements already have me halfway there again. In the blink of an eye, I've flipped from the workaday world of the library and its limited budgets and anxious borrowers and entered the pressure-cooker realm of Nemesis and his playful sexual mind-games.

Here, I can say anything. Do anything. Want anything.

'Do you really want to know?'

'Of course. I'm your friend, aren't I?'

Some friend . . . I glance at his hands, and imagine them on me. Then I seem to see his fingers holding a pen, or dancing across keys. It's on the tip of my tongue to demand the truth, but instead I simply say, 'OK then, I'll tell you how I feel. I feel horny!' His brows shoot up, but he smiles. 'There, is that friendly enough for you?'

'Well, that's one way of taking a man's mind off his head-ache.' He edges closer, and I take a hit of a luscious cologne. It's woodsy and spicy, toe-curlingly exotic. Down below, I feel myself flutter in response. 'Do you ... er ... want to do some-thing about it?' His thick dark lashes flutter down. Magnified by the lenses of his spectacles, they look like black velvet fans in the low light. 'Purely in the interests of friendship, of course. And it would give you something to tell Nemesis about.'

'Fuck Nemesis!'

I laugh as it dawns on me I'm almost certain that I'm about to do that very thing. He laughs too, and I know I'm halluci-nating because I seem to see a salacious sparkle bounce off his even white teeth.

'Indeed,' he concurs, his head tilting slightly. Did he wink then? He might have done. It's quite possible.

Indeed, indeed. He's so tempting, so delicious, and there's a quality about him that makes me feel powerful. He might have the upper hand most times, but right now he still looks a little bit frazzled around the edges and vulnerable. I surge forwards, making him start slightly, then grab him by the back of the neck to bring his face to my kiss. At the very last minute he snatches off his glasses and tosses them away across the confined space around the squashed settee. I hear the soft tap of them landing on the thin old carpeting. I hope they're not broken but the worry's like a minor tickle a million miles away. I love the feel of Daniel's curls in my fingers and the moist heat of his mouth around my invading tongue. I love the way he goes 'Mmm ...' and seems to swallow the very breath of my life.

His act of compliance is just that, an act. Even while I'm kissing him, his clever hands are at work. The tails of my blouse are out of my waistband before I know it, and hot searching fingertips are gliding up my back to the catch of my bra. He flips it open with suspicious deftness and the sensation of the garment sliding free against my skin is odd, but also sleazy and arousing. He compounds the sleaze factor by sliding his hand around, shoving up one of the cups and giving my breast a rough, demanding squeeze. In the same instant his tongue surges forwards, subduing mine, possessing my mouth with far greater assurance than I ever had.

I squeal silently and wriggle my hips when he pinches my nipple. The pain is tiny but acute, and it pierces my heart and my soul. How the hell did he know that would turn me on? I didn't even know it myself.

He does it again, not hard but with authority, and I feel the warm rush of arousal in my panties. Suddenly, I want to be bare down there. I want his hand again, touching, exploring, pleasuring. I want his fingers inside me, maybe not three but certainly two, pushing, pushing, pushing and readying me for the ingress of his cock.

Reaching down while he's still playing with my breast, I haul at my skirt, pulling it up, exposing my suspenders and stocking-tops. I pull with both hands, getting the cloth out of the way, bunching it at my waist, and then I start tugging at my knickers. Daniel abandons my breast as he feels what I'm doing, and helps. Between us, we drag my knickers off over my shoes, and then I'm partially naked from my bundled skirt to the tops of my thighs.

My eyes fly open, and I discover that Daniel's are closed, those heavenly lashes lying across the top of his cheekbones. He's savouring me in darkness, employing touch only as he flicks the lace and elastic of my garter belt, then slides his fingers along one suspender to the thick dark welt of my stocking. One fingertip slides under the nylon, delicately stroking, his nail hard against the soft bare skin that for so long has only felt my own touch as I wash ... and sometimes pleasure myself.

For about a minute he just dawdles around my stocking-top, teasing me. He's so close to my centre but he's staying away from it on purpose. I can feel myself oozing and flowing, my honey pooling on the cracked leather beneath my bottom. My sex is pouched and pouting, screaming silently for contact.

I lose my patience, grab his hand and jam it between my legs. I've had enough of this shilly-shallying about, and the low sound of appreciation that Daniel breathes into my mouth says he's not averse to my taking the initiative.

Immediately he assumes the perfect configuration, hand gently cupping my pussy, middle finger surging magisterially between my sex lips and zeroing in on my clit. He presses hard, as hard as he pinched me, and, almost as I register that, his other hand is inside my flapping bra again and delicately twisting my aching nipple. Twist, tug, press, rub. Twist, tug, press, rub.

My vagina flutters and clenches and I almost bite Daniel's tongue as I come. I'm glad he's got dominion of my mouth, because without it I'd be screaming – and, even though we're down here in the forsaken bowels of the library, somebody would be bound to hear me.

He works me right through my climax. He's merciless. I jerk and jiggle and clench and flow, performing for him. But inside I'm planning retribution. He commands my passion now, but soon I'll own his.

Still fluttering, I break away, set my hands against his chest and push him back against the settee.

'Condom? Have you got a condom?' I rasp, moving over him with little grace but a lot of breathless determination.

'Yes,' he gasps back at me, and, as his hands have been dislodged from my body, he scrabbles about in the back pocket of his jeans and pulls out a familiar small foil package.

Now isn't that convenient?

His eyes open for a moment, and he gives me a wry little smile and a roll of his shoulders.

You devil, you were planning this all along! I want to shake him, reprimand him, tell him he's an arrogant, presumptuous, teasing bastard of a manipulative pervert. But I don't, mainly because I want to fuck him.

Fixing him with a stern, admonishing look that he almost misses because he leans back and closes his eyes again, I attack his belt buckle, then his jeans button, then his flies. Astonishingly, he's wearing no underwear. More arrogant assumption that he was going to get his end away today. I should tell him that he's got a nerve, but I'm too dumbstruck by the glorious sight of his penis, rising like a rosy spear from between the dark denim wings of his jeans.

I'm almost faint with anticipation. I want him. I want him inside me. I want to have sex with famous television historian and all-round clever devil Professor Daniel Brewster. And I want it now.

'Give me that!' I grab the condom and wrench open the packet. The contraceptive inside is slick and silky, but nowhere near as silky as the head of Daniel's cock. Clear, silver fluid is seeping from the little eye there, his arousal just as eager and revealing as mine.

It's a while since I put a condom on a man, but it's one of those skills you never forget, because it comes with the perk of handling a man's delicious stiffness. I manage to achieve our goal without fumbling, but the heat in his mighty flesh is unnerving. As is the agonised beauty of his face as I enrobe him.

Finally, he's ready. Clad in rubber and even harder and higher than before, if that's possible. My pussy throbs and purrs in anticipation.

Now, how are we going to manage this? I have a strong urge to be on top. I need to assert myself. Kicking off my shoes, I climb astride, kneeling on the leather with my thighs straddling his. The ancient settee creaks ominously as I adjust my position, holding on to the back, almost pushing my semi-freed breasts into his face. My thighs feel as if they're creaking too, with the strain of holding myself above him. So I reach down, take hold of his cock and guide him into me.

My descent seems to take a long, long time. There's a universe of difference between looking at a big cock and having it inside me, and only now, as it's happening, do I truly apprehend the exquisite distinctions. He feels huge in length and girth, and he knocks my breath out of me. I gasp for air, still descending and still expanding to accommodate him.

At last I'm at rest, transfixed by that hot, sweet prong of flesh. I need to take a moment to absorb the fact.

I bend over him, breathing deeply and enjoying the sensation of being full of him. The feeling is intense, almost solemn, unexpectedly emotional. My eyes fill with strange, irrational tears. Just a fling? Oh dear, I'm in trouble.

My unfastened bra slides against my breasts as I move. Settling down further, and letting out a little gasp, I wrench off my blouse, tugging furiously at the still-fastened cuffs until the buttons fly. Once that's off, I fling it clear, then follow it with my bra. Now I'm naked to the waist, and filled to the brim with the gorgeous cock of the man I've got a horrible feeling that I've fallen in love with. I *am* in trouble.

I'm glad that Daniel's eyes are still closed, and that if he opens them the emergency lighting in this basement is forgivingly dim. The tears are still in my eyes and I'm certain that hopeless love is in my face.

His hands settle on the rounded curves of hips and bottom and the tenderness of his hold is more heartbreaking than ever. I hope to God that this is just infatuation, or it's going to be the hell of all hells when our fling-type thing is over.

I look at his face, his beautiful, famous, devious face, and my sexual sorrow transmutes shockingly into anger. Oh yes, this frolic doesn't mean nearly as much to him as it does to me. He must have scores of groupies. And while we're on the subject of the Professor's women, just who was that elegant, sophisticated vision he was chatting up in the lobby?

'Who was that woman?'

I can't believe I just spoke. What the hell is wrong with me? I'm drowning in the most sumptuous sensations, yet still my stupid jealous brain is screwing things up.

Daniel's eyes open, and for a moment they're unfocused and hazy. He blinks as if he's not quite sure who he's seeing – but I see red. Maybe he's even fantasising about her? 'You know, the one with the suit who you were snogging in the lobby.'

He frowns, still scrunching up his eyes, then seems to focus. Letting out an exaggerated sigh, he grips me hard round the waist, bucks up his hips and jams me down yet more firmly on his erection.

I let out a groan and feel as if steam is coming out of my ears. My body is stretched around him, the tension tugging hard on my clit. I forget that any other woman on earth even exists. There's only me sitting on Daniel, full of his cock. He thrusts up again and pulls me down, and it's not just the decrepit settee that creaks and groans.

'That woman ...' His voice is low and thrilling, his grip still hard. 'That woman is my cousin Annie, and she's the co-owner of the Waverley Hotel. Which is why I'm staying there.' Consolidating his grip with one hand, he swivels his wrist and slips his other between our bodies, finding my clit and flicking it. My pussy ripples around him and I see stars, my own eyes closing. He flicks me again and I start to come, still confused, still angry.

'Satisfied?' he growls and, taking my clitoris neatly between finger and thumb, he squeezes. When he gives my bottom a little slap, I *am* satisfied ... and I come. A scream bubbles in my throat, but at the last second I jam my fist in my mouth. Waves and waves of pleasure radiate from my clit where he grips it, holding on delicately even though I'm jerking and writhing all over the place.

He slaps me again and my orgasm surges. I half black out. I slump forwards and for a few minutes I just crouch over him, draped against his body, my chest heaving, my entire sex fizzing with aftershocks. His arms fold around me, cradling me, exquisitely gentle and tender where before he was domineering. It's as if I've been shot into space and now I'm floating down gently on my parachute.

Sex was never like this before. Maybe I've never even had sex before, just some pale and ineffectual simulation of it?

Eventually, I haul in a deep breath. I've touched down again. And the most pressing matter I have to deal with right now is the fierce erection that's still hot and hard inside me.

How on earth can this be? Does the man have superhuman powers? My ex or indeed any of my previous boyfriends would have finished long since. No way could they have withstood such an exciting ride, because surely it must have been as hectic for him as it was for me. And yet here he is, like a rock inside me, but a warm, blood-filled rock that pulsates with the force of his life.

I straighten a little, and look down at him. The devil! His smile is a picture. There *is* the tenderness, I wasn't mistaken – but shining through that is an infuriating male smugness. A 'look at me ... look at my powers of endurance ... you'll never beat me' expression which makes me want to do just that: beat him. I want to overwhelm him into shooting inside me, my helpless slave.

I shove back on his chest, bracing myself, adjusting my position. Then I lift and crash down again, taking him deeper. My pussy flickers dangerously again, another orgasm only a touch away, but I have the satisfaction of seeing Daniel's eyes open wide. And when I do it again he lets out a curse that's more appropriate for a merchant seaman than a highly educated and sophisticated academic.

'Shush!' I command him, leaning a little forwards again and covering his mouth with my hand.

Then I ride him, I really ride him, lifting up and pounding down on him again and again. Within seconds I'm coming, in a sudden, violent encore, but I work on through it, my body moving on auto while my mind sails among the stars.

And still he resists me, the bastard.

Enough already. I hunker down, squat really hard on him and clench my glowing sex around his cock. It makes me see those stars again, but I grit my teeth and grip him and work him as I've never gripped and worked a man before.

His hands grip my hips, digging into the too, too abundant flesh there, and I feel the tips of his nails threatening my skin. The fuck, he's still holding out on me! His beautiful face is a mask of strain and stubbornness, the line of his jaw hard as iron, his teeth clenched.

Bugger this!

Still tight on him, I rise up and crash down again. Two things happen simultaneously. No, three things. No, actually, four ...

Daniel snarls another seafaring oath. He comes, his hips pistoning crazily. I come again, the pleasure wrung from me almost as if it were pain.

And the ancient settee finally succumbs to the punishment we've inflicted on it and collapses under us with an almighty crash.

9 We Can End This

There's a moment of stunned, total silence, then I snap my eyes open and look right into Daniel's. They're brighter and happier than I've ever seen them, full of mirth and clear, despite the absence of his spectacles. We both start to shake, and laughter seems to gather momentum like that giant rolling ball that chases Indiana Jones. Just as I'm about to explode into howls of glee, another sound freezes us both to silence.

'Who's there? What's going on?'

It's Mr Johnson, the Borough Librarian, and, even though he must still be at the far end of the basement, it sounds horribly as if he's heading our way.

In a blur of movement, we disentangle, snatching up our gear like Special Forces reacting to an ambush. Acting purely on instinct, I grab Daniel's hand and drag him around the corner of the stacks and into a little hidey-hole I know of from tedious hours spent shelving down here. It's the one I've sometimes snuck away to for a few minutes' crafty porn reading.

Stolid footsteps approach.

'Is anyone there?' repeats the confused librarian, obviously confronting the thoroughly knackered sofa.

It's dark in our little niche. There's a wall light nearby but it's not on, and Daniel and I are huddled together next to a packing crate and a heap of old newspapers. As Mr Johnson tut-tuts in exasperation, our temporarily suppressed hysteria starts to bubble again, and both Daniel and I have to clap our hands over our faces and battle heroically against letting it out. I can't begin to imagine what will happen if my boss finds us, me half-naked and Daniel still with his deflated penis poking out of the front of his jeans. We can't sort ourselves out because even the slightest noise would lead to discovery.

After what seems like a protracted inch-by-inch examination of the settee, but in reality is probably just a cursory glance, Mr Johnson makes another little harrumph of befuddlement and then walks away, moving quickly between the stacks.

When we hear the door at the other end of the basement open and close, both Daniel and I first let out our breaths then collapse into uncontained merriment. This takes up several minutes, as we stagger out of hiding to tidy ourselves up and deal with the incriminating evidence of used condoms and missing blouse buttons. Eventually we're both more or less decent and back at Daniel's work table, but neither of us can stop smirking and breaking out into giggles now and again.

'That was mad. Just mad.' I roll up my sleeves to hide the lack of buttons on my cuff. Looks quite stylish and even more Fifties ... Maybe I'll set a trend among the staff? 'I've always imagined that there might've been naughty goings-on down here over the years, but I never thought I'd be one of them.'

'That was awesome, Gwendolynne.' Daniel gives me a smile from behind his newly restored glasses, but there's a hint of seriousness about him too. Have we gone too far? Got too intense? Burst out of the barriers of our fling arrangement? '*You* were awesome ... I feel as if you've just mopped the floor with me. But in a good way.'

I'm about to concur when out of the blue I start shivering in reaction. In shock. And it's not because I've just done something that could easily have cost me my job. No, it's what I feel. What I've so stupidly gone and let happen to me. Even though it's ridiculous, I'm now almost certain that I've fallen in love with Daniel Brewster and I want far more than just a bloody fling-type thing with him.

'What's wrong?'

I look up, and realise I've been in a fugue for a moment. Daniel's staring at me, his fine broad brow creased in a frown. He has a beautiful kiss curl that I want to reach out and touch and twirl around my finger, and the thought of doing that, in tender familiarity, calms me even though it shouldn't. I almost do it, but before I can he reaches out and takes my hand, squeezing it gently, and I don't need to. The warmth of his fingertips is just as soothing and reassuring.

'I was just thinking that we had a pretty close call there. It really *was* mad to have sex in a place where anybody on the staff could have discovered us at any moment.'

Daniel's mouth twists in a way that's not quite a smile. He looks perplexed, yet at the same time he's obviously still trying to be supportive.

'I'm sorry. It was my fault. I shouldn't have been so reckless. I put your job at risk. It was wrong of me.' He pauses, and his face become utterly serious. 'You know, we can stop this, if you want to. Just say the word. I love this thing we have. It's … well, it's very special. But I would never want to make life difficult for you, believe me. Not in any way.'

We can stop this …

For a second I teeter on the edge of tears again. He's sincere. I believe him utterly. He *does* care for me, even if only within the bounds of our present obsession. But it suddenly dawns on me: just what is it he's suggesting we should stop?

Gwendolynne and Daniel? Or Gwendolynne and Nemesis? Or have they always been one and the same thing?

'I don't want to stop.'

My words hang in the air. I can almost see them floating there, sounding far too vehement and desperate. Daniel eyes me from behind his glasses and, to my dismay, he looks distinctly wary. He's clever and intuitive. I bet he can read me like one of the old tomes in the archive, probably far more easily, and I could kick myself. He doesn't want more than a temporary relationship, and it must be written on my face that I want considerably more than that.

His broad intelligent brow crimps in a frown. He's framing his get-out clause, I just know it.

'Me neither.'

For a moment I think that I'm imagining things, just hearing what I want to hear, then the urge to leap up on the table and dance nearly gets me up there, before I stop myself. He *does* want to go on! There's still a chance! But before my grin gets too goofy and I do something that's even more deranged and besotted than I've already done, I get a grip on myself. Don't look too enthusiastic, woman, remember this is temporary. Just control yourself and enjoy what you've got while you've got it.

'Well, that's all right then.' I feign airiness and I know he sees through me, but I don't care about that *too* much. 'But I think we'd better behave ourselves down here in future, don't you?'

'Absolutely. There are plenty of other places for a nice fuck, aren't there?'

I'm about to ask where, then grab him by the hand and drag him off to one of them, when the grand old clock of Borough Hall chimes sonorously in the distance. With that, the outside world of not fucking and not playing mad games with Nemesis who is also Daniel claims me once more. My watch tells me that I've spent my entire lunch break down here and should be back on the clock. Immediately.

'Oh fuckadoodle-do! I should be back at work!'

I spring to my feet, and Daniel leaps up beside me.

'But what about lunch? You have to eat . . . I was just about to say, let's go out to the pub or a café or a restaurant.'

The idea is lovely, and I have a flash vision of us sitting at a table somewhere, just sharing food and a glass of beer, talking and laughing. Nothing particularly sexy, just good companionship. Closeness.

'Well, that's a lovely offer, Professor, but I've just spent my lunch hour, er, having you.' His puckish smile nearly slays me. 'I have to go, really. I have to.'

He nibbles his lip, then darts for his laptop bag. From one of its side pockets he produces a jumbo Snickers bar.

'Here. Lunch is on me.' He puts it into my hand and I feel as if I've just been handed a diamond necklace or an enormous lottery cheque. 'And I'll come up and collect you when you finish at teatime and we'll go somewhere. OK?'

For a moment I just gape at him, a haphazard angel with his dark, dishevelled hair, his serious spectacles and a face that seems at once infinitely masculine, infinitely sweet.

Oh shit, I have got it so bad for him.

'OK. Right. It's a date or whatever.'

Before I can do something immensely stupid, I give him a lightning peck on the cheek and turn and beat the hastiest of hasty retreats, away amongst the tall bookshelves, heading for the stairs. I carry my Snickers as if it's the Holy Grail, although I know that I'll still end up scoffing it. It's the nicest gift I've ever been given, but a girl's got to eat.

By teatime the Snickers bar is a sweet but distant memory. Sadly for my diet, I'm hungry again and loitering in the upstairs lobby, garnering some curious looks from Tracey, who's on evening duty on the Enquiry Desk. I've deliberately stood beyond the main doors and chatting distance, but it's drizzling outside so I'd be a fool to wait there, even for Professor Hottie.

What is he playing at? My watch tells me I've been stepping from foot to foot, trying to stay calm, for about fifteen minutes. Daniel knows what time I finish when I'm working a normal day, so where the hell is he?

Immediately, I feel guilty and worried in equal parts. Before we demolished it, he was lying on that settee for a reason. Another of his headaches or funny turns or whatever they are, I guess. Maybe he's down there now, slumped over the work table, wracked by a migraine or whatever it is he suffers from.

I'm just pushing the swinging door to the main Lending Library open when he appears from the door to downstairs, like a genie I've summoned from the land of dreams. He's set to leave, dark raincoat billowing around him as he walks, his laptop backpack slung over his shoulder and his briefcase in his hand. The perfect picture of the mad but sexy professor with his wild black curls, his glinting spectacles and his paraphernalia of academe.

'Sorry, some emails to deal with at the last minute. Hope I haven't kept you waiting too long.'

His complex smile makes every second of the fifteen minutes worthwhile. There's genuine penitence there, but also that impish twinkle I've come to love so much, the sexy spirit of Nemesis shining through the studious outward personality of Daniel.

How I wish we were back on that sofa again. Even if it is in bits and pieces on the basement floor.

'Oh shit!' he growls as we emerge together, followed by the scanning laser stare of Tracey, who was desperately trying to catch my eye as we left. Looks like at least a small portion of my 'secret' relationship will be common knowledge within the course of this evening's shift.

'I didn't realise it was raining.' He glances to and fro along the road. 'Where's the nearest place to eat?'

'Well, there's the West Side Fisheries ...' The diet, the diet! 'It's at the end of the road there.' I gesture, torn between visions of crisp golden chips and the pointer on my bathroom scales, swinging in the wrong direction. Showing bits of me now and again to an undeniably beautiful man has made me suddenly more aware of my size than I've almost ever been in the months since my divorce.

'Right, the West Side Fisheries it is.' He grabs me quite forcefully by the arm and hustles me through the teeming rain.

Soon, we're eating.

'This is good! We don't get them like this down south.' He bites a chip with his sharp white teeth, his face a picture of simple pleasure.

'Yeah, they're the best fish and chips in the Borough. But what with this and the Snickers, it really seems like you're trying to ruin my figure today. Maybe I should have had a salad?'

Daniel pauses, sets down his fork and reaches for his teacup. He takes a sip and gives me a very admonishing, professorial look from under his dark brows. After waiting until the waitress is well out of sight, he says, in a low voice, 'Your body is magnificent, Gwendolynne. It's sumptuous. Superb. I love every inch of it. You should be proud of your curves. They drive men mad.'

The words make me quiver. They're so husky, so intense, so hungry. He sounds as if he wants to eat me with just as much relish as he's bringing to his cod and chips and mushy peas, and his eyes flash behind his glasses to confirm his fervour.

Is this Nemesis speaking? Or Daniel? There really is very little difference between them, and any gap that there was is rapidly vanishing. He's just one man, but, like Janus, with two faces. Always tantalising me and never allowing me to know which to expect at any moment.

'Well, you know how it is ... it's just not fashionable to be a size 16 going on 18 these days.'

'Pish and tush! All this fashion business is meaningless. Men always have and always will adore women with luscious figures.' He forks up some chips and munches them in a way that looks vaguely rude. 'And you, my darling Queen of the Library, are the ultimate in lusciousness.'

And now I have confirmation. Nemesis calls me 'Queen of the Library' too. Daniel seems not to have noticed that he's given himself away. Although perhaps he has ...

'So, what's the latest from that old perv Nemesis? What's his latest challenge or forfeit or whatever? Did you have a chat last night?'

I eye him narrowly, but he doesn't crack one millimetre. His face is sexy and interested, and at the same time totally guileless. Or apparently so. For a moment, I experience a frisson of real fear at the thought of being involved with a man who's either demonically twisted and devious or the victim of a multiple personality disorder. But then the joy of the game kicks in again, and I wonder just how far I can push him towards giving in and admitting his trickery-freakery.

'Yeah, we had a chat.' I pause, pour some more tea, take a bite of buttered white bread, chew it.

Daniel shakes his head ever so slightly, acknowledging my two-can-play gambit. 'So?'

'Well, there was some of the usual stuff.'

His tongue slips out from between his lips and sweeps swiftly over the lower one.

'And then he issued a challenge.'

Daniel's eyes widen in a way that's worthy of Sir Laurence Olivier as I describe the forfeit and the call-girl-picking-up-a-john scenario.

'Are you going to do it? It sounds pretty risky.'

'Not really. You said you'd help me, right? Well, *you* can be the punter.'

He smiles, and a moment of perfect complicity passes between us. A delicious mutual awareness of the game and its pleasures. No need to speak of it, no need to acknowledge it or question it. In its own way it's as close as the sex is. All we have to do is play.

'OK, I'm up for that.'

'*Really?*'

He laughs. 'Hell, yes! Really!'

Right in the quick of me, I shudder. What's going on beneath that innocuous, immaculate red-and-white-checked table-cloth? Is he hard, imagining our next encounter? Has the thought of playing tart-and-punter games given him an erection right here in the West Side Fisheries?

'OK then, we need to choose a venue, and a night and a time. And then I have to let Nemesis know.' I'm trying to stay calm, stay organised, but all I can think about is Daniel's body. Visions of him naked, and of his cock, all hard and rosy, rampage through my brain, screwing with my concentration. 'I'm not sure if Nemesis wants to be there to spy on me, or just wants me to tell him about it afterwards. He seems to enjoy piling on the uncertainty.'

Daniel's head comes up and his eyes narrow. 'In which case, you needn't do any of it. You can just fabricate the whole thing.'

He's challenging me, of course.

'That's cheating.'

'But you don't owe this man anything. He's just a raving pervert. And he's manipulating you.'

Yes, *aren't* you.

'Actually, I think I do owe him.' As I say it, it hits me like a

139

chakabuku, that swift spiritual kick to the head they talk about in the movies. 'Without him, I wouldn't have … have seen the light.' He tips his head on one side, frowning. 'I would just have been forever wondering about sex, and the kinky stuff. Slyly reading erotica, daring to watch a video now and again … but I wouldn't have been *doing* it. And I certainly wouldn't have had the courage to fool about with *you*! So you owe him too.'

Daniel studies his fork, then glances back up at me. His lashes look a mile long behind his glasses. Then he gives me a smile of such beatific sweetness that I nearly swoon on the spot. It seems to say, *Well done! Now you understand, young Skywalker! The pupil has finally matched the teacher.*

'You're right, I do, don't I?' He laughs softly. 'Well, for that, I'd like to shake that man's hand.'

'Maybe you'll get a chance?' Right now I want to do more than shake his hand. Far more. 'So, where are we going to set this thing up? What about your hotel, the Waverley? It's got a lovely bar for the job. Or so I've heard. I've never actually been there.'

'Then you soon shall, my dear Gwendolynne, you soon shall,' he says roundly, reaching out to pat my hand as he does so. 'Now let's work out the logistics, shall we?'

Later, now, I'm thinking about our plan. Well, a bit. Actually I'm too confused, befuddled and frustrated to really do it justice. I'm also slightly worried, and more than a little miffed.

Daniel's gone to London.

For the next couple of days, and over the weekend, he'll be back in the metropolis, far, far away from the Borough and this librarian so sex-mad and lovelorn. And he'd never said a thing about it, not until we'd finished our meal and I was deep into the breathless 'will he, won't he want to see me tonight?' phase of our encounter. Upon which he told me he was going straight to the railway station. He's got an appointment, of some unspecified kind but one that made him frown, and he's visiting his parents, which also made him frown.

We parted with an exchange of phone numbers and his promise to call me. Does this mean *he'll* call me? Or will he call as Nemesis? And truly out himself?

For the moment, I don't really care. There was something off about our parting. As if he was hiding far, far more than his secret sexual peccadilloes.

I didn't push. Hell, I barely know the guy yet, even though I've had all sorts of sex with him.

Which is the root of my unease, I suppose. Like any kind of junkie, I'm craving my drug when it's not available to me. I keep clicking my 'check mail' button. I keep checking to see that my mobile is switched on. I keep wondering if I should have dashed back to the library before it closed to see if there was anything in the suggestion box for me.

But there's nothing for me anywhere tonight. Except for a bottle of cheapo Lambrini I bought on a whim at the super-market a few weeks ago.

Snickers, fish and chips and now another night on the booze – my healthy eating plans are shot to hell today, so I might as well just pig out on everything. I'll live on Slimfast for the next few days while Daniel is away. It won't offset the over-indulgence, but it might salve my conscience a little bit. A notion that makes me smile for the first time since he disappeared in the direction of the station. Who the hell am I kidding? I'll be comfort eating for Britain until he shows up again.

The wine is easy and sweet, and it doesn't take long until I'm mildly buzzed. I'm on late shift tomorrow at the library, so I'll have a few extra hours in the morning to recover.

I drift into a floating erotic fug, curled under the covers, still in my bra and pants like a total slut. I should get up, take a shower and sort myself out properly for bed, but I can't be bothered to summon the energy. And I don't want to wash away the faint essence of Daniel that lingers on my skin. It's a comfort, but also an odour of impropriety. A silken film covering my skin, lying thick between my legs and at my breasts and my throat, reminding me of him.

Bastard! Take what you want and bugger off, will you? I'll get my own back. One of these days, I'll make you crawl, Professor Hottie, I'll make you grovel and beg for just a sniff of me.

Once summoned, this idea gets a grip. I reach for my glass and knock down another belt of Lambrini. Not much left now, but I don't need it any more. The fantasies in my mind are far more intoxicating.

We're in a hotel room. It's quiet and luxurious, perfumed with potpourri. The décor is old-fashioned and chintzy. It's the Waverley, I suppose, the image culled from my notions of what it might be like and one or two pictures I saw in a brochure in our Tourist Information section.

I'm reclining on the traditionally patterned duvet in a sexy little red satin number, camisole and French knickers. I'm ten or even fifteen pounds lighter. Now *there's* a fantasy!

Daniel's kneeling before me, wearing just black jeans. His feet are bare and the lamplight makes his skin gleam like poured cream. His hair is wild and a bit mad as if he's been running his fingers through it. Or maybe I have? He isn't wearing his glasses, but I can't see his eyes because his head is respectfully bowed.

'Strip,' I command him, and he rises to his feet. As his fingers go to the button on his jeans, he looks up for an instant. He's either got his contacts in or he can see normally anyway in this dream, but his eyes are a furious blaze of defiance, even though he dutifully obeys me and unzips. As he shimmies out of the black denim, his cock bounds up and bounces meatily against his belly. He's hugely erect, his glans weeping fluid, the little eye so distended it appears to wink at me.

'Touch yourself,' I tell him as he steps out of his jeans.

He does as he's told, but his body is tense and his muscles are unyielding even as he gasps softly. His arousal must be hair trigger and I see him bite that sweet red lower lip of his as he fights to master a harrowing urge to pump and shoot immediately.

As he starts to weave his hips, and gets into a rhythm he's obviously enjoying, despite everything, I gesture imperiously.

'Never mind that. Time to service me.' I lounge back on the bed and nod downwards. 'Chop chop! Jump to it!'

He's livid with indignation and rampant desire, but his grace is faultless as he climbs on to the bed, kneels next to me and peels off my fragrant French knickers. I know they're fragrant because here in the real world of frowsty bed land I've got my hand between my legs and I'm playing in a puddle between my legs. And it *is* fragrant.

'Kiss them,' I command, and he presses his face to the aromatic red satin, nuzzling and savouring the contact. His eyes close rapturously. It seems to me, the goddess, that he's enjoying himself too much. He should be making love to me, not my knickers.

'Enough! Now make yourself useful.'

In my fantasy I lie back like an empress, parting my thighs and exhibiting all of my rather more slender than usual body to him. Despite his claims that he likes girls with flesh, he seems entranced, though he's still cross. With a diva-like gesture I point between my legs and, seeing that I'm in charge in every sense of the word, he moves in.

I expect him to lick me, or even slide into me straight away, but somehow something in my brain short-circuits and, even though this is *my* fantasy and supposedly under *my* conscious control, I lose my grip on it.

Daniel's strange eyes flash and he gives me one of his arch, knowing, 'I might be Nemesis' smiles. Slowly, he lifts his hand to his face and studies the tip of his middle finger. Then, indolently, with almost comic leisureliness, he licks the tip of it.

He *is* Nemesis now. In every fibre. He runs his tongue around his soft red lips, then does the finger-lick again. Then, staring into my eyes, he reaches down, works his finger deftly through the flossy curls of my bush and finds my clit. It's as if he's saying, 'This is mine. I control it. I control you'.

I'm touching myself now, but on autopilot, emulating the casual, insulting, manipulating action of fantasy Nemesis's fingertip. He just circles and circles, working the tiny bud of flesh, rubbing it this way and that. There's no other contact between us. He's kneeling, relaxed, his free hand resting lightly on his thigh as he plays my clit like the tiny joystick of some radio-controlled pleasure drone.

I bang my heels on the bed, in both worlds, and arch up from the mattress like a bow, my bottom six inches clear of the sheet.

'You like that, Queen of the Library, don't you?' he seems to say, his grin narrow and infuriating. 'You're a slave to your clit, aren't you? At the mercy of its throb, throb, throb between your legs.'

When I'm at the height of this arc of torment, he does that familiar little trick he knows I like so much. He pinches the tiny organ between his finger and thumb, holding me aloft by it.

I moan, in both realms, almost ready to come.

'You're a slut, Library Queen, aren't you? When you watch

men from that desk of yours, your clit gets swollen and tender, doesn't it, when you imagine them servicing you? Touching you ... licking you ...'

No! I want to say. *It's only you I get swollen and wet for, Daniel/Nemesis, only you.*

But is it? Aren't there others I've seen pass by that have tickled me a little? Cute Techno-Greg? The man with the muscles from Building Services who came to fix the window? Even tall, bluff Director of Finance Stone, the last time he visited the library for one of those interminable budget meetings? And the time I thought I saw him shagging in that alley ...

Yes, I've fancied all those men and, yes, I've felt it between my legs. Nemesis is right, I am a slut and, for the purposes of this fantasy, my clit controls me.

I toss my head and shake my hips, worrying the seat of my pleasure with thumb and finger, just the way I imagine – I wish, how I wish – *he* was doing. I'm so excited, I groan out loud, making a noise like an animal.

I come and holler 'Nemesis!' to the night.

10   The Infamous Waverley

So this is it, the infamous Waverley Grange Country Hotel?

Superficially, it looks perfectly normal. Quiet, luxurious and a bit old-fashioned, nothing at all like a sinister den of debauchery and perversion. Walking into the lobby, I'm greeted by the sight of a bunch of disappointingly ordinary, straight and rather well-heeled people, loitering around the reception desk or sitting in the posh upholstered chairs in the window nook, probably chatting about how ordinary, straight and well-heeled they all are.

One or two heads turn, making me feel self-conscious. I've hit my savings for a new frock for this little escapade, but I still feel out of place – even if this place is the local Sodom or Gomorrah. But as I saunter forwards looking soignée and confident, one or two men favour me with frankly lustful glances. So obviously my gamble on a cleverly darted black shift dress, a cleverly cantilevered bra beneath it, a pair of cleverly high heels and a sleek, clever chignon has paid off. Bye-bye sensible Ms Price from the library, and hello La Gwendolynne, sultry seductress.

I'm still nervous, though, and my eyes skitter about, seeking the Lawns Bar. And luckily there it is, across the lobby, an inviting, softly lit space reached through open and rather elegant double doors. Is Daniel here? Is he waiting for me? He said he'd try to be. But, according to his text, his trip to London took longer than anticipated.

We haven't really worked out how we're going to play

tonight. We're suspended somewhere between fantasy and reality, on a shifting borderline. Is it Gwendolynne and Daniel? Or Gwendolynne and Nemesis? I'm not sure if either of us really cares any more. We're just two people playing out fantasies in a temporary relationship. One person probably quite fond of the other, and the other, like a silly twit, in love. But I'm not going to fret and spoil the fun.

I really like the look of the Lawns Bar. It's warm and spacious and has a palpable sexy buzz. People are talking in low tones at the tables and at the bar, and there's Sarah Vaughan singing huskily in the background. As I walk in and look around, it's easy to believe the Waverley's reputation. Which, as a woman alone in a notorious place, only makes me more nervous. My skin prickles as if everyone's looking at me. And even though everyone isn't, some of them are. There's no sign of Daniel, so, trying not to reveal my inner quivering, I walk as confidently as I can to the long, backlit bar, very conscious of a kind of Sugar Kowalski hip and bottom sway, induced by unfamiliar high heels.

As luck would have it, in such a well-patronised establishment, I find a free stool and park myself as elegantly as I can. Not sure what to say if anyone other than Daniel propositions me, I focus on worrying about what drink to order. Something weak to keep my wits about me, or something strong to calm my nerves?

Pull yourself together, Gwen. Here comes the barman. And what a barman. A tall figure in a dark perfect suit glides towards me. He looks continental, a bit obvious, but still a stunner. His hair is jet-black and pulled back in a severe ponytail, he's wearing gold-rimmed spectacles and he has a deliciously pouty mouth. Another hot man in glasses. What is it about them?

'What can I get you?' His low Italian accent does nothing

for my equilibrium, even though he isn't really my type. He's far too smooth and 'look at me, I'm gorgeous' ... and he isn't Daniel. But he still strums my hormones, and when I don't answer straight away he suggests, 'Perhaps a glass of tonight's house white? It's rather good.'

'Yes! That would be wonderful. Thanks.'

He slinks away and returns with my wine. After offering a toast in Italian that sounds vaguely filthy but probably isn't, he retreats again.

I feel like swigging the lot down in one go, but I confine myself to sips. It *is* quite good, a soft yet sharp and apple-tasting Frascati, but I'm not really in a fit state to appreciate its nuances.

Where's Daniel? Nemesis? Whatever? I peer around the bar, trying not to teeter on my stool. Fortunately, I'm used to sitting on one at the Enquiry Desk every day, so I manage OK. In the absence of my faux-punter, I try to work out what gives this place its notorious reputation.

Just as in the foyer, all looks normal. At first. Then I notice one or two women wearing toweringly high heels and serious dresses. And even more serious makeup. A bit like my own outfit, only far more extreme. What are they, dominatrixes? The men they're with certainly look rather sheepish and in awe.

If Daniel doesn't turn up soon, maybe I'll give him a bit of that treatment when he does arrive. If I can work out what to do. It's all very well fantasising about these things, but actually having to perform is another matter entirely.

I try out that daydream again, the one where it's me in the mask and the leather. I get as far as him kneeling before me, without his clothes, and then annoyingly my mind starts to wander and worry about his absence. What if something's wrong? What if he's lying in his room, crippled with one of his killer headaches, too blinded by pain even to text me?

I'm just wondering whether I should make discreet enquiries, when a familiar face catches my eye and I turn to see Robert Stone, the Borough Director of Finance, heading towards the double doors through which I've just entered. He's looking as debonair as ever, and he's escorting a very beautiful young blonde woman in a slinky, crotch-skimming midnight-blue dress. As they pass me, I notice that his hand is wickedly low on her back, well, on her bottom really, and he suddenly glances my way as if he's noticed me noticing. He gives me a nod – either as if he recognises me from the library, or because he just can't help checking out women – and then a very strange, sly, sultry expression as if he knows something I don't. His large hand doesn't move from its low, caressing contact.

This all happens in the space of a millisecond, but it does make me wonder what the hell is going on here. One thing I do know, though. I'm almost certain that he *is* the man I saw in the alley the other night, and the lovely girl he's with is the one he was making love to. It's difficult to get my head around the fact that such a prominent local figure would do something so completely insane but, if he's a regular here, maybe he's fond of living dangerously?

Still no Daniel, but, when I turn back to the bar, I see the elegant older woman he met out in the library. His kissing cousin. She's with Signor Italian Stud, and it's immediately apparent they're an item. More than that: on closer inspection I note matching wedding rings, and a sweet cocoon of intimacy, although they're barely touching. She's chattering cheerfully about something, and he's watching her adoringly yet with an obvious, rampant hunger. It's a kind of lustful tenderness that makes me ache with twisting jealousy. Not for her gorgeous Latin lover, but for the close and easy love the two exhibit. I want that. With Daniel. But to get it, one needs a future, not a fling.

The Lawns Bar suddenly feels empty and cold, even though the place is crammed and the ambient temperature is tropical.

I said I wouldn't do this. I wouldn't pine for something that's not on offer. But here I am, going goo-goo over devious Professor Hottie again. Why can't I just accept what I've got for now, and make the best of it? Because I have got something many women would scratch my eyes out for. A series of stunning sexual frolics with a famous and intelligent man.

I straighten my spine, sit up straight and stick out my chest. A man a few stools away ogles me like a dog eyeing a juicy hambone. OK, it'll never be a picket fence and roses around the door with Daniel, but that isn't the end of the world, is it?

The Lawns Bar is a simmering hotbed of sensuality again. And, as if summoned by the heat, Daniel appears. Like the devil? I'm not sure how and when, but he's materialised at the other end of the bar and has his beautiful tight behind perched on a stool like mine. His cousin is already serving him a clear drink with ice in a highball glass, possibly a G&T or maybe vodka, I can't tell. As she chats him up, he catches my eye over her shoulder and gives me a long, level look. He's pretending he doesn't know me but, beneath the act and his well-polished glasses, his eyes are intimate.

I get a hectic feeling in my chest. Fear, apprehension, excitement – the thrill I always experience at the sight of him, only overlaid with warped and twisted piquancy.

Game on.

Not giving myself time to hesitate, I finish the rest of my Frascati, slip off my stool and head his way. Miraculously, or perhaps by some kind of cosmic design, someone's just vacated the stool next to his.

He watches me every step of the way, the devil, then pantomimes innocent surprise when I pitch up before him. His eyes twinkle behind his glasses as he courteously eases out the stool and then takes my arm to help me on to it.

'Good evening.' His voice is delicious, insolent.

My fears and frets seem to disappear like Scotch mist.

'Good evening.' I glance pointedly at his drink.

'What are you having?'

Everything, I feel like saying. 'A glass of the house white would be lovely.'

'How about champagne?' he counters, smiling merrily.

'Why not? Are we celebrating something?'

He waggles his eyebrows, signals to his cousin and speaks in low tones to her, requesting bubbly. I feel another pang of jealousy, despite her obviously blissful marriage to her Italian stud.

Daniel returns his attention to me and beams.

'So, *are* we celebrating?' I persist.

'Oh, most definitely ... it's not every day the most gorgeous woman in the room walks right up to me, without me even having to make an effort.'

'The view's better from this end of the bar.' I've absolutely no idea how to do this kind of championship flirting. It's all new to me, both the relationship and the game. But I still feel a shiver of pleasure, deep in my sex.

'It is now.' Daniel continues to smile while his eyes cruise unabashedly over the curves of my breasts. The neckline of my dress isn't low and the bodice isn't especially tight, but the clever cut makes my full shape look sensational. His lashes flicker in acknowledgement of my cleavage and he adjusts his position ever so slightly on his stool.

My heartbeat revs, and that lowdown shiver becomes a yearning, gnawing ache. I'm not the only one at this bar who looks sensational. Daniel has on a dark suit and a dazzling white shirt that accentuates his faint tan and makes it glow.

His wild hair is neatly combed for once, but there's still an untamed energy in his curls – and in everything about him. He looks strong and animal and dominant, a beast of sex.

'So, do you come here often?' I ask, and we both burst out laughing, dropping temporarily out of role. Our giggles raise a curious look from his cousin, who arrives with our champagne, but, the soul of discretion, she simply opens the bottle with a professional smoothness, then leaves us to it with a slight smile on her face.

Is she in on this? I suppose so. But it doesn't really bother me. I'm focused on Daniel, and Daniel alone. Oh, and Nemesis ...

'Yes, actually,' he says at length, still smiling, 'it's one of my favourite hotels.' He pauses, favouring me again with that sexy, blatantly undressing gaze. 'Probably because the women in here are always so beautiful.'

I laugh again. I can't help myself. I know we're flirting and playing games, but in my heart and my gut I know he really means it. Am I beautiful? Tonight, I choose to believe so. Not sure how to answer, though, I pick up my champagne flute and hold it towards him for a toast. The clink of glass is communication enough.

The wine is superb. I'm no expert, but somehow its smooth complexity connects on every level with my senses. Its delicate effervescence is the very embodiment of the excitement between Daniel and me. Watching him take a tiny sip from his glass makes me quiver and yearn to feel him deep inside me. His mouth touches the rim of the glass and a little of the champagne glistens on his lip. Slowly, his tongue sweeps out to lick the wine from the soft and sensuous curve. My body shudders and clenches hard, just from watching him.

'So?' he says softly, setting his glass down with a click on the bar.

Fuck it, I don't want to play games any more. Correction,

I just want to play *some* games. Sexy games with Daniel, up in his room. All this dancing around, pretending to be other people, it just gets in the way of me getting close to him.

Daniel's long fingers play up and down the stem of his glass, and he looks at me, slightly sideways, as if he's reading me.

'Don't you want to play?'

It's as if I've had the breath knocked out of me. I swig some champagne and only just avoid sneezing at the bubbles going up my nose. How the hell does he always manage to know what's going on inside my head?

'Yes, I want to play.' I put my glass to my lips again, then replace it on the counter. 'But just a simple game. Just you and me. Never mind all this argy-bargy with N–'

In a swift, accurate movement, he reaches out, places his fingers across my lips. They're warm and their touch makes me feel weak.

'Just a simple game, eh?' He looks at me intently, his eyes softly brown behind his glasses. For just a second a shadow moves in their depths and he frowns ever so slightly. Then it's gone in a flash, and he smiles. 'That works for me.' He strokes my lips very delicately, then withdraws and reaches for his glass again. He's very abstemious. He only takes a minute sip.

I take another sip of champagne too, determined that, no matter what the cost, I'm going to drink this stuff regularly. A bottle a month from Tesco – I'm sure I can afford that to rekindle memories of a special night like this.

Suddenly, things start to move rather fast. Daniel asks for the rest of our bottle, plus a second one, to be taken up to his room. I drain my glass, but he looks at his, leaves it and leads the way out of the Lawns Bar, across the foyer and into the lift.

It's just a short ride up, but it feels like an eternity. I want to touch him, kiss him, but he gives me a stern-playful look and retreats to the corner of the car, staring back at me, his fingertips pressed together and resting against his lips. I might have thought he was meditating if his eyes didn't burn so, behind his glasses.

It dawns on me that I'm not in control any more. I was, but, without registering the exact moment it happened, I've ceded it to Daniel. I have to dance to his tune, and the realisation makes me feel giddy, bubbly like the champagne. And filled with raw lust. Mad fantasies rage through my mind, fragmentary scenarios from the secret porn stash at the library and from dark depths of my subconscious that I wasn't aware of.

Daniel is Nemesis now, and I'm panting to do anything he desires.

When we reach his floor, he directs me along the corridor, still without speaking, and we pass several room numbers – 11, 15, 17 – until at last he pauses in front of number 19 and takes out his key-card.

He ushers me inside.

I shudder as I precede him into the room, finding it difficult to breathe. This feels like more, so much more than our minor escapades in the library archive and amongst the mops at my building. There's a sense of ritual and formality, and the image of Daniel in that leather mask rises up again from the murky depths of my imagination, bringing a fresh surge of yearning to my sex.

I open my mouth to speak, not knowing what I'm going to say, but Daniel sets his fingers very softly across my lips again.

'This is a simple game, remember? No reservations. No complications.' His hand, so warm and forbidding, is still across my face, so I just nod. 'I'd like to be in control. Total control. Is that agreeable to you?'

His power makes me feel fainter than ever and I nod again, feeling a wild whirling, as if I'm being lifted out of the realm of the real and the normal by a powerful twister. I've never been more afraid or more excited in my life.

He takes his hand from my face and retreats a few steps to sit in one of the large, over-stuffed, chintz-covered armchairs. He lounges back, his arms along the armrests, and seems perfectly relaxed. His eyes are still on me though, sharp and dark, like a raptor's. The eyes of Nemesis. Not the flattering cajoling Nemesis of the letters and messages, but a new one, who knows exactly what he wants.

In the absence of any formal instructions. I don't know what to do. I just stand there, clutching my little evening purse while I feel his assessing gaze slide over me. All I can do is listen to the silence, aware of the blood, hormones and fluids pumping and sliding around my body and my skin. Sweat prickles between my breasts and in the creases of my groin, and between my thighs I'm already wet.

'Show me your panties.'

His voice is quiet, matter-of-fact, but it still makes me jump. It's such a simple request but it feels as extreme and outrageous as if he'd asked me to lie down on the carpet naked and bring myself off with a vibrator. With shaking hands I place my bag on the bedside table and start to slide up my skirt. The action reminds me of when I did more or less the same thing in the library basement, but that seems to be a hundred years ago, and performed by an entirely different person.

Slowly, and still trembling, I display my red lace French knickers, and the elaborately decorated tops of my stockings where they attach to my garter belt.

His face remains very calm, very still, but behind the lenses of his glasses his eyes flicker with seething fires. I can feel the heat from where I stand, burning and burning me as he keeps me there, held in place by the weight of his stare for what feels like hour after hour after hour.

The sweat, and other secretions, gather and flow.

After an age, he says, 'Remove them, then bring them to me.'

It's as if there's a band round my chest. It's difficult to breathe, I'm so excited. I'm not sure I can peel off my knickers without falling over, never mind do it with any grace. But I've had my instructions and I have to comply.

I compromise by leaning on the bedside table while I reach round under the bunched folds of my skirt and pluck at my knickers' elastic. I'm not sure whether I'm supposed to seek support like this or keep my pussy exposed throughout the process, but Daniel remains superficially unmoved by my efforts to retain a modicum of elegance.

The flimsy lace is in danger of winding itself round the slim heels of my shoes as I grapple with it, but the gods smile and I manage to get my pants off without falling on my face or my backside. Defiantly, I let my skirt drop and cover me, then walk slowly towards him and hold out my offering.

'Are you fragrant?' His lips curl impishly and he lifts his hands and steeples his fingers in that sage academic way of his. What does he want? Does he want me to smell my own knickers in front of him? My decorum rebels, but I hold the red lace up to my nose for a moment and make a show of sniffing. They're already ripe with the oceanic smell of arousal, but that doesn't surprise me. Who wouldn't be soaked and aromatic under the spell of the beautiful man who sits before me?

He holds out his hand, and I dart forwards and almost throw my bundle into it. This wins me a wider smile, twinkly and familiar, much more the Daniel that I know and love so dearly. Unfolding the flimsy garment, he studies it as if it's an artefact he's uncovered in his research. His thumb slides over the lace, gauging its sheerness and assessing its texture, then he lifts it by the waistband and examines its construction. Which makes me blush furiously, not because they're my knickers and they're scented with the odour of my lust, but because to fit a girl like me they're not exactly tiny.

Daniel's eyes flick from my underwear to me, and it's as if he reads me completely.

'They're gorgeous. And so are you.' He tips his head to one side, doing that professor-despairing-of-a-thick-pupil thing again. 'Skinny women don't interest me. I like curves, flesh, womanliness ... as most men do, my lovely Gwendolynne, as most men do.'

'If you say so.' Although he's not said as much, I know I'm not supposed to speak, but I can't help blurting it out. I'm happy that he's said what he said. I sort of knew that in my heart already, but it's good to hear it straight from his lips.

He gives me a stern little look, and seems just about to reprimand me, when there's a soft knock at the door.

'Ah, that'll be our champagne. About time.'

Moving faster than seems possible, he leaps to his feet and gives me a hard kiss on the mouth, then sort of tangos me back to the bed and makes me sit down. He gives me another lightning-fast kiss, then calls out, 'Come in!'

11 Games

The door swings open. Oh, God, it was unlocked throughout the whole business of me taking off my panties. What if room service had done just the cursory knock-and-enter thing? Fortunately at the Waverley they have a little more decorum, and there's a short tactful pause before a tall, very dignified woman with beautifully coiled black hair pushes a trolley into the room.

'Your champagne.' Her smile is discreet, neutral, unreadable. 'And strawberries, courtesy of the management.' Next to the jumbo-sized ice bucket, with our existing half bottle of bubbly plus a new, unopened one, there's a silver bowl full of large succulent-looking strawberries. Two tall flutes stand alongside, delicate and sparkling. All very *Pretty Woman*.

'Will that be all, sir?' enquires our waitress. Although, come to think of it, I see that she really isn't a waitress at all. She's wearing a very elegant and severe black suit, with a discreet name badge on her lapel saying 'Saskia Woodville, Assistant Manager'.

'Yes, thank you.'

She proffers a folder with a chit to sign, and, as Daniel's back is to me, I don't see the transaction, but I see a faint, complicit smile warm the Assistant Manager's face. Is she part of the charade too? After all, this is Daniel's cousin's hotel.

The tall woman turns her smile on me, and it's pleasant, open and genuine. 'Good evening, madam,' she says quietly, then retreats. At the door she pauses and, for just a second, her eyes flick to the chintz armchair where Daniel was sitting a moment ago. The corners of her red-painted mouth curve fleetingly, then she's out of the door and gone, closing it soundlessly.

Only when I follow the track of that quick last glance do I realise that my red knickers are lying there on the seat, clearly visible. My face burns pink with mortification, but then I relax. What's the big deal with a pair of naughty knickers on show? The Waverley is a wicked hotel with a wicked reputation. And I'm a wicked woman in a wicked relationship. Ms Woodville probably wouldn't have turned a hair if I'd been stretched out on the bed naked. Or even if Daniel had been stretched out on top of me, giving me his all.

'You're not embarrassed, are you?' Daniel returns to his armchair, picks up my red lace frippery on one tapered fingertip and lets it swing slightly. 'They see much naughtier things every night in this place,' he adds, confirming my suspicions as he flings himself back into his chair, and begins to fondle my knickers again in a slow contemplative way that only makes me wish he was fondling me with such deliberation. Now that my crotch is naked I feel my sticky, silky fluid begin to well and seep, and as Daniel gives me a puckish little smile, accompanied by a waggle of his dark eyebrows, a thick trickle of it slides tellingly down my leg until it reaches the lace top of my sheer stocking.

'I'm sure they do.' I'm getting nervous again now. Edgy, energised, popping with readiness, but not sure what I should be readying myself for. Anticipation is like thin bands of steel wound around me, hampering my breathing, controlling my body, my limbs. I try not to gasp and give myself away.

'Pour me some wine,' says Daniel casually, still handling my underwear.

Am I supposed to serve him? Act as his handmaiden? A part

of me rebels at such a subservient role, but most of me thrills to it in some ancient, primal way. Another dribble of hot honey wets my stocking-top.

Trying not to shake, I cross to the trolley and pour champagne into one of the tall, pretty glasses. When I pause and look across at Daniel, the bottle hovering over a second glass, his eyes narrow warningly behind his spectacles. Clearly I have to earn my champagne, but in what way I'm not quite sure yet.

I serve him, and he drops my panties on the chair arm before taking the glass from me. He takes a very small but very lingering sip again. He's barely drinking tonight, and for some reason I get the impression it's not really of his choosing. I start to wonder about that, but all the while his eyes are locked on mine, and I can almost imagine that he's forbidding my speculations. Having drunk only the tiniest amount of the fine wine, he puts the flute on the table beside his chair.

Still looking up at me, he gestures for me to move in closer, the action tiny but imperious. As I take a step, he opens his legs wider to allow me to stand between them. I'm not sure whether I'm even supposed to look, but I can't help staring down at his immaculately suited crotch, where he's hard, his erection prominent.

'Take your frock off, Gwendolynne,' says the voice of Nemesis. And, as I reach for my zip, he casually cups himself and adjusts his penis in his trousers. Arrogant sod. But I love it.

I shimmy out of my chic new dress, then step out of it and kick it aside. At one time, I would have felt mortified at exposing my ample body like this, especially if I wasn't wearing any pants. But looking into Daniel's hot eyes, and then seeing the way his wicked-thick eyelashes flutter and his fingers roll over his hidden cock, I feel the power in my own flesh, and I revel in it. He's playing the ascendant role here, but somehow he's also in thrall, at the same time, to my curves, to my breasts, to my hips and my bottom. He wants my abundant flesh just as I want his sleek muscularity and his fantastic, jutting hardness.

I stand before him in my red bra, my red garter belt and my smoky lace-topped stockings, with the sheen of my arousal clear and shining on my inner thighs. Without warning, he leans forwards and throws his arms around my waist, pulling me to him. At the same time, he presses his face between my breasts, rubbing his cheeks against their soft, lace-clad slopes, like a child or a puppy nuzzling for comfort. Not stopping to think, I cradle his head, slipping my fingers into the black silk of his thick curly hair.

It's a strangely asexual moment. A deeper communion. Daniel makes a sound like a gasp, almost a groan, and nuzzles deeper. He *is* seeking comfort. I feel strange. My body is still completely turned on and primed for him. I can smell my arousal, and so must he be able to. But the urge to nurture floats atop the lust, sharp and poignant. Does he have one of his headaches? His action suggests a yearning for some kind of solace. I hold his head lightly, in case it's tender in some way, and without a word he reaches up, one hand still holding me round my middle, but the other settling over my hand where it's resting on his hair. Our fingers lace and he emits a faint sigh.

I daren't speak, but I so want to ask if he's OK. These headaches come often, I can tell, and that suggests something serious. I want to know what troubles him, even though now is a strange time to ask, when I'm half-naked in his hold, my exposed crotch pressed lightly against his shirt.

'Is anything wrong?'

Did I speak? I must have ...

Daniel doesn't move or respond for a moment, then he slides his hands off me and puts me away from him a little.

Shit! Shit! Shit! Now I've spoilt it all. Men don't like to seem weak. Especially when they're playing the sexual master.

He frowns, and a look of irritation flits across his face. At me? Or at himself? I sense the latter.

'No, nothing at all,' he says crisply, 'especially not with you.' His lips curve; they look reddened and hungry. 'There's nothing whatsoever wrong with you, beautiful Gwendolynne. You are truly a sight for sore eyes.' That angry look returns momentarily, then he reaches for me again, pulling me forwards with his left hand while his right slides arrogantly between my thighs, then my sex lips, searching for my clit. When he unerringly finds it, it's my turn to gasp, but he shushes me softly.

'You must be a quiet, good girl, my Queen of the Library. No moaning and groaning while I play with you.'

There it is again, that title. The one that unequivocally proves he's Nemesis. But I don't care who he is or where he came from. I can only think, if that's what you'd call it, about what he's doing in the wet furrow of my sex. He presses hard on my clit, flicking at it and playing with it, and I experience a harrowing urge to wiggle my hips and bounce on the fulcrum of that maddening fingertip. But I don't, because I know he wants me to be still.

Biting my lips, I suppress a groan. Intense yet frustrating sensations are gathering. I close my eyes, unable to look at his dear, tantalising countenance. But he tuts softly, and I have to open them again. His face is sublime, strong yet exquisite. Utterly masculine and pleased with himself, yet as beautiful as a devil-angel from an Old Master.

His touch is outrageous, like sin incarnate. He coaxes me closer and closer to orgasm with every stroke, then time and again backs off just when I'm about to come.

Just when I'm on the point of screaming at him to finish me, he withdraws his fingers entirely. Then, slowly and lasciviously, he first takes another tiny sip of champagne from his glass, then dips his forefinger and middle finger into it and reapplies them, wet with the precious wine, to my clit. I shout hoarsely as the effervescence tips me over and I come hard, almost painfully, my empty sex pulsing and grabbing at nothing.

My arms grab him, encircling him, holding on to him, clamping around him like a vice as I throb and flutter and climax. Lost in sensation, I curl over him, pressing my face against his black curls and breathing deeply of his intoxicating blue-herbal shampoo. I kiss his scalp and, deep in the heart of my pleasure, a maternal yearning wishes I could cure the pain that sometimes ails him.

Eventually he pulls me on to his lap. Although I automatically start to protest that I'm no little slip of a girl and too heavy, he ignores me. Reaching for his champagne glass again, he feeds me the last of the golden fluid and I quaff it down as if it were lemonade, thirsty from coming.

I'm still pretty shocked and shaken up, but it doesn't take long for me to start thinking again. And noticing things that are rather hard not to notice. Like the enormous erection beneath me, poking at my still-glowing sex through the fine worsted of Daniel's suit trousers.

'You're very hard,' I remark inanely, and he laughs.

'Yes, I like being hard.'

'Don't you want to do something about it?'

'Presently.' He strokes me under the chin as if I were a kitten, his eyes merry and playful behind his glasses. 'But not just yet.' He licks his lower lip as if savouring something delicious. 'I like to prolong the anticipation sometimes. Wait until I really, really want it, before I get off. And I know that when I get inside you it's going to be really spectacular, and well worth the wait.'

For a fleeting second he touches my clit again, and I whine without being able to help myself, almost ready to come again.

'Let's watch the telly for a while,' he says as I try to wriggle back on to his fingertips, in vain. Putting me from him with a phenomenal ease and strength, he sets me on my feet again, then rises beside me and leads me across to the bed. He plumps a pillow, then says, 'Sit down' in quite a stern tone.

My heart thudding, I slide on to the chintz quilt, not sure what to do. Daniel cocks his head on one side, then carefully, and almost completely by touch, removes the grips that are holding my hair up, sets them aside, then fans out the heavy locks over my shoulders, touching and adjusting.

'Lie,' he instructs me, nodding towards the pillows, and I comply, trying to arrange my limbs in an alluring configuration. The fact that my crotch is bare, framed by the narrow lacy bands of my garter belt, just seems to shout at me. I can't look anywhere else than at my uncovered sex. It's sort of obscene, but seductive and exotic. The heat in Daniel's eyes seems to say he thinks the same.

He pours more champagne and places our glasses at either side of the bed, on the bijou little bedside cabinets.

'Relax.' Grinning down at me and looking inordinately pleased with himself, he arranges me, taking my wrists and settling my arms above my head on the fat pillows, hands loosely clasped, then nudging my sticky thighs slightly apart, opening my pussy.

'Relax,' he murmurs again, his voice more gentle, as if he's trying to coax me out of the sudden 'rabbit in the headlights' mode I've lapsed into. I have free will here, but I feel just as immobilised as that little bunny faced with a juggernaut.

His fingers move reverently over the side of my face, then smooth my hair against the pillows. That does relax me. As does the sight of him shrugging off his jacket, unfastening his tie and flinging them both away, before heeling off his shoes and almost dancing around to the far side of the bed.

The springs bounce lightly when he flings himself down beside me, just as if we were calmly going to watch the football together. When he snatches up the TV remote and presses the on button, I half expect the set to spring to life with *Match of the Day*. But no, it's just a menu with the Waverley logo. Daniel eyes his champagne glass briefly, then seems to decide not to drink and begins to scrolls through the televisual options, using the handset.

I can't believe this! Even in this most exotic and hothouse of circumstances, he's just like any other man. He can't resist channel hopping! And then it's my turn to laugh out loud when we reach UK History and his own familiar face smiles out at us. He's sitting on a dry-stone wall somewhere, talking about the Norman Conquest.

'Yuck! I hate that guy! What a ponce.' With a chuckle he stabs at a button and we're back at the menu.

It feels downright peculiar, and vaguely perverted, to be lying here, draped across the bed, while Daniel surfs the channels, but I'm a telly addict too and I can't help but watch the screen, even though I'm half-naked and on show, like an odalisque.

He flicks through a few things. Movies. A concert. Boxing, ugh. And then, inevitably, he finds the porn. First we drop in on a pair of busty but sylphlike blondes, kissing each other messily and writhing against each other like snakes. But this doesn't appeal to Daniel and he jumps back to the menu and scrolls down a little.

Next we find a guy I know to be the famous Ron Jeremy, putting it to another blonde in a vigorous doggy fashion.

'Seen this one,' says Daniel, surprising me. Whoever knew that everyone's favourite academic was into skin movies?

Back to the menu again, and flick, flick, flick, he highlights 'Live Feed'. What the hell is that? Unfortunately all the screen shows us is the legend 'Channel scrambled'.

'Oops!'

Before I can ask what exactly 'Live Feed' entails, Daniel bounces off the bed, fishes in his jacket pocket and pulls out a key-card, much like the one that admitted us to this room. He jams it in a slot on the front of the television, then stabs the button again as he sprints back to the bed and flings himself alongside me, his eyes on the screen rather than my partially clothed body. Great.

The image snaps to a strangely familiar one. Chintz. Soft light. Two lovers. One dressed, one partially naked. It's a webcam feed. Not of us, thank God, but clearly streaming from somewhere inside the hotel.

'Oh no, it's him!'

Daniel's attention flicks back to me and he looks at me curiously.

'Do you know him?' He nods at the screen, on which a masked yet recognisable man is looming over a woman I've also seen before, and recently. In a room much like ours, the suave yet obviously insanely reckless Robert Stone, Borough Director of Finance, is about to spank his blonde beloved, the pretty girl I saw him with just a short while ago. He's sitting on the edge of the bed, wearing a leather domino-style mask, which makes something go thump inside me, reminding me of my fantasies. It's the sort of thing that would probably disguise his identity ... unless you already knew it. His partner is draped across his knee, wearing a basque, a similar but more dainty mask, with a fine lace trim, and not much else.

The colour definition of the scene is surprisingly good, given the lighting conditions, and it's easy to see he's already been spanking her for a bit, because her enviably slim and toned bottom is pink and seriously hot-looking. She's shaking too, as if she's snivelling in pain. But, when she turns her face, allowing us to see her expression but not her disciplinarian, her eyes are sparkling with excitement within the frame of her exotic mask, and she's smiling a happy little smile to herself. She loves it!

'Jeepers! Spanking! That's hot,' murmurs Daniel beside me, echoing my thoughts entirely, and adjusts the way he's sitting slightly, as if the kinky scene is already getting to his nether regions. As it's getting to mine.

Stone gives his lady-love's rump a lazy slap and she jerks across his lap, swirling her hips. Her mouth moves as if she's moaning, but there's no soundtrack, presumably allowing the couple to retain some degree of privacy in a blatantly exhibitionistic scenario. I have to bite my lips to stop myself moaning, and, when I tear my eyes away from the screen for a second, I discover that Daniel's actually watching me, not them.

'Does that sort of thing excite you?' His eyes flash behind his glasses, telling me that the idea of that excites *him*. He inclines over me, his glance darting from the screen to me and back again, to and fro. As Robert Stone lays on a couple more whacks, in quick succession, Daniel reaches over and slides his hand between my thighs. Testing me.

He finds what I expect he was expecting, and this time I can't prevent myself moaning. I'm wet and slippery, hot and ready for his touch. When I wriggle and try to press my hand over his own, he says, 'Uh oh!' and gives me a stern little look. It's complex, full of humour, yet slightly forbidding, and

I wonder if I'm in the presence of just as skilled a disciplinarian as the one who's going about his business in the webcam feed.

It's an effort, but I return my hands to their former position, lightly clasped and brushing my fanned-out hair. It's like being bound and yet not bound, and even though I've never done bondage and all I know of it is from pictures and stories, I instinctively know that it's probably far harder *not* to be fastened up in this sort of situation. There might actually be a relaxation in being in shackles. At least that way you don't have to fight your own urge to move, to struggle. Especially when a beautiful man you adore is stroking your clitoris with the tip of his finger.

I gasp and my hips work of their own accord, just like those of Robert Stone's beautiful companion. He's stopped hitting her for a moment, and she's writhing across his sturdy knees, working herself against him, trying to stimulate herself.

'You're as naughty as she is.' Daniel moves closer, his mouth inches from mine. 'I bet it does excite you. I bet you read all sorts of wicked books down there in that library basement of yours, don't you? I've seen them. I know what's down there.'

And still he's flick, flick, flicking me, and I'm compelled to gyrate my bottom. But that doesn't knock him off target, no way. It's as if he's laser-guided, surgeon-precise.

'But that means you've read those books too,' I gasp, still trying to fight him because somehow I know that's what he wants. It's part of the game, one of the figures you have to go through in the course of this dance. 'So you're a pervert too.'

'Shush!' He gives me a hard kiss, the classic romantic, punishing kiss, all the time circling his finger where it matters. My body gathers itself, but he snatches his hand away and puts it over my mouth as he breaks the kiss, still scented from me. 'We're talking about you, Ms Gwendolynne Price, not me.

And about all the dirty little secrets you hide behind that prim, professional librarian's façade of yours.'

I want to tell him that I've never affected a prim façade, even when I was relatively inexperienced, but I'm too close to coming. And anyway, his strong hand is still firmly across my mouth.

As one, we return our attention to the screen. Although that's not such a good idea for me, on the brink as I am, because in the interim Robert Stone has manhandled his lover on to the bed and moved her into the doggy position, her bare, rosy bottom raised high and her slender thighs parted. I gasp behind Daniel's fingers as our exhibitionist friend unzips himself and reveals an impressive penis to match his height and build.

For a second, I glance up at Daniel's face and he laughs at me, much more himself suddenly, no longer Nemesis.

'I'm not intimidated. I'm not intimidated. I'm not intimidated.' He rolls his eyes behind his glasses, and, as I can't speak, I tell him with my eyes that I have no complaints about him in that department. I'm more than delighted, thrilled and awed by *his* splendid cock. He gets the message and gives me a wink. We turn back to the action, neither of us unmoved. I'm still dying to come, and Daniel's sporting a monumental bump in his trousers.

The lovers are fucking now. Stone is powering into his darling with majesty and enthusiasm, going at her like a piston, yet somehow almost tenderly. It's in the way he holds her hips, and the way that, from time to time, he reaches forward to lay his hand on her shoulders, her neck. There's love in their union, wild sweet love. Oh, how I want that! I want the exquisite cherishing way he curves his body over hers as she's clearly about to come. The way his mouth moves, the silent words unmistakeable as he reaches beneath her and strokes her to embellish her pleasure.

They jerk and rock, their lips framing cries of ecstasy and love, their hips heaving and juddering until at last it's over and Robert Stone executes a sort of sideways roll, taking his sweetheart with him, pulling her to lie sideways with him instead of just collapsing his not inconsiderable post-coital weight upon her. The last thing I notice, just before Daniel clicks the remote, is that their linked hands are both wearing wedding rings. I can't imagine them being anyone's but each other's.

'Crikey, she's his wife. It's married kink. They could be at home bonking, but they obviously like to show off.'

'Some couples do, I suppose.' Daniel's frowning slightly, and he sits up, pushing his hand through his hair, scrunching his eyes up behind his glasses.

Alarm bells ring in my heart. Is he OK?

Then, an instant later, he's smiling again.

'So, those naughty exhibitionists ... did they turn you on?'

'You know they did!' He obviously wants me to say it. 'Surely you could feel it?'

'Yeah, you're fabulously wet, my little Library Queen. There's quite a pond down there.' He lays his hand over my bush in a slight curve, middle finger dipping but not making contact. I could shout and kick, it's so frustrating, but somehow I hold the pose he seems to have assigned me.

'Little? You must be joking.'

'Tut-tut, we're not going to have this discussion yet again, are we?' He gives me a stern little shake of the head and his finger ventures a little closer to the hot zone. Then his eyes change and become open, sincere, strangely innocent. 'Gwendolynne, it's not a lie, or a line, when I tell you that you have a fabulous body. It's true. It's what I believe. You have the most beautiful, glorious shape I've ever seen.' For a split second, he looks totally stricken – and terribly afraid – but then, just like before, he's back to normal. Almost. 'Or am likely to ...'

I open my mouth, on the point of begging him to confide in me, tell me what's troubling him, but then he touches me and we're back in the lush world of drowning sensuality again, because he's touching my clit and bending over me to press his lips to my throat, and then to the upper curve of one of those ample breasts he's so fond of. My hips rise to the contact, and my skin burns beneath his mouth.

'So, what's it to be, goddess?' he breathes, a zephyr of heat against the slope of my bosom. 'A spanking? Or a fuck? Hell, I know what I want!' He shimmies his body, twisting so he can press his erection against my bare hip. He's huge and hot and, hell, I know what I want too. Let's save the bottom-centric antics of the devoted Stones for another day, eh?

'Me too.' Breaking the secret bondage pact, I reach down and cup him and he gasps, rocking into it. His finger rocks too, on my clit.

Then we're a whirl of motion, an unspoken agreement to get naked. I pull and snap at bra straps and garters without taking my eyes off the emerging beauty I first saw the other day, down in the library washroom. My stuff comes off in double-quick time, but Daniel is more circumspect, especially when, very hesitantly, he plucks off his glasses and lays them aside. Immediately, he blinks, then tears off the rest of his things and just throws himself at me, as if anxious to make up in skin-skin contact what he loses with his less than perfect vision.

Kissing me, he rubs the full length of himself against me, much the way he rubbed his face against my breasts a little while ago. It's as if he's 'seeing' me with all of himself, absorbing the texture of my skin, the resilience of my flesh, the frisky rub of my pubic hair. His own pubic hair and the mighty penis that springs from it are pretty frisky too. His erection slides and pushes and silently dominates me.

We slither and wriggle against each other for a while, teasing and tantalising and upping the ante. Eventually he grabs me and holds me tight against him, his cock like a bar of fire against my soft rounded belly.

'I want you like he had her,' he growls in my ear, nudging, pushing. 'I want you on all fours. I want to see that sensational bottom while I'm fucking deep inside you.'

Ah, such coarse, delicious words from the erudite and sophisticated professor. What would his swooning lady fans think if they could hear what I'm hearing?

'Come on, sex goddess, I *need* to fuck you!'

He rolls away slightly, then grabs me by the middle, turns me and lifts me with impressive dexterity and masterfulness. Like an obedient she-animal, I come up on my elbows and knees, my hair dangling down around my face. I hear him open the bedside drawer, fish around and shut it again. Obviously the Waverley is well stocked with condoms. Then he dims the light and we're in faintly lit near-darkness. Well, if he can't see too well anyway, what's the difference ... and me, I can feel, I can feel!

The air in the room is warm and balmy, the surface of the quilt crisp beneath my knees and elbows. The faint scent of potpourri tickles my nostrils, and the stronger smells of our blended colognes and my sex, ripe and musky.

Daniel moves against me, and his skin is very hot. He's not a gorilla, but I feel the rub of male hair on his chest, and on his legs and thighs as he moves over me and grabs me by the waist again, not entering me, just working his entire body against mine, making me know it by touch and heat and scent. His lips settle on the back of my neck and, as he kisses me there, he reaches underneath me and roughly fondles my breasts, switching from one to the other, squeezing and revelling in the abundance and springiness of my flesh.

'You're beautiful, Gwendolynne,' he murmurs again, the sound muffled because he's licking and kissing at the same time. He can barely see me in this diminished light, but the raw quality of his voice convinces me there's beauty in the tactile contact alone.

I sway, rub back against him as hard as he's massaging me with his torso, his thighs, his latex-clad cock. I'm in an ecstasy of heat and body-scents and strong male flesh.

And then he's at me, at my entrance, probing gently with his fingers, adjusting my soft folds, making space for his hard, high erection. I feel the swollen glans pushing and pushing, and it's as if it's all brand new, even though it's been there before. He moves right over me, even further, rests the side of his face against the crook of my shoulder and neck, and edges inside me. I can feel his beautiful dark curly hair tickling me, and the faint hint of stubble scratching my skin as he jerks his hips and tries to shove for full penetration.

So close and so frantic, it's a bit of a fumble. He backs up, comes up on his knees, grabs me by the hips and, adjusting his angle, places himself better with his fingertips. Pitching on to one elbow, and falling forwards to press my face amongst the pillows, I reach around to clasp his muscular thigh and brace myself against him.

Bingo! He slides in, really deep. Now we're fitted together, he drapes himself over me again, as if seeking maximum contact. His heated body feels like a blanket across my back, and tears spring into my eyes, just from the sense of closeness. For a few moments, as we're still against each other, it almost doesn't feel like sex at all.

I know I love him. It's crazy. Unwise. And I don't think there's a future for it. But still I don't regret the feeling. Didn't somebody once say in a film, 'A life lived in fear is a life half lived'? Well, I'm not going to hold back on loving Daniel Brewster for fear of it ending or not being reciprocated. Life's too short. I'll take this emotion while I can.

'You feel amazing,' he says softly, his breath sweetly stroking the back of my neck. 'Such a perfect fit ... It's never felt like this before.' He gives a little push and the fit's better than perfect.

Men, they'll say anything, but his words still move me. I rub my face against the pillow, ineffectually drying my eyes and probably wrecking my makeup. I push myself back against him, wishing he could climb inside my skin, my brain and my heart, so I could know his secrets.

But we can't go on like this forever. Inevitably, he begins to move, and it's ineffable. He's big. He stretches me all ways, in and out. Each thrust tugs diabolically on my clitoris. I hold out against the sensations, but they dazzle me. I want to come, and to be touched as I'm fucked.

Daniel reads my mind as if he actually *has* crawled inside it. Taking his weight on one arm, he searches around beneath me, into my bush, and finds my clit. Considering how skewed his concentration must be now, from raw male lust, he still manages his usual breathtaking pinpoint accuracy. I think momentarily of the clumsiness I've experienced in the past, and acknowledge he's a most superior lover. He times his delicate strokes with the big thrusts of his powerful hips, and not once does he waver or miss the beat.

I shout. Growling, 'Oh God! Oh hell! Oh shit!' or something equally banal, I grind my hips back against him as my sex clenches around him and my mind fills with white light. It's as if my loins exist in another space, and my brain is in short circuit. My only awareness is of rapture, rapture, rapture ... and the heartbreaking warmth and beauty of Daniel's body.

And then I'm in a sort of heap beneath him, still slightly coming, but aware again, and trying to do my bit to make it good for him, rather than lying here like a selfish heap of insensible protoplasm. I jerk against him, trying to syncopate, and at the same time clasp at his thigh, his buttock, holding him to me and trying to draw him in even deeper. My reaching fingertips brush his anal furrow and he gives a raw and aching cry. I stroke it again, the best I can, and his hips lurch out of control and he starts to pound me, coming furiously.

We collapse in a muddle of heat and limbs ... and tears.

12 In the Dark

A while later, we're lying silently in the darkness. The light's out, the condom is disposed of and our hearts are gently thudding at a normal resting rate. We lie side by side under the quilt and all's quiet and cosy, but I'm painfully aware that I might have said, 'I love you' among all the 'fucks' and 'hells' . . . and I'm wondering if Daniel heard it, and what he thinks. He seems relaxed, but with men you never know.

'That was nice,' he says at length, although I get an inkling that he knows that's an understatement. It certainly understates what I felt. That must have been the best instance of lovemaking I've ever experienced in my life. I can't call it a fuck because it was much more than that.

'Yes, it was . . .' I'm at a loss to express the impact he had upon me. I've probably said far too much already, in the throes.

The room is all sooty shadows, because the curtains are very thick. The only light comes from the illuminated numbers on the bedside clock, like tiny glow-worms in the darkness. I feel Daniel turn on his side to face me, then his fingers settle on my cheek, so lightly that they might be made of moth's wings.

'It was more than nice,' he says, and then the touch of his lips on my brow is even lighter.

There's a great sense of something breaking inside me, and all my protestations to myself about risks being worth it start to falter. The idea of being without him, after being with him, takes my breath away and, unable to stop myself, I reach for his head, dig my fingers into his silky curls and pull his face down to mine for a proper kiss. He tastes of the delicious strawberries that we guzzled hungrily after we'd finished fucking. Urges that ought to have been well and truly sated start to stir again.

'I was going to spank you, you know,' purrs Daniel in my ear as we draw apart, 'like Stone and his lady love in the video feed. I really fancied that.' He pauses, pushes my hair back from my face where it's hanging in hanks across my cheek, then kisses my throat. 'But then somehow, when we started, it just seemed enough to fuck ... to make love.'

I want to grab him, pull him over me, get him inside me again. Bind him to me with desperate lovemaking, so he'll never want to let me go. Instead, I just say, 'Yeah, I thought it was going to go that way ... then it sort of didn't, did it?' I take a deep breath. 'We could try it now if you like ...'

I don't really feel like doing anything kinky at the moment, but for Daniel I'll give it a shot. Funny, I never wanted to go the extra mile like this with my husband. But, of course, he simply wasn't the man for me. And Daniel is.

'That's an exquisite offer, my sweet,' he says, kissing my brow again. 'And God knows I'm tempted, but somehow I just feel like lying here and being normal for a while, don't you?'

I do. And I tell him so. Then add, 'Although I suppose Nemesis will be disappointed if I don't report any ultra perv –'

Daniel laughs, a warm, happy sound. 'Yes, he does sound as if he's the type to enjoy the kinkier byways, doesn't he?' A strong arm slides around me and, to my surprise, I discover I'm light enough to be hauled bodily into a man's arms. 'A man who sends explicit sex notes and emails must be a complete and utter freak, mustn't he? The dregs of humanity.' The laughter is still in his words, and it's right on the point of bursting out again. In spite of my qualms, and my love, my own mirth bubbles.

'Oh, he's awful! A sick monster. Depraved and repulsive. I don't know why I bother with him.' I pause, and the flickers down in my loins start to gather momentum again. As I press sideways I discover Daniel's got flickers of something too. 'It must be because he's so masterful. He tells me what to do, and I like it. I never did before, with other men, but I like it with him.'

Too much information? It seems not. I can't see Daniel, but I can sense his smile, twinkly and impish, and almost see the gypsy-wicked look upon his face.

'So? You like all that domination stuff, do you? I thought you did ... Was that why you were such a hot and randy little bitch earlier?'

'I suppose so.'

'In that case ...' He releases me and rolls me on to my back again. 'Spread your legs. Wide apart. Do it now.'

I feel a surge of something. It's like a twist in my heart, a spike of fear, yet it's delicious, like the champagne we drank earlier and never finished. I feel as if my free will is melting, out of control, and making me giddy.

'Now, I want you to part the hair of your pussy. Comb it with your fingers and expose yourself. Really open yourself, bare your clit and your pretty little sex-lips.'

Hello, Nemesis.

I obey him, trembling all over. I thought I was sated, maybe ready to sleep a little, but suddenly all my neurons and pheromones are firing. I reach down and start digging in my sticky, flossy pubic hair. I'm a bit matted from the way I've flowed and sweated in our previous coupling.

A larger hand than mine comes down, checking for my obedience. I peel myself further open, allowing him to dabble and flick and play. He toys with me a minute, then nudges my own hand into position.

'Now play with yourself. Really go at it. Be a bit rough.'

I gasp, suck in air. It's hard to breathe. I feel pinned to the bed. As I begin to finger myself, his hand folds over mine, doubling the pressure, the action. I'm slippery and getting wetter. The onslaught is intense, overwhelming. The sensations gather so fast and hard they're almost painful, and when the pleasure comes it's so sharp and compressed it's close to anguish. I cry out, like a bird in the night, my vagina clenching. I feel as if I'm floating up to the ceiling.

Then, while I'm still in shock, Daniel's on the move. He flings the duvet off us, then climbs astride me and holds himself above my body. It's an awkward position, but somehow we manage it. I'm all spread out like a washed-up starfish on a beach, and he's kneeling over me, strong thighs wide and braced on either side of my ribs. Pressing his hands on either side of my breasts, he makes a deep groove between them and inserts his penis into it.

'Oh, that feels divine,' he groans, beginning to swing his hips a little and slide back and forth in my cleavage. He rocks and slides, rocks and slides, and gradually I surface from my temporary inertia. My pussy is on its own, out of the field of operations for the moment, but somehow a tingle gathers again.

I grab his thighs, feeling the muscles tensing and relaxing as he thrusts, loving the feel of the light veil of wiry masculine hair on his skin. I slide my fingers upwards, stroking the inner slopes of his bottom, teasing his groove the way I did before ... with predictable results. He shouts aloud, jackhammers his hips, rains warm salty semen on to my chin, my cheeks.

And all this in the dark. I wish I could see his beautiful face as he comes, but I console myself by licking his essence from my lips, sampling and savouring it.

He sways, fighting for control, resisting his natural male inclination to slump across me satisfied and sleepy. Instead, he flings himself to one side, gasping in the black night, then reaches back to hold me, his arm damp with sweat.

'Thank you,' he pants, 'thank you, thank you, thank you ...'

For a few moments he breathes heavily, his arm weighty across my middle. Then he shakes his head as if to clear it, his hand slides down my damp belly, and his fingers dive into my cleft again. As his middle finger begins to move, fast and hard at the heart of the matter, I lick my lips again and again, tasting him.

'No! No! No!'

I fly up out of sleep, jerked awake by Daniel shouting and struggling and flailing about. I reach for the bedside light, catching sight of the time as I snap it on. It's the early hours and we've been asleep, snuggled together, like old lovers.

'What is it, love?' I try to put my arms around his shoulders, but he's shuffling into a sitting position, his shoulders turning this way and that, his hands across his face. The room is warm but he is shaking wildly. I try to pry his hands free, but he makes an anguished sound and turns away from me.

I can't work out whether he's awake or asleep, but, when I put my hand on his bare shoulder and feel his skin soaked with sweat, he doesn't flinch. Thankfully.

'Daniel, what's the matter? Are you all right?'

He doesn't answer, but his chest lifts in a huge gasp. He's still clasping at his face and keeping it turned away, but he lets me slide my hand around his back. He feels cold and clammy.

I don't know what to say. What to do. I just hold him and

absorb the shaking. And the fear. He's so afraid, desperately afraid, of something.

Gradually the shudders begin to subside, but he still won't take his hands away from his face. It's as if he's hiding from something. Behind his fingers his eyes are scrunched up, and his brow is wrinkled in a heavy frown.

'How about a glass of water?' Well, that's what they always suggest in the movies, isn't it?

Another gasp. Then, 'Yes ... yes, thank you, I'd love one.'

I give him a squeeze, then rise naked from the bed and pad to the mini-bar. There are several kinds of water, and I pick a still Malvern, pour it into a glass and bring it to him. He's still hiding his face, but I manage to pry his fingers loose and put the glass into his hands. He sips gratefully, but not once does he open his eyes.

There's something wrong with his vision. I've worked that one out. But what? And how serious? Has there been a crisis all of a sudden? Can he even see?

'What's wrong, Daniel? Please tell me. How can I help you?'

He lets out his breath as if he's been holding it and, still clutching his water glass, he opens his eyes. Blinking, he peers at the glass and his own hands holding it, then scrunches his eyes up again.

'Bad dream,' he says in a low, flat voice, then just stares at the water as if he's never seen a glass before. It seems that he's finished with it, though, because he lets me take it away from him and set it aside.

I reach for his hand and he clasps mine, quite hard, almost desperately.

'What was your dream about, love?'

I'm not sure I should be calling him that, but it seems right for the moment. And at last he looks at me. His expression is strange, complex, stricken, yet I can see he's fighting to get back in control, pull himself together, be the man. And his eyes don't look quite right. They're hazy, not quite focused.

'I dreamt that I woke up and I couldn't see. Everything was black.' He stares at the bed-sheets, then glances at me, face full of troubles.

'But it's the middle of the night, and the curtains are thick. Everything *was* black in here.'

He shrugs. 'No, this was different. Believe me . . . I know.'

'How?' I bring our clasped hands to my lips and give his knuckles a quick kiss. It seems to comfort him and he gives me a crooked smile.

'This was blackness inside, Gwendolynne, not the room. I know it . . . I recognise it.'

A cold hand grips my heart. God, I was hoping that there wasn't something wrong. That he was just having tension headaches, or suffering from stress, or whatever.

'Have you got something wrong with your eyes, Daniel?' I ask firmly. I'm not going to shilly-shally about any more. If he's got a problem, it has to be faced. And if it's something that can be better faced by two, I want to be the one he can rely on. I need to be that one, because he's the one for me.

The words 'in sickness and in health' flash through my mind. They were just words in a ceremony at my wedding. Now I mean them.

He still seems unable to look at me, but he begins, hesitantly.

'Well, it's not so much my eyes as in here.' He rubs his head, at the back, ruffling his curls. 'There's something in here that shouldn't be. I've been having tests, and scans . . . and I have a tumour. They think it's benign, but it's got to come out.' He drags in a deep breath. 'And soon.'

At last he looks at me again. His eyes are more focused now, but I can see both acceptance and fear in his expression. The cold hand squeezes harder. I fight not to give in to it, but it's hard not to be swamped by horror. For him. How it must gouge at him . . . the fear, the prospect that he might go blind . . . that he might die. The cold hand throws me into a surging sea of terror and grief and anger.

No! Not this man! This can't happen to him! Not now I've found him! Maybe we won't have more than his fling-type thing, but still, I don't want any harm to come to him ever. Because I love him. And I don't even care if I can't have him forever. I just want him to be well and to be happy. But at the same time I don't want to drown him in pity and woefulness. Men don't like that sort of thing.

'That's hard. A tough thing to deal with, Daniel,' I say cautiously. 'I'm sorry to hear it. Is there anything I can do? Any way I can help you complete your research or anything? Type up notes, whatever?'

Miraculously, his eyes sharpen, and he turns to me. Gives me a slight smile, his head tilted on one side.

'You're a very special woman, Gwendolynne.' This time it's his turn to kiss my palm. He does it once, twice, then he rubs his stubbly cheek against the back of my hand. 'A very special woman indeed.'

His smile is in his eyes now, and I know that right at this moment he can probably see me perfectly.

'How do you mean?'

'Most women would go all smothering and Mother Teresa on me about now, but you, you're all calm and practical and no-nonsense.' He kisses me again. 'And I like that. I'm grateful for it.'

In spite of his world-shaking revelation, I feel a bubble of something great, something wonderful. A real communication between us that's not just to do with sex. 'Well, I didn't think

you'd want fuss and pity and mothering and all that. I … um …'
I pout, not sure how to express what I mean. 'I don't want you
to think that I think you're less of a man because you've got
some health thing going on.'

He laughs, and it's a pure, sweet sound.

'I swear that you must be a genius or a psychologist or
something, my lady librarian.' He shrugs again, and gives me
the fondest look. An expression that makes my heart turn
somersaults, despite everything. 'That is exactly how I was –
am – feeling.' The look turns serious. Intense. 'I want you,
Gwendolynne. I desire you, and I care for you. And I want
you to desire and care for me. The last emotion I want from
you is pity.' His eyes narrow. 'I'm still a man and I still get
horny, regardless of whether I've got a lump of God knows
what in my head.'

'Yeah, I get that.' I look at him, so beautiful, so tousled, so
male. He's just dropped a massive bombshell into our relationship, but we're still sitting in a bed, naked, together, and he's
still the most gorgeous man I've ever met. Am I some kind of
sicko to suddenly be wanting him all over again? 'You don't
want any pity fucks.'

He laughs again, then gives me a sly, narrow look. 'No, none
of those …'

But what about the other sort? I can't tell, the sheet is across
his hips. The threat of darkness and mortality hangs over him,
but the human spirit and the male libido are notoriously
defiant in the face of adversity.

I wonder though. An uncertain future explains his desire
for a temporary relationship, his wariness about deeper
commitment. Might it also explain his strange way of initi-
ating a liaison? Being Nemesis gave him distance, clandestine
thrills, a chance to have perverse fun with a woman without
direct involvement. It's the product of a devious mind, but

then, he is Professor Hottie, as brilliant as he is charismatic and handsome.

He frowns slightly. 'What? What are you thinking?' He might have problems with his vision but he can see right through me. He knows I'm working things out.

'I can see now why you might employ some, er, shall we say "unorthodox" methods to seduce women, to keep things at a distance. Not get in too deep.'

He cocks his head at me, and a dark kiss-curl dangles on his brow. It looks so perfect, so tantalising, that I have to reach out and touch it, smooth it back. But it only flops down again.

'I don't know what you mean, Gwendolynne,' he says archly, grasping my wrist. He has hold of me by both wrists now. Not too hard, but there's a definite masterful quality to his grip, and it intensifies when he gently presses me back on to the pillows and looms over me.

'You won't admit it, will you?' I stare back, taking the game to him.

'Admit what?'

'You know.'

He's laughing again, in my face, low and deliciously evil.

'You're a wicked girl, Gwendolynne, making vague, unfounded accusations.' His body is pressing against me, hard and vital, up for it in all senses of the word. My heart swells, happy to feel it, even as my own body revs up again, seemingly inexhaustible in its desire.

'Not vague! You're N–'

I can't finish because his lips come down hard on mine and his tongue is in my mouth, suppressing the word I tried to utter. We both know what I nearly said, though, and we both acknowledge it's the truth. The kiss itself proves it.

He moves on top of me, his rock-hard cock jabbing at my belly. With crafty dexterity he manages to grab both my wrists in one hand, while with the other he makes an insolent progress down my flank and my thigh, then cups my bottom, his fingers between me and the mattress. He grips hard, squeezing the cheek, threatening in a way that only makes me more breathless.

Holding me, pinioning me, he slides against me, skin on skin. I feel his packed muscles and his mighty erection. My jaw starts to ache from the force of his kiss, but I welcome it. I revel in his energy. I submit to it, and to him.

When he's thoroughly quelled me, at least for the time being, he breaks the kiss and growls, 'Any more accusations, library girl?' He doesn't allow me to answer, just punishes me again with another kiss, more seductive this time. His tongue stirs and tastes, dabbing at mine, flicking it. He does a thing with his hips, compelling me, if that were needed, to acknowledge his cock.

'Nothing to say?' he persists, his voice throaty and devilish.

'No, I don't need to. You know what I was talking about.'

'You won't back down?' His eyes look furious, wonderful, sharp and clear. I cannot imagine a man less whole.

'No!'

'I should punish you then. You deserve it. You won't take no for an answer.'

My innards quiver, and all thoughts of Daniel's uncertain future fly away in the excitement of the moment.

'Do your worst, Professor Hottie, do your worst!'

13 Lessons with Professor Hottie

He almost barks with laughter. '"Professor Hottie"? Why, you cheeky little cow! Is that what you call me behind my back?'

'Yes. Me and all the girls in the library. I thought you knew that.'

'I bet you encourage them, don't you? I bet you speculate endlessly about me and that you always come up with the wildest stories and fantasies.'

'I might have done a bit. Well, a lot really ...'

Still chuckling, he rolls off me and sits up.

'Turn over. Show me that gorgeous arse of yours.'

Something breathtaking stirs inside me. A sense of weakening and melting, a mutinous pleasure at being ordered about and at giving in to those orders. I never wanted this before. I resented it before. But now it's delicious, irresistible. So exciting it makes my pussy flutter and flow. My head fills with images of leather masks, dark rooms, the perspective of kneeling before a stern but beautiful master. This stern but beautiful master, none other.

'You need a damn good seeing-to, madam,' he says in the tones of a dictatorial schoolmaster, then adds, 'And I don't just mean a fucking.' Which rather spoils the impression of an august and serious scholar.

Slowly I comply, rolling over, my heart racing madly as he lifts the sheet away from my lush, rounded bottom and flings it to the end of the bed. I bury my head in my arms because somehow I daren't look at Daniel. He's suddenly become too awesome in my imagination, too dazzling. I shudder, shaking like a racehorse as he begins to stroke the curves of my backside, exploring the meat of me, the muscle and the softer dimples. He tracks his fingertips over every inch, bringing hot blood to my face as he explores my anal furrow and the rosy little hole that nestles there. He spares me nothing, dabbling and probing and causing me to wriggle, mashing my crotch against the sheet beneath me. I'm his creature. He can do anything he wishes.

'Touch yourself. Do it now,' he growls, leaning over my back, still playing with my bottom.

I moan involuntarily. The idea is so shaming and delicious.

'Gwendolynne,' he says ominously, pushing at me.

Gasping for breath, I squeeze a hand beneath me, probing for my sex. When I find my target, the amount of simmering wetness is astonishing. I'm creating a little puddle of sticky fluid beneath my pussy.

'Finger on your clit.'

'Nooo ...' I wail.

'Why not?'

'I don't know ... It seems so dirty to be turned on while you're playing with me like that.'

'That's because you're a dirty little girl, Ms Price. I know you masturbate.'

I narrow my eyes. Ha ha! How do you know, Professor Hottie? I've only told Nemesis. But then I remember how he nearly caught me in the garden behind the library. What I'd been doing there must have been unmistakeable, even if he feigned not to notice.

'Yes, I know I do, but so what, everyone does.' I grit my teeth as he presses harder, testing my resolve, my resilience. 'You certainly do!'

There's dead silence for a moment, even though he continues his wicked play, slithering his own free hand beneath me to make sure I'm obeying him.

'And how would you know that?' His voice is in my ear, his breath caressing my face, ruffling my hair.

My clitoris seems to tingle beneath my fingertip as I imagine that exquisite scene I witnessed. Daniel touching and caressing himself in the tiny library washroom. I see again the pure, agonised lines of his face, the tension in his back and thighs. His cock spurting and his semen sliding down the porcelain base of the wash-basin, white on white.

'Because I've seen you do it.'

More silence. His fingers are behind mine, increasing the pressure on my clitoris.

'Ah,' he says eventually, the word quiet against my skin. 'I had a suspicion that I was watched that day.' His lips settle and kiss, ever so lightly. 'And a suspicion that it was you ... at least I hoped it was.'

'You'd have been in big trouble if it'd been Mr Johnson!' I want to laugh. It's just a reaction. A defence mechanism.

'How so? I'm sure a visiting celebrity can be allowed his little foibles.'

'That's some big foible.' I nudge the side of my hip against his mighty erection. 'And what if old Johnson had been gay? He might have started making overtures.'

'That's an impertinent thing to say about your boss ... and about me.' He nudges back with his cock, pressing it into my flesh. 'I'm more and more convinced that you should be disciplined, you saucy minx. Don't you agree? Aren't you ashamed of your own wickedness?'

'No! Not in the slightest!'

Daniel laughs again, rubbing his face against my hair and my cheek, then kissing and nibbling.

'I adore you, do you know that? Even if you are the most teasing and tantalising woman I've ever known. I'm going to have to spank you, you know that, don't you?'

I squirm against him, wanting it, scared of it. Excited beyond measure. I could almost come on the spot, I'm so close. He's still tickling my anus and my groove.

'Yes,' I hiss, as he first prods, then pats me. 'As long as you know what you're doing. Have you spanked someone before? I would imagine it's quite an art.'

He bites my earlobe, gently but with authority.

'I've spanked a girlfriend or two in my time. I think I can manage.' The tips of his fingernails ever so lightly dig into the inner slope of my bottom cheek.

'That's all right then,' I gasp, feeling lightheaded as the tiny pressure increases. 'Get on with it, why don't you?'

'I should tan your hide.' He drops a light pat on my left buttock. It's nothing. Just playing. I barely feel the impact, although my sex responds by fluttering.

'I should wallop you with a leather belt or a teacher's cane or something. Then you'd know.' He slaps harder, and I do feel it this time. It's like fire, soft fire, and, though my bottom cheek doesn't seem to like it and makes me try to squirm away, the nerve endings in my pussy seem to think it's delectable. Another ripple of pleasure makes me moan more than the pain does.

'You like it, don't you, you kinky little girl?' He sounds so happy, so relaxed, so far from his troubles. Part of me rejoices in this, while the rest of me goes slightly mental when he smacks me again and again. My brain doesn't really know what's happening. It registers the fiery beat of his hand, tries to process it as unpleasant and to be avoided, but there's some rudimentary seat of animal intelligence that dwells much lower down, which is telling me it's fabulous, it's thrilling, it's pure sex.

I wriggle and writhe, grinding against my fingers, and his, as I move.

'Little? You're joking, surely,' I gasp at him when I can spare a breath. 'I bet I'm the furthest from "*little* girl" that you've ever gone out with.' I pause to squeal as he gives me a very sly slap on the inner slope of one cheek that stings like a firecracker. 'A man like you can have his pick of gorgeous supermodels, I'll bet.'

'Don't be stupid, Gwendolynne,' he says amiably, as he really whacks me one and I shout like a madwoman. 'I would say, "Fuck supermodels", but I don't actually *want* to fuck them. I only want to fuck you and your luscious, magnificent body.' He whales me again, really hard, and I have something that I think is a mini-orgasm, although the signals are so scrambled I don't really know what it is. 'Why don't you believe me when I tell you that you have the most beautiful figure I've ever seen? For an intelligent woman, my love, you can be wilfully and mulishly thick!'

He's really smacking hard now, and I *am* coming. My sex clenches in hot, violent spasms in time to the loving blows, and silky honey flows out across our fingers. I groan and snarl and rock myself against the fulcrum of my own middle fingertip, but not once does Daniel miss his target, or the beat. The fucker, he's spanked more than a couple of girlfriends, that's for sure. He knows how to do this. I'd swear he's an expert.

I'm mangling the pillow, I'm gouging the sheets with my toes, I'm all over the place. But he's still in control and he's still smacking me. My bottom feels as if it's swollen hugely and has turned fluorescent red, and the incendiary heat in it is spreading to my quivering sex. Suddenly I want more. I want him. I need him inside me. I squirm free, roll over and begin to plead.

'Please, please fuck me. I can't bear to be empty. I want you inside me.'

His eyes look strange, dark, full of emotion. Can he see me? I think so. Even if his vision is choosing at this moment to be recalcitrant, he's seeing me with other senses, in perfect clarity. He leans sideways, fishes in the bedside drawer without looking and brings out another condom. He rips off the foil, rolls it on quickly, then parts my legs and plunges inside me up to the hilt.

I grab him, scrabbling at his shoulders and back, then his buttocks, wanting him closer, ever closer, as close as can be. He's filling me, but I want him inside me even more, inside my cells and nerves and consciousness. I heave my hips up to meet his, crushing our sexes together just as he meets me with equal and opposite force. Hot twinges streak from the soreness in my bottom, only adding to the intensity, the pleasure.

The chaos of our thrusts and our jerking and struggling makes it impossible for us to kiss, but he jams his mouth against my neck, lips parted, teeth scraping my skin, nipping, almost feral. That drives me even crazier, it's so basic. Tilting my pelvis, I lock my ankles round the back of his waist, taking him deeper.

We strive and rock against each other, making wild, not quite human sounds. If thunder suddenly cracked and rolled outside, it wouldn't surprise me. The storm's already raging and crashing inside our bodies and our hearts. Even if he doesn't feel what I feel, I can't believe that he's left unmoved by our union.

Tumult like this can't last for long. It's too furious, too intense to sustain. Orgasm hurtles through me like a blazing, falling star, and with a great cry Daniel joins me in the heart of it. I shudder on the edge of a blackout, dragging in great breaths, my chest heaving and Daniel's heaving against it.

We're a tangled heap of limbs and sweat and fluids and shredded consciousness, but slowly we disengage, my legs flopping open against the mattress, allowing Daniel to lever himself free. He just lies between my thighs for a few moments, as if gathering strength to move, then with a gasp he lifts his weight from me, our sticky skin peeling apart as he heaves himself to one side, and collapses alongside me.

I don't know what to say, and I sense he doesn't either. But as he reaches for my hand and laces our fingers, my heart turns over.

For the second time tonight, we drift into sleep.

14 Bombshell Time

When I awake, it's proper morning and Daniel is at the door of the room, taking possession of a laden tray of breakfast. I glance at the clock and see it's ten thirty, which makes me sit bolt upright in a panic, until I remember that I've prudently made sure I'm not working today.

Daniel's eyes widen appreciatively behind his glasses as he brings the tray to the bed, his attention zeroing in on my frontage. He looks fresh and rested in a dark-blue towelling robe, and his curly hair is wet from a recent shower. I feel slightly irritated that he's got up without waking me, but I suppose he only did it out of consideration for my obvious state of totally shagged-out exhaustion. Because I feel as if I've run a dozen marathons, and I have tiny subversive twinges nagging me in most unlikely places. Or likely, when you consider our sexual exploits. Strangely, though, my spanked bottom seems OK.

'Coffee?' Daniel suggests, lifting the pot, his glance still lingering on my nipples or thereabouts. Oh, men, they're so transparent, so focused on flesh.

Me, I'm focused on flesh too. Professor Daniel Brewster's. I can't see as much of him as he can see of me this morning, but I can remember every inch I saw last night. I can remember how it looked and how it felt. And how I felt feeling it. Which is much as I feel now, although I'm too tired and suddenly too shy to do anything physical about it.

I remind myself of the inconvenient truth of the matter:

that, like an idiot, I've fallen in love with him. How typical of me to fall too hard and far too soon for a man who in many ways is pretty much unattainable. I'm under no illusion that I'm anything other than a diversion for him while he's here researching at the library.

And yet somehow, something in his expression has altered even while I was waking up. Those eyes, whose vision some-times lets him down, are full of shadows that don't seem to be anything to do with his increasingly unreliable sight. I see doubt and uncertainty in them that mirror my own. Is he regretting the soul-stripping intimacy of last night, just as I am? And, if so, is it for a different reason than the one that's beginning to plague and torment me?

I've given too much. I've plunged too deep. I've given my heart too thoroughly to ever get it back without leaving pieces behind. Does he feel the same, or does he just regret getting a little more entangled than he'd anticipated?

'Gwendolynne?' he prompts, his fine mouth twisting slightly. He's definitely troubled.

'Yes, please pour me some.' I snatch a second robe that he's thoughtfully placed within my reach, wriggle out from beneath the covers and slip into it. 'I'll be back in a minute. I just, um, need to use the bathroom.'

'OK. Milk and sugar?'

'Just milk,' I request, and scoot for the haven of the bathroom as if I've been scalded. Maybe I have, in a way. My fingers are metaphorically but very definitely singed and burnt. I've reached for a flame, a beautiful flame, and these are the consequences.

I do what I have to in the bathroom, strangely reluctant to leave my temporary sanctuary. I feel shy, ridiculous as it seems after all he and I have done together. But loving the man, and not being sure what he feels for me, just makes the situation seem more and more precarious.

Eventually I slink out, closely bundled in my robe and a thick cloak of wariness. Daniel is sitting up on the bed, a coffee cup cradled in his hands, staring at his feet. I take my own cup and perch next to him. I stare at his feet too. They're very nice feet, quite big, but well shaped and immaculately kept.

'I've got to go away again. Later today. For an operation.' His words drop like a piano into a pond, so sudden and momentous that I wince. This is an even bigger shock than last night, if that were possible.

'Oh ... right ...' I can't think of anything to say, but inside I'm screaming. Obviously I knew that he would be having treatment. He can't *not* have any. But the actuality of it, and the fact it's now, straight away, forces me to confront the horror of what's happening to the one I love.

'I've got to get this thing sorted.' He pauses and rubs the back of his head, ruffling his curls. Where the damn thing lurks. 'And the sooner the better, or the brutal fact is I'll go blind ... or worse.' He draws a great breath, and I know he's fighting a tidal wave of fear. Who wouldn't be? I fucking well am! For him.

'I've got to return to London, to the clinic, for a few more tests ... then, in two or three days, I'll be under the knife.'

There's a loud moaning, which I realise, to my horror, is coming from me.

'Hey, don't worry! I'm young and fit and a pretty tough bastard for an academic.' Cup abandoned, he puts his arm round me. I put my own cup shakily to my lips and try to drink. The coffee is excellent but I spill some of it down my robe, fortunately avoiding any naked flesh.

The spectre of him blind, or gone, is too horrible to comprehend. It's as if everything inside me is crushed. Letting him take my cup too, I feel numbed yet frantic. And I start making deals, in my head, with the higher powers.

I'll give him up, never see him again, just let him be all right.

Do something to me instead, just let him be all right.

I'll give up all pleasures of the flesh and donate everything I own and earn from now on to the poor, just let him be all right.

'Can I come with you?' I hear myself say. 'I can get time off work. I can be around. Do errands or whatever for you. I, um, I don't mean in a serious-girlfriend sort of way with any claims or anything, just a helper or something.'

I feel the muscles of his arm around me tense and stiffen. I've said something stupid, I know. But I just want to be there for him, so I'll know, as soon as is possible, that he's all right.

When I turn to him, he looks worried and perplexed. He sighs heavily again.

'I need to do this on my own, Gwendolynne.' He shakes his head slightly, as if he's not quite sure what he's saying and actually thinks he's being a fool but can't help himself. 'I ... I ... don't want anyone I care for around me. I don't want people to see me weak.'

'Oh, that's just bloody stupid!'

Shocked by my outburst, he actually flinches. His beautiful mouth compresses, and I realise that, even at a critical time like this, a brilliant scholar like Daniel Brewster can be as stubborn as a caveman. Mercifully, his arm remains around me.

'Maybe it is, Gwendolynne, but that's the way I want it.' His angry look softens. 'It's not you, love, it's me. I just need to do this alone. To prove to myself I can.' He gives me a squeeze. 'I do care for you, a lot, a helluva lot, but ... I can't explain it, this is the way I need it to be.' Touching my face, he makes me look into his eyes, dark and shadowed behind his glasses. 'Please. I've got to do this my own way.'

'But it doesn't make sense. If it was me, I'd want someone there.'

Then I think ... would I? For the fear and the darkness, yes. But presumably there'll be head-shaving and tubes and all sorts of medical gruesomeness. Nothing like that would ever diminish what I feel for Daniel, not in the smallest degree, but there's a vain, silly part of me that would cringe at him seeing *me* that way. And men can be vain and silly too, when it comes down to it.

We cling to each other for a while, at an impasse.

'Are you *sure* I can't come with you?' I say eventually in a small voice. It's not a whine, except inside my head.

He's silent for a while. His arm and his body are very still against me.

'Look, there isn't anyone else who's going to be there, if that's what you're thinking,' he says suddenly, taking my hand in his free one. 'There's no one in my life but you, Gwendolynne, I swear it.'

It had crossed my mind. Indeed it had. As an explanation for the fling-type thing, originally, and now for his reluctance to let me support him through his coming ordeal. I should be grateful, but my own stubbornness won't let things lie.

'I believe you ... but all the more reason for me to be there then. If there's no one else.'

'No!' he says sharply, his mouth settling into a stern, immovable line.

I feel pretty stern and immovable myself. I want to insist. I open my mouth to protest, to insist on being heard and say any damn thing to make him concede, then I bite my tongue. The man I love is under duress. How can a person think straight and logically in the face of what lies ahead of Daniel? If I love him, I have to indulge him and let him deal with his operation and its perils in his own away. No matter how much it pains me.

'OK,' I say softly, 'I get it. You want to deal with this on your own.' I feel deflated, lost, wanting still to be there for him. As if the breath has all gone out of me, I slump against him, and he puts both arms round me, holding me against his body.

'I'll be OK, Gwendolynne. I'll go in, and get the op, and I'll be right as rain again in no time.' He strokes my hair, slowly, rhythmically. 'And as soon as I get the all-clear, maybe we could have a holiday or something? Somewhere nice and warm and luxurious where we can laze on a beach and you can go topless and I can spend all day ogling you with my restored vision.'

Ah, the dream holiday with the perfect man. Something I've always fantasised about and never quite achieved. Why does the prospect of it finally happening have to have such a terrifying rider attached to it? To reach our idealised getaway we first have to pass through the valley of death – and Daniel won't even let me hold his hand while we traverse it.

I shake and sob and wish that life wasn't so complicated. It's as if I'm crashing somehow, and I'm the one facing horrendous surgery. Daniel holds me tighter, and his hands are, oh, so tender. But after a few minutes of falling apart, I'm strengthened by his warmth and his presence. I should be strong for him, his rock, not act like a lily-livered ninny. I should accept the truth of the matter, and be there for him in whatever way he needs me to be. Even if that means me *not* actually being there.

And I need to give him the best possible send-off. I seek his mouth with mine, find it and initiate a kiss. I feel his firm, coffee-scented lips curve beneath mine. He gets what I'm up to. Our tongues duel for several minutes, hot and slippery. I try to push him back against the mattress, intending to blanket him with pleasure in any and every way I can think of, but he holds firm.

'No, my way,' he says in a fierce voice, holding me by the

shoulders and attacking my mouth again, forcing it open, plunging in his tongue in a way that makes the pit of my belly flutter and melt.

I push away all notions of condemned men and hearty meals and just allow myself to succumb, thrilled by his strength and his take-charge handling of me. When he sweeps over me, forgetting the darkness becomes sweet and easy.

He kisses hard, the onslaught so exciting it's almost like being fucked before we've even got our robes off. His long, elegant hands start to rove, caressing me roughly through the towelling, using its texture as an extra stimulant. Eventually, though, he rips my robe open and bares my body. Then, jerky and impatient, he pulls the sash roughly out from beneath me and grabs my wrists and pushes them over my head. In a series of loops and knots that a Boy Scout would be proud of, he secures my hands to the brass head-rail of the bed and tests the bonds to ensure that my wrists aren't too uncomfortable.

A sense of wild panic crossed with delicious, submissive weakness sluices through me. I didn't expect this, not at all, not at this strange, emotional juncture. I'm just not ready for it, yet I've been waiting far too long. Automatically I start to wriggle, and a smoky fire begins to smoulder in Daniel's eyes at the sight. My compulsion to test my bonds seems to please him, and his beautiful mouth curves devilishly. His obvious pleasure makes my skin feel hot and tingly.

Still robed himself, he leans over my exposed form, bringing his face close, and I realise that somewhere along the line he's removed his glasses. He doesn't seem to be having too many problems seeing me, though. In fact he's happily ogling everything he wants.

Without warning, he dips down and licks my nipple, his tongue warm and tricky as it caresses the puckered tip. The sensation shoots down to my clitoris, making it throb, and as he bites lightly, and at the same time slides his thumb into the dent of my navel, I moan and whimper.

'Hush,' he mutters against my breast, then closes his teeth again, ever so lightly. They feel very sharp and very threatening. He lifts and tugs and circles, drawing out the soft flesh like a little cone. I bite down hard on my lip to suppress my groans, while my pussy protests silently, burning and aching to be touched.

For a while he plays intently with my breasts, handling them, cupping them, fussing with my nipples until they stick out lewdly like fat dark studs. As I fight not to go crazy – and occasionally fail dismally, hefting my hips about on the bed – his fingertips sometimes stray to other zones, before returning to my navel, prodding and probing in a way that makes me jerk and wriggle. Sometimes he just draws the tips of his nails up and down the groove between my belly and my thighs, the indentation of my groin.

Studiously, and very scrupulously, he avoids my sex.

But I can't avoid it. It seems to have taken over my entire consciousness. It feels swollen, tense, open, stretched by agonising desire. It seems to pout between my thighs, glistening with juice and almost steaming, it's so hot, hot, hot for his attentions.

I'm almost dying to come, and to feel anything of him down there. Finger. Tongue. Cock. Yet, somewhere in the still, cool heart of my consciousness, I recognise that, even though I'm on fire for him, this interlude is about Daniel, about him being in control, about him losing himself in the game and forgetting what lies ahead of him. My intense frustration, the torment of temporary denial – these are sweet gifts I can give him to distract him.

I open my thighs wider, twist my hips against the sheet, lift my pussy, show myself to him, offering total submission, letting him know that my flesh is his, completely, to do with as he will.

Finally, he sits back. His eyes look hazy, but I don't know whether it's from lust or the hateful thing that afflicts him. He throws off his robe and he's hugely erect, his cock vital, powerful, full of magnificent life and strength. As he inclines over me again, kissing along the lines of my collarbone and circling my nipples with his thumbs, the hot bar of his masculinity drags silkily across my thigh.

'I wish we had more time,' he says in a low, hard voice, then reaches into the drawer for a condom. 'I'd like to drive you insane with pleasure. Spend hours on you. Make you come and come ...' As he speaks, quietly and with suppressed anger at his fate, he rolls the sheath on to himself. 'I'd work you into such a pitch of lust that you wouldn't be able to remember your name and you'd scream your throat raw when you came.'

Before I can stop myself, I suddenly break out of my role and say, 'I'll take a raincheck ...'

There's a moment of utter silence, in which I would kick myself if I could do it successfully, then Daniel roars with laughter and virtually throws himself between my thighs.

'Oh, my beautiful Gwendolynne, you are priceless. What would I do without you?' He gives me a quick hard kiss on the lips, then positions himself at my entrance and starts to push in. 'We are going to have so much fun when all this crap is over. We're going to fuck like bunnies and play all the sex games we've ever dreamt of ... and then some.' He gives a determined and happy grunt and shoves himself home.

For a moment, my longed-for orgasm is in danger of sliding away, out of my reach, distracted by renewed thoughts of Daniel's coming ordeal. But then the sheer beloved presence of him, his weight, his smell, his hardness, his hot breath against my neck, all conspire to recapture it and urge it into being. My pussy blooms around his cock and, unable to hold him in my arms, I hook my legs round his, lift my hips and push and push and push my pelvis and my spasming sex against him.

Daniel pounds me in return, sliding a hand beneath my bottom, powering into me as if working out all his apprehension and uncertainty with the force of his thrusts. We jerk against each other like animals, just as we did before, revisiting the bright, cleansing space of mutual pleasure, mutual desperation, mutual orgasm.

Of course, at this sort of pace it could never last long. I rise to another jolting, breath-catching climax and, just as I grab and secure it, I feel Daniel reach his peak too. He sobs and roars as he empties himself inside me, and the sound is a mighty shout of dark emotion.

Afterwards he unties me and we uncouple.

We're both quiet, lost in our thoughts, survivors of a hurricane. And a bombshell. Daniel seems like someone I barely know, which he is really, and my head feels full of thoughts and confused emotions that are difficult to process.

I focus on the sequence of events, trying to make sense of it. One, I get involved in a kinky sex game. Two, I fall for a beautiful, brilliant, glamorous man in the course of the sex game. Three, I begin to wonder if there might be some serious, long-term chance for me with said beautiful, brilliant, glamorous man. Four, I discover said beautiful, brilliant, glamorous man is in peril of his life, and, because there's been no time to really get to *know* him, I have no claim on him, no lover's rights to insist that he lets me help him.

I want to scream and throw a tantrum and break things in this lovely room we've shared so much in. But I can't. I must be calm and quiet, not make a scene, play it sensible and make allowances for Daniel, who surely can't be thinking straight himself at a time like this. I compromise by having a secret little snivel in the bathroom, but when I emerge, cleaned up and smartened up but uneasily aware that I'm wearing last night's frock and no knickers at all, I offer Daniel what I hope is a calm, supportive, but not too pushy smile.

He's in his robe still, but his suitcases are out and he's packing. His expression is complex and wistful, yet tinged, even now, with a little desire.

Oh, if only our timing hadn't been so utterly crappy! Who knows what possibilities would have beckoned?

'Wh–where will you have the operation? How are you going to get there? I assume you can't drive.'

He heaves a sigh but, to my relief, doesn't get all distant on me. We sit together for a while and he tells me, in general terms, what will happen to him. What he won't tell me is where the hospital is, but it is, apparently, a world-renowned centre of excellence, a private clinic where he'll receive the finest care.

I want to push again, beg for the details, beg to be allowed to come with him, but we've been through all that, and, though it's the most horrible, painful thought in the world, if these are to be our last moments together, I don't want them to be full of strife and conflict.

'You're a good woman, Gwendolynne,' he says suddenly, taking my hand in both of his. 'I can tell how much it's costing you not to ask questions and probe and get in a strop because of the way I am. And God knows, I adore you even more because of it.'

He lifts my hand to his lips, kisses it with infinite tenderness.

'You're rare and special, and when this is all over I think *we* can have something rare and special too.' He presses his warm face against my hand, and I can feel the delicate prickle of his stubble. He continues to speak, not looking at me, his breath brushing against my skin. 'But we must get past this first, so we can start clean. I don't want what happened to my mother to happen to you. My father's illness extinguished her life, crushed her creativity.' He pauses and his fingers tighten almost painfully around the bones of my hand. 'And I swore that I'd never inflict that on a woman I cared for, never. He's been a capricious and ungrateful patient, and he's blamed her for his misfortunes.' He kisses my skin again. 'And I can't guarantee that I won't turn out like him when the crunch comes.'

I want to tell him that I know in my gut that he won't be a bit like his father, but I'm struggling with such misery inside me that I just can't speak. Instead, as Daniel straightens up and I see the shimmer of ferociously suppressed tears in his eyes, I just put my arms around him and envelop him in a hug. We kiss and embrace for a while. It's strangely asexual, given what we've been through in this room.

Presently, though, it's time. The house phone rings and from Daniel's side of the conversation I can tell that there's a car coming for him in less than an hour – and he still has to shave and dress and pack his belongings.

We're on our feet, both a little awkward.

'I'll walk you down to the foyer, get you a taxi,' he says, reaching for a pair of jeans on top of his suitcase.

'No, it's all right. I'll be fine.' There's an ice axe hacking at my heart, but I manage to keep it together. 'You finish your packing and whatnot. It's probably better if I just go.'

I make as if to head for the door, not sure how long I can maintain this, but instead of the jeans he snatches up a shirt, 'Here ... a sort of jacket. Slip it over your dress.'

I nearly do lose it then. He's so thoughtful, trying to make me look less conspicuous in a dress that's obviously for evening and cocktails and so forth. When I slip my arms into the shirt, his fragrance wraps around me.

At the door, another fierce kiss, and as we hug again he whispers in my ear, 'It won't be long. They think it's straightforward. I could be sorted in two or three weeks, and on the mend. I'll call you then.'

My heart screams: but what if I don't get a call, what does that mean?

But I stay silent, savour the last moments with his arms around me, and after a final lingering kiss I open the door. He watches me down the corridor, and the sight of him as I turn for one last look, so handsome and so boyish in his dark robe and his bare feet, nearly kills me. We give each other a little wave, then I hurl myself round the corner and run for the stairs rather than the lift. I don't stop running until I'm out of the Waverley, and I grab the taxi that's waiting on the gravel drive. Fortunately, it seems to be for me, and the driver remains sympathetically quiet as my pent-up tears begin to fall.

15 Best Intentions

I'm in a haze. I feel as if I've had an operation too. Surgery to detach me from reality, from the everyday ebb and flow of my existence.

Like an idiot, I've taken some leave, because I didn't think I could concentrate on work. But now I've got too much free time on my hands. I should have gone into the library anyway, to keep myself occupied, but instead I'm at home, just mooching around the flat, trying to recreate in my imagination all the things that Daniel and I did together. If I can immerse myself in gorgeous memories of life and sublime sensuality, maybe I can squeeze out thoughts of what's about to happen to him, or may already have happened.

I can't even take comfort from the fact that pining for my beloved has put me off my food and I'll lose some weight. Just the opposite. The fridge is a constant temptation, and finally I have to get myself out of the flat and away from it, walking the streets aimlessly with no particular destination, staring at passers-by and shop windows, but seeing only Daniel, Daniel, Daniel.

Finally, I find myself watching a daytime episode of *ER* that I'd intended not to watch ... and I crack. I don't care what he says. I have to go to him. Deep down I'm sure he wants me there, or at least that's what I tell myself as I dial the number for the Waverley Grange Hotel and ask for the one person I know who might be able to tell me which clinic or hospital he's in.

'Annie Guidetti,' says a warm, pleasant voice that immediately makes me feel almost tearful with relief. Not Daniel, but someone who knows him, someone of his blood.

'Oh, er, hello, you don't know me, but I'm a friend of your cousin Daniel Brewster's and I wondered if you knew how he was getting on.'

'Gwendolynne? Is that you? I was just about to ring you. What a coincidence.'

She knows me? She was going to ring me? Black fear grips my gut. I flop into the chair.

'Yes, that's me. Daniel and I have been sort of seeing each other. I was at the Waverley last week.' I feel myself veering dangerously towards panicking and snivelling and I make a huge effort to pull myself together. 'I know he's having or has had an operation, and he said not to contact him, but I've just got to know how he is, even if he doesn't want me to know.'

My voice sounds desperate, ridiculous, bordering on hysterical, but Annie Guidetti speaks kindly.

'Daniel's a brilliant man, but in this instance he's a damned idiot. And it's very cruel of him not to keep you in the picture. I told him that, but he's such a mule and a stoic, determined to do his own thing . . .' She pauses momentarily. 'Oh, my dear, I am sorry. I'm chattering on. Yes, he's had the operation. He had it the day before yesterday and it went marvellously by the sound of things. Straightforward, no complications, and the surgeon was able to remove every bit of the tumour so it shouldn't come back.'

I can't speak. Tears are streaming down my face. My heart flies up and I feel as if I'm flying too. Even though I'm weeping profusely, I'm grinning like an idiot at the phone.

'Are you all right?' asks Annie. 'Did you get that? Daniel is going to be fine. I spoke to his nurse and he's recovering well. There's post-operative pain, and he's exhausted, of course, but all that's normal, apparently. His really bad headaches have stopped and the early signs are that his vision won't be affected in the long term. He'll still wear glasses, but then he always has done.'

'Oh, that is such a relief.' I manage those few words, and then I'm off again, blubbering like an idiot.

Annie lets me get some, if not all, of it out of my system, then says, 'Look, why don't you come to London with me to visit him? He told me not to as well, but I've decided to go anyway. And I'm sure if you turn up he'll be thrilled to see you, regardless of his silly macho ideas of "going it alone" and all that nonsense. Do come. I could do with some company on the drive. Valentino's arranging a room for me at a hotel run by one of his friends in the trade, but he can just as easily book two rooms as one.'

I see Daniel's face, serious, grave, determined to get his own way. Well, bollocks to that, mate! I don't mind you ordering me around sexually, in fact I love it, but in this I'm going to do what *I* want and you're going to accept it!

'That would be wonderful, thanks. I'd love to travel with you. I've got to see him, whatever he says. I don't care if he does get cross with me. I'll take my chances.' And I'll take my chances ringing old Johnson at home as well, and telling him I'm going to visit a sick friend for a day or two. 'What time are you setting off? Shall I come to the Waverley?'

No, she'll pick me up and we'll set off in a couple of hours.

When I put the phone down I dance around the room, singing incoherently. Daniel's alive! He's OK! And he can see!

Annie Guidetti turns out to be an amazing travelling companion. To take my mind off my remaining worry about Daniel – how he'll react to my turning up now – she regales me with tall tales of the friskier goings-on at the Waverley Grange Hotel.

It turns out that it doesn't have its naughty reputation for nothing, and most of the rumours about sex parties, exotic activities and 'special' rooms with 'special' facilities are only the surface of the wildly outrageous truth.

'I was pretty much an innocent until I met the Stones and my husband,' says Annie brightly, 'but now I'm a dirty old woman and I like it!' She flashes me a smile and a wink, then returns her attention to the road, accelerating confidently and smoothly.

I point out that she's not old, and reflect on what it must be like to be married to such an exotic and highly sexed man as her husband Valentino, the gorgeous continental stud who served drinks to me in the Lawns Bar what seems like a hundred years ago.

What would it be like to be married to a glamorous and highly sexed man like Daniel? a sly, dangerous voice inside me asks before I can suppress it. It's ridiculous. I still barely know the guy. We've only ever interacted in the library and in our crazy erotic games. Face it, I've never even got him to admit that he's Nemesis, much less explore any deeper, lasting feelings. Although there was hope, wasn't there, in those last minutes before he left ...

'What does Daniel think of the Waverley?' I say, trying to distract myself from my thoughts. 'It must be rather weird running a sort of sex hotel and having your own cousin come to stay.'

'Well, Daniel's barely a proper cousin. He's actually the son of my mother's second cousin, so technically I'm an aunt of some kind. I didn't even know the Daniel in our family was the Daniel on the telly until he rang up, saying he was researching up here and did we have any rooms?'

'Oh, right.'

'He took to the ambience of the old place straight away.

He's definitely a player.' She gives me another swift sideways glance, very challenging. 'And he hadn't been here more than a couple of days before he was talking about this gorgeous woman he'd met at the library, one he wanted to get involved with, and bring to the Waverley to spend some time with.'

Wow.

'When you say he's a player ... could that include sending anonymous sex notes and emails, perhaps? Explicit challenges, that sort of thing?'

'Oh, definitely. I'd say that was right up his street. He's a very sexy man, but also subtle and mischievous. Why, has he sent you some?'

In carefully edited terms I describe some of the Nemesis communications and she laughs delightedly.

'Oh, how delicious! That sounds like glorious fun. But it's very naughty of him not to own up. I think you're going to have to take him to task for that when he's better, don't you? Turn the tables on him. Men like that now and again. Even the most macho and alpha males like a woman to be the strong one for a change.'

How would that be, I wonder? Annie puts some soft jazz on the in-car mp3 player and we fall into a companionable silence for a while. I give the idea of taking Daniel to task some thought. Some serious thought.

I don't feel like taking him to task when I finally see him, though.

It's evening by the time we pitch up at the clinic, which is private, dazzlingly clean and a haven of quiet and almost hotel-like luxury. Not quite like the Waverley, of course, but still pretty swish.

As Daniel's doing so well, he's already back in his private room, although under careful monitoring. When I'm allowed in to see him, after first sitting in on Annie's reassuring chat with the senior nurse, and then a quick once-over with the hand sanitiser, I find him lying on his side in a big white bed, looking like a wounded war hero. The light is subdued and there's a television on low playing one of my favourite cop shows, but Daniel seems to be asleep, his eyes closed. He has the fixings for an IV still taped to his arm but other than that I see no worrying tubes or wires.

In the muted flickering light from the box, his complexion appears a bit pale and ethereal. He's wearing a soft white stockinette skullcap, to secure his dressing, I suppose, and I feel a moment's pang for the loss of his beautiful black curls. His face looks a bit odd and drawn, with purple shadows under his eyes, but otherwise he's still the handsome sexy man I fell in love with. The pallor of his skin and the whiteness of the cap somehow make his thick, sooty eyelashes look even longer than ever, and they lie like luscious black arcs on his pale cheeks. The room is warm, and his chest is bare above the bedclothes that cover his lower body.

I tiptoe to the side of the bed, not wanting to wake him.

'You're a very wicked and disobedient girl, you know. I wish I had the energy to spank you for defying me.'

I flinch in surprise. I'm sure he never opened his eyes. His familiar voice sounds husky and a bit reedy, but still full of fun. In spite of what he says, I can tell he's happy that I'm here. And I know it even more when he opens his eyes, and there's joy in their brown depths, clear and unclouded.

'You know me . . . I never can do what I'm told.'

I want to smile and smile because I'm so happy to see him, and I just know that he's going to be well. Tentatively I reach for his hand, but he anticipates me, grabbing mine. His fingers are hot and his grip reassuringly strong.

He smiles too, and it lights his face, making him look less

knocked about, more normal. More deliciously and intoxicatingly handsome, despite his little white hat and the absence of his curls.

'What do you think of the new headgear? Sexy, isn't it?' He waggles his black eyebrows. 'And I'm afraid my flowing locks have gone too. I decided that all off was more butch than just half and half.'

'I bet you look very macho. A veritable SAS hard case. I'm sure you'll be ready to go out subduing insurgents or something in a day or two. Or mugging someone.'

'I couldn't mug rice pudding, the way I feel at the moment.'

'You'll soon feel better. The nurse says you're doing great and you'll soon be out of here.'

I still can't stop smiling and looking at him and drinking him in. And loving him. I don't know what the future holds, and whether I'll be in it for him. But he's survived, he's going to be OK, and that was what I begged for.

His fingers tighten around mine, strong and vital despite his ordeal.

'I'm glad you came,' he says simply. 'Forget what I said. Forget my stupid ideas about dealing with this on my own and not wanting you to see me weak.' He lifts my hand to his lips, and brushes them briefly against it. There's not a great deal of force in the action, but I can sense his heart in it. 'I feel as weak as the proverbial kitten, but I've still never been happier to see anyone in my life before.'

I'm dumbstruck. Lost for words. Not so much from what he's said, but from the look in his eyes, where his feelings now shine through with a clarity I've never seen before, even though I would imagine I'm probably still a bit of a blur to him.

He *does* care. He cares for *me*. He maybe even loves me.

I give him a befuddled smile and place my hand over his hand that's over mine. I want to hold him, hug him, embrace him, but, just for the moment, and temporarily, he's fragile and I can't be manhandling him. But that will pass, and when he's well I'll give my all to him and more, in any way he wants.

'Your cousin's here. She gave me a lift down. Do you want to see her too?'

'Yes, I want to thank her for bringing you to me. And when I've had a chat with her, I want you back in here again, pronto.'

He's getting stronger now, sounding cockier. My sexy confident Daniel is fast returning.

'But they said we could each only have ten minutes, and that was all for the night.'

'Fuck 'em,' he announces cheerfully, rubbing his thumb against my palm in a decidedly rude and lascivious way, not at all what you might expect from a patient recovering from a brain operation. 'I'm paying a fortune for this room. The least they can do is indulge my whims a bit.'

Desire stirs low in my belly, even though I'm appalled at myself for getting horny in a situation like this. He could have died, and here I am entertaining lewd fantasies about lifting the sheet and climbing on top of him right here in his room. Oh dear, I am turning into such a nympho.

Daniel's brown eyes twinkle. They're bright and clear and I can almost read his thoughts. And I'm certain that he's just read mine.

He winks. 'Yeah, I know. I've always had kinky fantasies about sex in a hospital bed too, but, alas, I'm too closely monitored, having had the old skull drilled into.' He shrugs, strokes my hand again. 'And I'm not sure I'm up to it, even if they didn't keep checking up on me what seems like every five minutes. The spirit is willing, and certain bits of the flesh are showing interest.' He flicks his gaze down to his groin. There's not much to see beneath the hospital bedding, but my imagination supplies a delicious picture of his magnificent sleeping penis beginning to rouse itself. 'But the rest of me feels as if it's been run over by a steamroller, and I wouldn't want to disappoint my beloved Queen of the Library with a less than stellar performance.'

'I can wait. I've got self-control ... sort of.' And I can play with myself tonight, in the privacy of my hotel room, anticipating the happy day when Daniel's back on form again.

'I don't doubt that you have, Miss Price,' he says archly, letting our linked hands drop on to the bedspread. I can see he's exhausted, but he still looks uncannily well and alert, given his post-operative condition. It's as if a great burden has been lifted off him and he has everything to look forward to. 'But what are the odds that you'll weaken when you're on your own again? I know what a deliciously sensual woman you are, Gwendolynne. You won't let the small matter of the lack of a man stop you doing what has to be done.' His head sinks against the pillow, but he still has the energy to wink and grin.

'I don't know what you mean, Professor Brewster,' I say primly, then narrow my eyes accusingly at him. 'And you do realise that "Queen of the Library" is Nemesis's name for me, don't you? What conclusions am I expected to draw from that little slip?'

He gives a weary little chuckle. 'Conclude what you will, my dear,' he says softly. 'But making assumptions and jumping to conclusions are very rash activities. They can get you into a lot of trouble. Trouble I might have to attend to, as soon as I'm back to full fitness again.'

Excitement flutters in my belly. I imagine him restored, fit, powerful, smacking my bottom the way he did back at the

Waverley. My sex aches and yearns for his hand, his strength, his cock, and I know that his threat about the spanking, when I first came, wasn't an empty one.

'I'll look forward to that . . .' I'm breathless, and all he's done is make a suggestion. A promise. I'll be a melting jelly of lust by the time he's back in business.

'And what about tonight? Are you looking forward to tonight?' He's still holding my hand, and he turns it over, then plays around in my palm again, doing that suggestive thing with his fingertip. 'Alone in your hotel room . . . I do hope you're staying in town?' For a moment, he looks a little bit lost, as if the idea of me leaving hurts him. 'Aren't you?'

'Yes, Annie's husband made the arrangements. Got one of his hotel contacts to give us really, really nice rooms at a moment's notice.'

'Good,' says Daniel, perking up again, 'because I'm going to imagine you in your really, really nice room tonight. I'm going to picture you naked and magnificent, sprawled on your bed, masturbating and fantasising about what I'm going to do to you when the doc gives me the all-clear.'

I'm speechless, I want him so much. This is crazy. He's an invalid in a hospital sickbed and he can still turn me on more than any man ever in my life.

His beautiful lashes droop. I can tell he's tired, despite his puckish naughtiness and that sly, subversive little smile of his.

'I'm not joking, you know,' he purrs, his voice low. 'I'll expect you to play with yourself tonight, in my honour.' He runs his pink tongue over his lips. 'And when you've done, I think you'd better write it all down, and send it to our friend Nemesis, for when he next gets a chance to check his email.'

I want to play with myself now. I want to do lewd and rude

things, to cheer up my wounded hero and make him feel better soon. I want to satisfy the delicious lust he inspires in me, again and again and again.

'But I don't have my laptop with me.'

Daniel's eyes are closed now, but my hand is on my thigh, fingers splayed as it inches towards my groin. It creeps closer and ever closer.

'Well, you'll have to go old school then, pen and paper. That's how he started.'

Visions of hot words dancing on blue paper almost make me moan aloud, but then a sharp knock at the door sends me jumping inches into the air, and Daniel's eyes fly open and he laughs, taking in everything.

Daniel's nurse pops her head around the door.

'Time up, I'm afraid, Ms Price,' she says cheerfully. 'I'll let Mrs Guidetti in for a few minutes, and then it's time for sleep for you, young man.' She's very middle-aged, very British, very brisk. She probably has a heart of gold, but I don't expect she'll take any nonsense from her patients, no matter how persuasive or gorgeous they are.

Daniel kisses my fingers, then, with astonishing, almost feverish strength, hauls me towards him and reaches up to bring my lips down to his. His mouth is hot as it makes contact with mine, and his tongue presses for entry, probing and sensuous, despite the presence of our audience. We're probably really, really not supposed to kiss like this, for infection-control reasons and all that, but for a few seconds he totally dominates me from his bed, tasting and teasing.

'Professor Brewster! Really! That's enough of that,' admonishes the nurse. Her outraged words break the spell, and we part. With extreme reluctance.

A moment later, I'm at the door, looking back. Daniel seems drained by our fierce kiss, but his eyes are lambent, crystal sharp, exquisitely dominant. 'See you later, library girl,' he murmurs, 'and don't forget that letter.'

'See you later, Professor Hottie.'

He laughs quietly as I scuttle from the room, close to tears, longing to stay.

Forever.

A little later, after some time spent in the visitors' lounge thinking, thinking, thinking and getting progressively more hot under the collar, I'm allowed back in to see Daniel again. For two minutes only, and strictly no more than that, because they have nurse things to do before he goes to sleep.

This time we're not left unattended, presumably in case Daniel might get randy again.

He's still awake, but I guess he's in need of his rest now. The nurse told us that the process of healing drains the body's energy as much as taking exercise. Despite that, there's a wicked glint in his eyes still as he turns to greet my arrival.

'I told them I wouldn't go to sleep until I'd seen you again,' he murmurs, his voice all soft and affectionate around the edges.

'I should think so!' I squeeze his hand and he squeezes back, quite hard.

'God, I feel knackered, though.' Those sublime lashes drift down again, and it does seem as if he's as spent as if he's just run a marathon. Even so, he still clings to my hand.

I lean in, touch his dear face, stroke his skin. I wonder what his scalp feels like, all shaven and velvety, but I know it's irresponsible to investigate and the nurse would probably frogmarch me out immediately if I started messing with the cap. So I console myself with running my fingertips over his stubbly jaw. He mutters something about 'should've shaved there too ...' and opens his eyes and smiles again.

When I kiss his cheek he just quietly accepts it. I whisper, 'Good night, sweet prince,' into his ear, thinking how stupid and soppy I must sound, and how when he's back on top form he's perhaps not going to be too keen on such sentimentality.

Behind me, the nurse says, 'Time to go, Ms Price. You can come back in the morning.'

But just as I release Daniel's hand, touch his shoulder and step back again, he whispers quietly but intently, 'Good night, my love. See you tomorrow.'

When I turn back at the door, his eyes are still on me, bright with meaning.

16 Billet Doux

In my room at the Whitford Hotel, which is extremely luxurious, I discover that the guests' writing paper is blue. Eggshell blue, the exact colour that Nemesis always uses. It must be a sign, or an omen, or something.

After a long, hedonistic soak in which I used almost all the rich complimentary bath essence and sipped at a split of Zinfandel Blush from the mini-bar, I settle down on my wide, soft but achingly Daniel-free bed with my pen and my sheets of blue paper. In spite of the supposedly relaxing bath, I feel mixed up, edgy and a little hyper. I feel as if I'm the one who's had a brain operation and it's difficult to process all the events and the emotions of the last week.

I yearn for Daniel, but I feel slightly guilty to be having lustful thoughts about him at a time like this. I know I'm being silly, but it just seems peculiar and a little bit sick to be entertaining sex fantasies about a man recovering from a serious operation.

And it feels even more twisted to masturbate, thinking of him. But I've had my instructions, and who am I to argue? Well, not with him ...

Casting aside my paper and pen, erotic masterpiece unstarted, I unfasten the thick white robe provided with the compliments of the Whitford. I'm naked beneath it. The room is warm and my skin is a little pink from the steamy bath and a little shiny from the vitamin-enriched body lotion I slathered on after it, imagining I was preparing myself for Daniel.

I close my eyes, trying to summon him, and suddenly it's easy. In my mind he's with me, knowing and beautiful, dressed in dark clothing. His wild, black gypsy hair is just as it was before the operation, and as it will be again. And he can see. No spectacles obscure the wicked magic in his eyes.

Sinking into that magic, I imagine him touching me, fingertips tracking over my breasts as I lie inert and unmoving like a piece of statuary designed for his entertainment. He investigates every bit of skin he can reach, then peels off my robe and explores every inch and nook that was covered too. He owns every zone he lays hands on. Breasts, belly, bottom, thighs, sex, it's all for him. And as I imagine his scrutiny, I imagine how I might describe it in my letter.

He tweaks my nipples, rolling them between his fingers and thumbs, making me squirm and rub my legs together.

He sticks his forefinger in my navel and it feels like he's fingering my sex.

He examines my bottom and my anus, turning me over and making me show him everything, and I burn with as much lust as mortification.

He plays in the moist groove of my pussy, gently plying the soft lips, my swollen clit, my entrance.

And when he's done this, he sticks two fingers right inside me.

In the real world, it's just me doing all this and me beating at my clitoris as I thrust and thrust with my fingers in a poor imitation of his penis. But because I'm doing this for him, the pleasure soars quickly and I come, crying out, 'Daniel!'

It's quick and hard and disorientating. My flesh is satisfied, but my heart and mind still feel disjointed and somehow out of phase, because he's not here.

I lie for a while, just breathing, settling myself, quietly re-iterating to myself that this is just temporary. Soon Daniel will be well and not only will we be able to have a proper, delicious fuck – and more – but we'll also be able to sit down and talk, and, in my case at least, put our cards on the table.

But I'm impatient. I want to commit now. I know it's stupid, but still.

So I cinch my sash, top up my wine, climb into bed and take my pen and the hard-backed leather folder containing the hotel's expensive stationery.

And I begin to write.

Dear Nemesis, I have something to tell you. Some of it you're going to like, and some you may not. But here goes . . .

Here I am in a London hotel room and I've just been masturbating. I wish I could tell you that I was thinking about you, but I wasn't. Not really. I was thinking about another man as I touched myself. The one I spoke of in one of our earlier exchanges. You know the random man who I chose to show my pussy to? It's him.

I've come to know him, and I've fallen in love with him.

I hope you're not cross?

He's beautiful and intelligent and he's funny. And he makes me feel all those things too. With him, I feel like a goddess. Exactly the goddess that you describe me as, too. Only he does it with the power of his touch, his eyes, his voice, his laugh . . . and his incredible body as he fucks me and caresses me.

Just now I was lying here in this wide bed, touching myself and imagining it was him. I'm wearing a thick, fluffy towelling robe, but I unfastened it and opened it wide, so that I could believe that he was studying my body and touching it. His gaze was like molten heat flowing over it, and the brush of my fingers became his, gliding and exploring.

He made me touch myself everywhere. On my breasts, and my nipples. My thighs and bottom, right in the groove. In between my legs in the cleft of my pussy. I got dripping wet just thinking about him, dreaming of his clever hands examining me, his fingers paddling in my moisture. I played with my clit, just the way he plays with it, and I pushed fingers inside me, just the way he does.

And when I came, it was for him, shouting out his name.

I hope this doesn't distress you? But I can't help myself, I love him.

I love him for his body, and for the way he fucks and plays with me. I love him for his mind, because he's clever and playful and unusual and like no man I've ever met before. I want to do things with him, to him and for him that I've never wanted before. Strange things, that only now seem wonderful and right.

Can you understand that? I think you can. I think you know him just as well as I'd like to. I think you know him far better than you do me, and than I do you.

I'm in too deep, Nemesis. I can't pull back now.

And I would never want to, even if he doesn't love me as I love him.

Will I ever post this? Or hand it to the person it's intended for? Somehow, I think I will. I'll be bold. I'll be brave. He's worth the risk.

17 Somewhere Luxurious

I'm in the bedroom, in the villa, preparing myself, my heart thudding.

On the bed lies a letter, written in a familiar hand on blue notepaper. It's explicit and delicious, and it makes me hot. Not that I'm not hot already, in more ways than one.

Here I am in a tropical paradise, somewhere nice and warm and luxurious, and my companion is the man I love and lust for, Daniel. He's completely well now, fully recovered from his operation and from the threat that prompted it.

The instructions in the letter are quite specific.

Scent yourself with lily of the valley.

Done.

Trim your pubic fluff just the way I like it.

Done.

Put a bit of lip tint on your nipples and play with them until they stand up.

Done ... ooh, yes, very well done.

Wear your corset again, your beautiful white one with the white lacy-topped stockings and those white high heels.

Good job I had the intuition to bring them, isn't it? But how could I not, given the reaction they got last time I wore them?

The Caribbean twilight is multicoloured and balmy and, obeying my beloved, I hook myself into the lace-trimmed white satin basque that he's so passionately fond of seeing me in. Despite Daniel's protestations about my perfection, there's just a tiny bit less of me to cram into it. He said that I was very naughty and he'd punish me if I went on any silly diets and lost weight, but there are just some special days in a girl's life when she really needs to be more svelte than others. There's still plenty of me, though, and likely to be a tad more before long, given the luscious island cuisine and its abundance.

A perusal in the mirror is both necessary and a secret pleasure. I like looking at myself in all my snowy finery. Well, I like looking at myself anyway. I love studying my body and imagining Daniel's hands roving all over it, worshipping it and savouring it and giving it pleasure, oh, so much pleasure, in a score of different ways.

I love the way he looks at it too, seeing it without hindrance now and enjoying every detail.

My reflection makes me giggle. Pretty as the corset and its accoutrements are, they do impart the aura of a naughty 'Like a Virgin' lap-dancer, although in the better clubs I would imagine the girls don't have their boobs balanced quite as precariously on the edge of exposure as I do. And they probably wear G-strings too, whereas my neatly trimmed bush is still on show in all its glory.

I grab a brush, reach up to tidy my hair and, whoops, a nipple pops out from one of the dangerously shallow bra cups. It's pink and rosy, just as specified, and as I lever it back into place a jolt of pleasure courses through me and my clit glows and tingles. I've felt so wanton since we got here that I'm ready for sex every hour, every minute of the day or night. I don't know whether it's something in the tropical flower pollen that perfumes the air that's acting as an aphrodisiac, or just that I love Daniel so desperately that I want to fuck him all the time.

Or do other things.

I run my fingers over the back of the classic and very expensive wooden hairbrush he recently bought me. And that makes my clit tingle too.

Still holding it, I make one last inventory.

Hair gleaming and tumbling over my shoulders? Check.

Acres of ripe cleavage almost bursting out of my basque? Check.

Carefully groomed pubic hair already slightly glistening with arousal? Check.

Eyes huge and bright with exquisite and deliciously fearful anticipation? Check.

My hips swaying, I walk slowly through the secluded private villa we're renting, my excitement and desire gathering with every step. Between my legs I feel engorged already, and my slippery honey is on the point of welling over. But I know Daniel loves the fact I'm so juicy. He tells me off for being such an easy and wanton trollop that I'm permanently wet for him, but he really adores it, and of course it gives him a perfect excuse to discipline me.

The sky that arcs over the ocean beyond our veranda is streaked with pink and aquamarine, and the colours blend into the darkening tropical night. Lamps flicker at either end of the open, board-floored expanse, attracting fluttering moths, and there's a rough wooden table and a couple of high-backed planter's chairs. At the far end of the veranda there's a low, broad daybed, spread with a cotton throw striped with cheerful, primitive colours.

In one of the high-backed chairs sits my beloved, perfectly relaxed, staring out to sea. He too is wearing white – a pair of loose, drawstring linen trousers – and both his lightly furred chest and his elegant feet are bare and tanned.

But it's what he's wearing on his face that makes my sex clench and flutter.

Oh, it's the mask . . . the leather mask from our frisky letters and our sex play.

Wicked arousal roils in the pit of my belly and the juice that's been gathering overflows and slides down my leg, moistening the white lace tops of my stockings.

As if he's smelt it, he turns, both Nemesis and Daniel, one and the same. As if I hadn't known that subconsciously from the beginning.

His eyes glitter in the frame of the dark leather that surrounds them and his velvety, sensuous mouth curves for just a second in a little smile. He still wears glasses some of the time, but tonight he's got his contacts in. The island breeze ruffles his glossy dark hair, which has grown again, although he doesn't wear it quite as long as before. His black curls frame his head like a halo, giving him the look of a debauched cherub, angelic and infernal.

Especially in the mask.

'Who said you should bring that?' His voice is soft and full of laughter, even though it's clear that he's trying to sound stern.

I look down and realise I've brought the brush with me. Wishful thinking, obviously . . .

'Nobody. I . . . I forgot I was carrying it.'

I feel giddy, light-headed, almost floating, as if I'm on some incredible high. Which I am, of course. I'm flying. I clutch the brush, holding it tight as a way to focus myself and stop myself rocking to and fro, swirling my hips or reaching down to touch myself. Anything to assuage the intense, congested feeling in my sex. Part of me wants to throw myself down on my back on that daybed and just spread my legs wide so he can plunge straight into me. But part of me craves our delicious, twisted games.

He affects a sigh, as if I'm that vexingly dense student again, the one who just won't learn. But it's all an act. Inside I know he's laughing. I'm grinning myself, inside, though for the purposes of this interlude my face is solemn and respectful. Well, it is for now. I have a woeful habit of cracking up at critical moments, which sets him off too, resulting in delicious chaos.

'Well, put it on the table. There's a good girl.'

So professorial. So nearly stern. So full of love.

I teeter to the wooden table, my heels clattering on the boards and my breasts threatening to spill out of the lace-edged corset, a fact that doesn't escape his masked eyes. They flare with undisguised excitement, and, when I steal a glance at his crotch, I can see stirrings already under the white linen.

On the table are other objects that make my mouth go dry and my crotch get wetter. Toys for our play, familiar items we both enjoy.

'Come here now.'

I obey, starting to feel faint. I can never get over how wonderful he is. How glamorous. I don't think I'll ever get tired of the fact that such a special man is mine. That so rare a creature as he is believes that I'm just as special, and has the power to make me believe it too.

His mouth looks very red beneath the mask, his nose noble and powerful. I want to fling myself on to my knees and worship him. I want to pull down his trousers and mouth his cock. Something that might very well happen before the night is out.

He lounges in his chair, just looking at me. I stand trembling, just looking at him. I get stickier and more aroused by the second.

'Show me your breasts, library girl,' he says, clearly relishing the words. 'I want to see those lovely, rosy nipples.' He's smiling now. Is he going to lose it first this time?

Self-conscious, but in a good way, I pop myself out of the top of my corset. The upward pressure of the stern boning makes my bosom look more voluptuous than ever, and seems to present my ample curves for his perusal. His tongue flicks out and sweeps his lower lip as if he's already tasting me.

'Play with them,' he commands, shifting slightly in his seat, then, with a shrug, laying his hand across his crotch. He knows I know he's got a hard-on. I'd have to be blindfolded not to notice. So why hide it?

Really shaking now, I touch my nipples. With caution. I'm so turned on that even the tiniest bit more stimulation might tip me over. As it is, silvery darts streak from my breast tips to my clitoris and, unable to stop myself, I churn my wayward hips.

'Tut tut,' warns Professor Nemesis.

Apparently beyond my conscious control, my pelvis still sways.

'Now stop being a naughty girl and behave yourself,' he continues in his best scholarly tone, still gently squeezing his cock. 'Play with your nipples properly and stop waving your pussy around, or there'll be trouble.'

Trouble like you wouldn't believe! Trouble that I long for, crave and beg for.

The night is like magic, otherworldly in its beauty, yet so real. It's all real. I pinch my nipples hard to remind myself I'm not dreaming. Then yelp from both the pain and the pleasure.

He gives me a warning glance from behind the mask and I melt. Silky honey slides out of me again and I let out a helpless whimper of lust as it trickles downwards.

'That's it, you hussy! I've had enough of this lack of self-control.'

Then he's on his feet and manhandling me to the veranda rail.

'Stay there. Stay still.'

I know it's just a game, but his voice is so fierce it almost makes me come on the spot. I can hardly contain myself and stop myself from masturbating there and then as he strides away to the table for a moment and comes back with a silk scarf and the cushion from his chair. This he folds over the rail, then he manhandles me over it, so that my head and arms are hanging over the other side. My breasts spill even further out of my corset, and the pressure on my belly drags on the tender root of my throbbing clit. I'm almost ready to climax when he slips the scarf between my teeth and fastens it behind my head as a gag. I tend to make a lot of noise when we play, and when he's fucking me.

He nudges my ankles apart to improve his view, and the gentle balmy breeze tickles my sex. I feel so lewd, so wanton, so exhibited. It makes me ache and squirm and moan behind my gag. He rewards me by reaching over to tweak a nipple with one hand, while with the other he pushes two fingers deep inside me. I begin to surge, but he withdraws, murmuring, 'Not yet.'

He returns to the table. I wait, aching for him. When he returns, he penetrates me quickly, peremptorily, almost violently. But not with himself.

No, it's a toy, a pair of weighted glass spheres on a silk cord. One of my favourites. Unable to hold out any longer, I come hard, my inner muscles grabbing hard at the sexy intruders, while my groans are an uncouth gurgle behind my gag.

'I warned you about your lack of self-control, didn't I?' His voice is like velvet in my ear. He pinches my bottom cheek and at the same time strokes my clit, and I come again, making the spheres rock inside me.

Mewling around the obstruction between my teeth, I feel something hard and slightly prickly as he moves against me that isn't him. I realise he's got the brush tucked into the waistband of his trousers. It doesn't stay there long. A moment later, as my sex is still quivering, still almost convulsing, he starts to spank me with it. I wriggle and jiggle about, holding on to the rail with one hand and daringly stroking myself with the other. I don't think he minds; in fact, he probably likes it. He's not hitting me hard, it's just a game, the taps are playful. But still they sting, and create heat. More heat. Sizzling warmth that settles and gathers and burns in my streaming pussy.

And then he's had enough of play. With a muttered but laughing 'Oh hell!' he flings the brush aside, then rudely wrenches the little glass orbs out of my sex. A second later, as I reach around to try to caress him, he drags down his white trousers, fits his cock to me and enters. He fills me in a swift ruthless rush and I come again, clenching him now, not the cool inanimate glass. In transports of bliss, I grip the rail with one hand, and with the other reach around blindly to grab at the flexing muscles of his thigh. He too grips the rail while fishing round beneath me to find my clit.

It's not an elegant congress. In fact we must look quite a sight in the tropical twilight, jerking and pushing and sliding against each other, me with my bosom dangling out of my basque and him with his bare buttocks flexing as he shoves and fucks and thrusts. In the midst of the mêlée he tugs the scarf free and my cries of pleasure assault the vivid evening sky.

Eventually, and fairly quickly, we reach the inevitable, and I'm not the only one shouting and groaning and calling out 'I love you'. I'm not the only one coming and coming with the one I adore.

Later, we stare at the stars in a navy-blue sky, sprawled on our daybed, both naked beneath the cheerful throw. Well, almost.

I've still got my stockings on, but the basque is lying somewhere on the boards, along with my shoes, Daniel's trousers, the hairbrush and the love balls.

'Home tomorrow then?' I touch his dear face in the darkness, awed as always by his regal profile. The lamps went out a while ago, but it's so romantic out here that neither of us cares.

'Yeah, but we'll come back,' he says, which adds another warm happy glow to the ones I already feel. His arm tightens across my middle in an affectionate squeeze.

It'll be nice to go home, back to our ordinary but also quite extraordinary life. Me back at the library, Daniel working on his documentary and his book and then settling down to a new job, a prestigious newly created chair of history at the local university – which is glad to get such a distinguished and high-profile figure on its academic roster. For the moment we're living in my flat, which is a bit of a squeeze, but when we get settled we'll start looking for a house.

He turns to me and even in the indigo shadows his eyes are bright. I think of what might nearly have happened to him and I bite back tears for a moment, then slide my arms around him and hug him as tight as he's hugging me.

'Are you OK, love?' he asks, dropping a kiss first on my brow, then my cheek, then my lips.

'I'm fine, Professor Brewster, just fine.' In fact I'm more than fine, because against my hip I feel his ever-randy cock hardening yet again. The daybed is OK, but inside we've got a magnificent four-poster with crisp fresh linen provided daily by the maid service.

'Shall we go inside and, um, deal with this in more palatial surroundings?' I touch his cock and he makes a low, hungry sound. He pushes against me for a moment, then flings back the throw, gets up off the bed and reaches down to draw me gently to my feet.

'Good idea, Mrs Brewster, as ever. Good idea.'

'OK, just a minute.' I strip off my sagging white stockings, fling them to join my bridal basque, then reach for my husband.

Arm in arm, naked in the balmy night, we walk together into our honeymoon villa ... and the future.

Visit the Black Lace website at
www.black-lace-books.com

LOOK OUT FOR THE ALL-NEW BLACK LACE BOOKS – AVAILABLE NOW!

All books priced £7.99 in the UK. Please note publication dates apply to the UK only. For other territories, please contact your retailer.

THE STALLION
Georgina Brown
ISBN 978 0 352 34199 0

The world of showjumping is as steamy as it is competitive. Ambitious young rider Penny Bennett enters into a wager with her oldest rival and friend, Ariadne. Penny intends to gain the sponsorship and the very personal attention of showjumping's biggest impresario, Alister Beaumont. The prize is Ariadne's thoroughbred stallion, guaranteed to bring Penny money and success.

Beaumont's riding school is not all it seems, however. Firstly there's the weird relationship between Alister and his cigar-smoking sister. Then the bizarre clothes they want Penny to wear. In an atmosphere of unbridled kinkiness, Penny is determined to win the wager and discover the truth about Beaumont's strange hobbies.

To be published in October 2008

THE DEVIL AND THE DEEP BLUE SEA
Cheryl Mildenhall
ISBN 978 0 352 34200 3

When Hillary and her girlfriends rent a country house for their summer vacation, it is a pleasant surprise to find that its secretive and kinky owner – Darius Harwood – seems to be the most desirable man in the locale. That is, before Hillary meets Haldane, the blonde and beautifully proportioned Norwegian sailor who works nearby. Intrigued by the sexual allure of two very different men, Hillary can't resist exploring the possibilities on offer. But these opportunities for misbehaviour quickly lead her into a tricky situation for which a difficult decision has to made.

TAKING CARE OF BUSINESS
Megan Heart and Lauren Dale
ISBN 978 0 352 34502 8

After leaving the wrong man, Leah Griffin's not ready to look for the right one. All she wants to do is survive the conference she's planned and spend time with her best friend, Kate Edwards. But she never expected the conference services manager to be so tall, dark and handsome … or so eager to please. It's Brandon Long's job to make Leah happy and, after a scorching interlude in her hotel room, neither can deny that business has become pleasure.

Smart, driven and successful attorney Kate Edwards has spent her life making the right choices. Directly counter to those right choices, she's involved in a long-distance, secret love affair with a co-worker. And Charles Dixon is a bad choice she can't help but make – over and over. A conference and a promotion bring Kate back to Pennsylvania and suddenly Dix wants far more than a few nights in random hotel rooms. He wants something permanent and Kate has to figure out if some-times a wrong choice is exactly what a woman needs.

To be published in November 2008

THE NINETY DAYS OF GENEVIEVE
Lucinda Carrington
ISBN 978 0 352 34201 0

A ninety-day sex contract wasn't exactly what Genevieve Loften had in mind when she began business negotiations with the arrogant and attractive James Sinclair. As a career move she wanted to go along with it; the pay-off was potentially huge.

However, she didn't imagine that he would make her the star performer in a series of increasingly kinky and exotic fantasies. Thrown into a world of sexual misadventure, Genevieve learns how to balance her high-pressure career with the twilight world of fetishism and debauchery.

THE NEW RAKES
Nikki Magennis
ISBN 978 035 234503 5

The New Rakes are known for the hot, dirty electro music they play in basement gigs all over the city, but lead singer Kara has ambitions beyond underground success. Fuelled by her sexy performances and the love-hate relationship with her guitarist Tam, the band is poised on the brink of stardom. And when Mike Greene, the charismatic head of a record company, offers them a deal, it seems all their hopes are about to be realised.

But Kara and Mike have a history – and this time he wants more than a professional relationship. Kara is seduced by his glamorous promises and, despite the attempts of his manipulative ex-girlfriend, she becomes Mike's lover.

Meanwhile, The New Rakes are plunged into the capricious world of the music industry, where Kara's tempestuous relationships threaten to spoil everything. As she gets tangled in a web of sex, power and deceit, Kara learns the hard way what success really means and must finally choose between the limelight and true love.

ALSO LOOK OUT FOR

THE NEW BLACK LACE BOOK OF WOMEN'S SEXUAL FANTASIES
Edited and compiled by Mitzi Szereto
ISBN 978 0 352 34172 3

The second anthology of detailed sexual fantasies contributed by women from all over the world. The book is a result of a year's research by an expert on erotic writing and gives a fascinating insight into the rich diversity of the female sexual imagination.

Black Lace Booklist

Information is correct at time of printing. To avoid disappointment, check availability before ordering. Go to www.black-lace-books.com.
All books are priced £7.99 unless another price is given.

BLACK LACE BOOKS WITH A CONTEMPORARY SETTING

❏ THE ANGELS' SHARE Maya Hess	ISBN 978 0 352 34043 6	
❏ ASKING FOR TROUBLE Kristina Lloyd	ISBN 978 0 352 33362 9	
❏ BLACK LIPSTICK KISSES Monica Belle	ISBN 978 0 352 33885 3	£6.99
❏ THE BLUE GUIDE Carrie Williams	ISBN 978 0 352 34132 7	
❏ THE BOSS Monica Belle	ISBN 978 0 352 34088 7	
❏ BOUND IN BLUE Monica Belle	ISBN 978 0 352 34012 2	
❏ CAMPAIGN HEAT Gabrielle Marcola	ISBN 978 0 352 33941 6	
❏ CAT SCRATCH FEVER Sophie Mouette	ISBN 978 0 352 34021 4	
❏ CIRCUS EXCITE Nikki Magennis	ISBN 978 0 352 34033 7	
❏ CLUB CRÈME Primula Bond	ISBN 978 0 352 33907 2	£6.99
❏ CONFESSIONAL Judith Roycroft	ISBN 978 0 352 33421 3	
❏ CONTINUUM Portia Da Costa	ISBN 978 0 352 33120 5	
❏ DANGEROUS CONSEQUENCES Pamela Rochford	ISBN 978 0 352 33185 4	
❏ DARK DESIGNS Madelynne Ellis	ISBN 978 0 352 34075 7	
❏ THE DEVIL INSIDE Portia Da Costa	ISBN 978 0 352 32993 6	
❏ EQUAL OPPORTUNITIES Mathilde Madden	ISBN 978 0 352 34070 2	
❏ FIRE AND ICE Laura Hamilton	ISBN 978 0 352 33486 2	
❏ GONE WILD Maria Eppie	ISBN 978 0 352 33670 5	
❏ HOTBED Portia Da Costa	ISBN 978 0 352 33614 9	
❏ IN PURSUIT OF ANNA Natasha Rostova	ISBN 978 0 352 34060 3	
❏ IN THE FLESH Emma Holly	ISBN 978 0 352 34117 4	
❏ LEARNING TO LOVE IT Alison Tyler	ISBN 978 0 352 33535 7	
❏ MAD ABOUT THE BOY Mathilde Madden	ISBN 978 0 352 34001 6	
❏ MAKE YOU A MAN Anna Clare	ISBN 978 0 352 34006 1	
❏ MAN HUNT Cathleen Ross	ISBN 978 0 352 33583 8	
❏ THE MASTER OF SHILDEN Lucinda Carrington	ISBN 978 0 352 33140 3	
❏ MIXED DOUBLES Zoe le Verdier	ISBN 978 0 352 33312 4	£6.99
❏ MIXED SIGNALS Anna Clare	ISBN 978 0 352 33889 1	£6.99
❏ MS BEHAVIOUR Mini Lee	ISBN 978 0 352 33962 1	

☐ PACKING HEAT Karina Moore   ISBN 978 0 352 33356 8   £6.99

☐ PAGAN HEAT Monica Belle   ISBN 978 0 352 33974 4

☐ PEEP SHOW Mathilde Madden   ISBN 978 0 352 33924 9

☐ THE POWER GAME Carrera Devonshire   ISBN 978 0 352 33990 4

☐ THE PRIVATE UNDOING OF A PUBLIC SERVANT   ISBN 978 0 352 34066 5
    Leonie Martel

☐ RUDE AWAKENING Pamela Kyle   ISBN 978 0 352 33036 9

☐ SAUCE FOR THE GOOSE Mary Rose Maxwell   ISBN 978 0 352 33492 3

☐ SPLIT Kristina Lloyd   ISBN 978 0 352 34154 9

☐ STELLA DOES HOLLYWOOD Stella Black   ISBN 978 0 352 33588 3

☐ THE STRANGER Portia Da Costa   ISBN 978 0 352 33211 0

☐ SUITE SEVENTEEN Portia Da Costa   ISBN 978 0 352 34109 9

☐ TONGUE IN CHEEK Tabitha Flyte   ISBN 978 0 352 33484 8

☐ THE TOP OF HER GAME Emma Holly   ISBN 978 0 352 34116 7

☐ UNNATURAL SELECTION Alaine Hood   ISBN 978 0 352 33963 8

☐ VELVET GLOVE Emma Holly   ISBN 978 0 352 34115 0

☐ VILLAGE OF SECRETS Mercedes Kelly   ISBN 978 0 352 33344 5

☐ WILD BY NATURE Monica Belle   ISBN 978 0 352 33915 7   £6.99

☐ WILD CARD Madeline Moore   ISBN 978 0 352 34038 2

☐ WING OF MADNESS Mae Nixon   ISBN 978 0 352 34099 3

BLACK LACE BOOKS WITH AN HISTORICAL SETTING

☐ THE BARBARIAN GEISHA Charlotte Royal   ISBN 978 0 352 33267 7

☐ BARBARIAN PRIZE Deanna Ashford   ISBN 978 0 352 34017 7

☐ THE CAPTIVATION Natasha Rostova   ISBN 978 0 352 33234 9

☐ DARKER THAN LOVE Kristina Lloyd   ISBN 978 0 352 33279 0

☐ WILD KINGDOM Deanna Ashford   ISBN 978 0 352 33549 4

☐ DIVINE TORMENT Janine Ashbless   ISBN 978 0 352 33719 1

☐ FRENCH MANNERS Olivia Christie   ISBN 978 0 352 33214 1

☐ LORD WRAXALL'S FANCY Anna Lieff Saxby   ISBN 978 0 352 33080 2

☐ NICOLE'S REVENGE Lisette Allen   ISBN 978 0 352 32984 4

☐ THE SENSES BEJEWELLED Cleo Cordell   ISBN 978 0 352 32904 2   £6.99

☐ THE SOCIETY OF SIN Sian Lacey Taylder   ISBN 978 0 352 34080 1

☐ TEMPLAR PRIZE Deanna Ashford   ISBN 978 0 352 34137 2

☐ UNDRESSING THE DEVIL Angel Strand   ISBN 978 0 352 33938 6

BLACK LACE BOOKS WITH A PARANORMAL THEME

- BRIGHT FIRE Maya Hess — ISBN 978 0 352 34104 4
- BURNING BRIGHT Janine Ashbless — ISBN 978 0 352 34085 6
- CRUEL ENCHANTMENT Janine Ashbless — ISBN 978 0 352 33483 1
- FLOOD Anna Clare — ISBN 978 0 352 34094 8
- GOTHIC BLUE Portia Da Costa — ISBN 978 0 352 33075 8
- THE PRIDE Edie Bingham — ISBN 978 0 352 33997 3
- THE SILVER COLLAR Mathilde Madden — ISBN 978 0 352 34141 9
- THE TEN VISIONS Olivia Knight — ISBN 978 0 352 34119 8

BLACK LACE ANTHOLOGIES

- BLACK LACE QUICKIES 1 Various — ISBN 978 0 352 34126 6 — £2.9
- BLACK LACE QUICKIES 2 Various — ISBN 978 0 352 34127 3 — £2.9
- BLACK LACE QUICKIES 3 Various — ISBN 978 0 352 34128 0 — £2.9
- BLACK LACE QUICKIES 4 Various — ISBN 978 0 352 34129 7 — £2.9
- BLACK LACE QUICKIES 5 Various — ISBN 978 0 352 34130 3 — £2.9
- BLACK LACE QUICKIES 6 Various — ISBN 978 0 352 34133 4 — £2.9
- BLACK LACE QUICKIES 7 Various — ISBN 978 0 352 34146 4 — £2.9
- BLACK LACE QUICKIES 8 Various — ISBN 978 0 352 34147 1 — £2.9
- BLACK LACE QUICKIES 9 Various — ISBN 978 0 352 34155 6 — £2.9
- MORE WICKED WORDS Various — ISBN 978 0 352 33487 9 — £6.9
- WICKED WORDS 3 Various — ISBN 978 0 352 33522 7 — £6.9
- WICKED WORDS 4 Various — ISBN 978 0 352 33603 3 — £6.9
- WICKED WORDS 5 Various — ISBN 978 0 352 33642 2 — £6.9
- WICKED WORDS 6 Various — ISBN 978 0 352 33690 3 — £6.9
- WICKED WORDS 7 Various — ISBN 978 0 352 33743 6 — £6.9
- WICKED WORDS 8 Various — ISBN 978 0 352 33787 0 — £6.9
- WICKED WORDS 9 Various — ISBN 978 0 352 33860 0
- WICKED WORDS 10 Various — ISBN 978 0 352 33893 8
- THE BEST OF BLACK LACE 2 Various — ISBN 978 0 352 33718 4
- WICKED WORDS: SEX IN THE OFFICE Various — ISBN 978 0 352 33944 7
- WICKED WORDS: SEX AT THE SPORTS CLUB Various — ISBN 978 0 352 33991 1
- WICKED WORDS: SEX ON HOLIDAY Various — ISBN 978 0 352 33961 4
- WICKED WORDS: SEX IN UNIFORM Various — ISBN 978 0 352 34002 3
- WICKED WORDS: SEX IN THE KITCHEN Various — ISBN 978 0 352 34018 4
- WICKED WORDS: SEX ON THE MOVE Various — ISBN 978 0 352 34034 4
- WICKED WORDS: SEX AND MUSIC Various — ISBN 978 0 352 34061 0

BLACK LACE NON-FICTION

To find out the latest information about Black Lace titles, check out the website: www.black-lace-books.com or send for a booklist with complete synopses by writing to:

Black Lace Booklist, Virgin Books Ltd
Virgin Books
Random House
20 Vauxhall Bridge Road,
London SW1V 2SA

Please include an SAE of decent size. Please note only British stamps are valid.

Our privacy policy
We will not disclose information you supply us to any other parties. We will not disclose any information which identifies you personally to any person without your express consent.

From time to time we may send out information about Black Lace books and special offers. Please tick here if you do <u>not</u> wish to receive Black Lace information. ❏

Please send me the books I have ticked above.

Name

Address

Post Code

Send to: Virgin Books Cash Sales, Random House,
20 Vauxhall Bridge Road, London SW1V 2SA.

US customers: for prices and details of how to order
books for delivery by mail, call 888-330-8477.

Please enclose a cheque or postal order, made payable
to Virgin Books Ltd, to the value of the books you have
ordered plus postage and packing costs as follows:

UK and BFPO – £1.00 for the first book, 50p for each
subsequent book.

Overseas (including Republic of Ireland) – £2.00 for
the first book, £1.00 for each subsequent book.

If you would prefer to pay by VISA, ACCESS/MASTERCARD,
DINERS CLUB, AMEX or SWITCH, please write your card
number and expiry date here:

Signature

Please allow up to 28 days for delivery.